"Why would anyone believe I'd cave to this kind of intimidation?" Julia said.

Mitch preferred the defiance in her eyes. "Every contact so far implies the stalker intends to use you as an inside source."

"Yeah, I got that loud and clear." Julia pursed her lips. "We both know I can't do what he wants. What happens then?"

"We'll burn that bridge *if* we get there." Somehow he'd make sure the stalker didn't push things that far. "You won't have to face that dilemma."

"*Hmm.* Your confidence is impressive, Mr. Galway."

He shot her a grin. "Hopefully it's contagious, too, Miss Cooper. Take all you want."

She smiled, genuinely amused despite the lingering worry shadowing her green eyes. "Thanks."

As they walked back, she slid her hand into his. That expression of budding trust slipped over him, made him feel ten feet tall and invincible. This wasn't the first time he'd made a promise with no foolproof plan for how to back it up.

He wouldn't let this be the first time he let someone down.

* * *

Be sure to check out the next books in this miniseries. Escape Club Heroes: Off-duty justice, full-time love

* * *

Dear Reader,

Welcome to Philadelphia, Pennsylvania, and a new adventure into the world of my Escape Club Heroes. The Escape, a riverside nightclub owned by a retired police officer, is known for hot bands, but it maintains a quieter reputation for helping people with problems that fall through the cracks of typical law enforcement.

When she becomes the object of an aggressive stalker, Julia Cooper seeks help from the Escape to unravel the threats to her career as well as her life. Unfortunately, she can't decide if being under the watchful eye of Mitch Galway makes things better or worse. Julia has hidden her true motivations for her career success from the world for so long that I knew it would take a special kind of hero to crack through the wall around her heart.

Mitch, a Philly firefighter currently moonlighting as an Escape bartender, is a remarkable guy and he intrigued me from the start. Firefighters are vital, everyday heroes in our communities and they have a place of honor in my heart. I am forever grateful for the swift response, expertise and compassion of the crew that saved our family home during a New Year's Eve party when I was a kid.

Julia and Mitch felt like dear friends to me as I was writing their story and I hope you'll soon feel the same way. Enjoy their story and keep an eye out for more Escape Club Heroes on the horizon.

Live the adventure,

Regan Black

SAFE IN HIS SIGHT

Regan Black

HARLEQUIN® ROMANTIC SUSPENSE

Recycling programs
for this product may
not exist in your area.

ISBN-13: 978-0-373-28196-1

Safe in His Sight

Printed in U.S.A.

Regan Black, a *USA TODAY* bestselling author, writes award-winning, action-packed novels featuring kick-butt heroines and the sexy heroes who fall in love with them. Raised in the Midwest and California, she and her family, along with their adopted greyhound, two arrogant cats and a quirky finch, reside in the South Carolina Lowcountry, where the rich blend of legend, romance and history fuels her imagination.

Books by Regan Black

Harlequin Intrigue

Colby Agency: Family Secrets (with Debra Webb)

Gunning for the Groom
Heavy Artillery Husband

The Specialists: Heroes Next Door (with Debra Webb)

The Hunk Next Door
Heart of a Hero
To Honor and To Protect
Her Undercover Defender

Visit the Author Profile page at Harlequin.com for more titles.

To Mark, for twenty-five years we've held hands through life's roller coasters, speed bumps and temporary derailments. You've offered your belief when mine wanes, your humor when I'm frustrated and your superb lasagna when I'm on deadline. Thank you for being my forever hero every day!

Chapter 1

The crisp autumn breeze of a clear, late September day kissed Julia Cooper's cheeks as she exited the Marburg Law Firm. It still gave her a happy thrill to know she belonged here in this historic limestone building with the impeccable Philadelphia-proper address.

Once again, as she walked up the street toward the Liberty Bell Center to have her lunch, she startled passersby with her persistent smile. Despite her valiant efforts, the expression couldn't be muted when she was out of the office. It was a side effect of being unexpectedly added to the major criminal case old man Marburg himself had just picked up.

State and federal authorities had been working for over a year to crack open a highly organized car-theft ring operating out of the docks on the Delaware River. The FBI had Danny Falk, a man purported to be one of the higher-ranking locals in the operation, in an undisclosed safe house. Julia hadn't recognized the name, only that Falk apparently had enough clout or money—or the right connections—to have Marburg canceling two of his three weekly golf games.

She found an empty bench in a swath of sunshine and opened her lunch bag, pulling out her usual blend of fresh salad greens topped with shredded chicken and a light drizzle of dressing. Eating lean and healthy in law school might have made her a little boring, but it had given her an advantage over her boozing and pizza-loving peers. The advantage carried over to her demanding job. She dug into her meal while she skimmed local and regional headlines on her phone. At a prestigious firm like Marburg, it paid to stay on top of current events.

The chime sounded for a text message and she swiped her screen to check it. The number wasn't familiar, though the area code was local. Her assumption about a wrong number evaporated instantly.

Hello, Julia. Are you having vinaigrette or ranch on today's salad?

More than a little uncomfortable, Julia returned her fork to the bowl, glancing around for the person messing with her. None of her fellow associates at the firm cared how she dressed a salad enough to find out even for the sake of a prank. They all thought she was odd for leaving the building most days to eat outside. The true benefit of taking her lunch break in the park was the daily boost of sunshine, another rare commodity for a new hire at Marburg.

Ignoring the juvenile stunt, she resumed her lunch and headline search.

You look better in blue. And I prefer the skirt.

This text message arrived with a picture of her in yesterday's charcoal skirt and white sweater.

A rush of nerves skated over her skin. Who had been watching her and how had she missed it? She forced herself to chew and swallow the peppery greens that had turned to tasteless mush in her mouth. Quickly she packed the remainder of her salad and prepared to head back to the office.

Don't go. I'd like us to be friends.

Fat chance, starting off like this, she thought. Knowing better, she sent a reply. Who are you? What do you want?

Who I am is irrelevant. I want what most men want when they look at you: insider access.

What did *that* mean? Was that some sort of sick innuendo? Her hands trembled. She lowered them to her lap to hide her reflexive fear. Glancing around, she searched again for the jerk behind this ill-mannered trick.

Let's take a walk, Julia.

She refused to play his game. Pulling her tote close to her side, she leaned back on the bench and stretched

out her legs, pretending to watch a group of schoolkids
having fun on their field trip to the Liberty Bell Center.

I said walk. You should cooperate with me. Your choices
today will have long-term consequences.

She ignored those texts. Another arrived, this time
a photo of her moments ago, sitting on the bench, eyes
on her phone eating the salad that was now souring her
stomach. She followed the angle of the picture, frustrated
when no one seemed to have any undue interest in her.

I'm walking, Julia. Get up and join me.

Stubborn and feeling a modicum of safety among
the numerous people in the park, she remained on her
bench. The phone was blissfully quiet for several minutes. Maybe he'd moved on to someone willing to satisfy his bid for attention.

You don't want to be late.

He might know about her lunch hour habits, but he
couldn't know anything about her wants. She spotted a
policeman on patrol and gathered up her tote. Hoping
she wasn't being too obvious, she aimed that direction.

The cop is a mistake. Talk to him and he'll die as quickly
as the other witnesses.

She stutter-stepped at that message as her gaze raked
wildly over the people in the park. There was only one
local case with witnesses who had dropped dead within

days of cooperating with the authorities: the Falk car-theft ring. She changed direction, pausing at the next trash can, making sure the cop moved by without any exchange with her. This time as she looked around, she saw a man in an orange ball cap with the city's hockey team logo standing a few yards behind her. Her heart pounding, she raised her phone at him and pressed the camera icon.

The man in the cap didn't react. Maybe she'd guessed wrong and he was unfortunate enough to be the object of her swelling paranoia. She crossed at the light with a group of pedestrians, picking up her pace as she neared her building, thankful she didn't have far to go.

Relax, Julia. I need you alive.

She could hear the unwritten threat: for now. Almost to the front door, another text popped up on the screen.

Save my number, Julia, and keep me informed. I need to know the names your client is dropping.

She couldn't divulge that information under any circumstances. Her personal and professional ethics wouldn't allow it. Unsettled, telling herself it was a lousy attempt at intimidation, she hurried into the building, grateful for the sturdy shelter of limestone and the friendly, weathered face of the security guard standing by at the information desk. "How was lunch, Miss Cooper?"

"Great." The word sounded too bright, too sharp, and it bounced off the marble columns and floor of the first-floor gallery. She forced her lips into a smile. "The fresh air always perks me up, Arthur," she replied in a calmer tone. She caved to the mounting pressure to look over her shoulder. She hadn't been mistaken at all. The man in the hockey cap was there, on the other side of Walnut Street, boldly aiming his camera at the Marburg building.

Just a gutsy reporter, she told herself, not believing it for a second as she hurried toward the elevators. Out of his sight at last, she took a deep breath and forced her racing thoughts to slow down. Her attachment to the case wasn't yet in the public record. Reporters had no reason to fixate on her. A reporter wouldn't threaten a cop's life because she'd been tempted to seek help. Whoever had rigged this stunt wanted to scare her.

She was mildly ashamed it had worked so well. Upstairs at her desk, she took several minutes to document the text messages, a limited description of the man in the ball cap, and her gut feelings about the whole mess. She did save the number, to add it to a potential police report rather than out of any sense of obedience. The small, positive actions eased the tension in her shoulders and enabled her to sink into the Falk case, studying the raw statements the team had gathered so far.

When her phone chirped with an email alert from her personal account, she ignored it. She ignored the next two alerts, as well, and set the phone to vibrate. When the fourth alert came through within three minutes, she gave up. Saying a quick prayer her bad day wouldn't get worse with some pseudoemergency request from her mother, she checked her inbox.

The emails appeared to be from the notifications address of her favorite cosmetics store, but instead of a graphic or coupon, the attachments were pictures of her. Julia's breath backed up in her lungs as she examined the numerous images from the past week. It took a moment for her to realize the pictures were labeled Day 1, Day 2, etc., matching the time line precisely to how long she'd been on the Falk case.

Her stomach clenched. How had she missed this jerk following her to and from work, out to lunch and to the gym in the evenings? Pulse skittering, she clamped her lips together, biting back the scream building in her throat. Thank God she didn't have an exterior office with a view. She was safe in here, two rows of cubicles between her and the windows.

Still, it required a significant effort to stay in her chair when she wanted to cower under the desk and hide from the man on the street below. She flexed and stretched her hands, bunching up the fabric of her slacks in her fists and smoothing it out over and over again, until the anxiety subsided. She was strong, capable. When she regained a measure of calm, she downloaded and saved each photo attachment from her email account, adding them to the file she'd created less than an hour ago.

She enlarged the single picture she'd caught of the man in the ball cap, searching out any details in the shadows of his face for possible identification against Falk's known associates. There just wasn't enough to go on with the shadows from the bill of the cap and the dark sunglasses that blocked his eyes. Although he seemed of average height compared with the nearest passersby on the sidewalk, the blue windbreaker hid his real build.

Julia swore when yet another email arrived. No picture this time, just one sentence: You will keep me informed.

Her temper quickened and she fought the urge to send back a scathing reply. He might not realize it, but she would never jeopardize her career or the safety of a client over a random stranger's overblown sense of power. Having learned the hard way that pride and temper could negate strength and capability in a challenging situation, she carefully considered her options.

She couldn't go to the police without talking to her bosses first. Discussing this with one of the investigators on staff would have the same result. Both options would likely get her dumped from the case. While leaving the case might make her less valuable to the stalker, opportunities like the Falk case didn't come along every day. There were fifty other associates ready to snap up her spot if she was removed. And what was there to say? *A man found my personal number, followed me and took pictures of me around the city.* So what? It was an inconvenience, a nuisance, not a crime.

She could wait him out. He'd proved he had access and he was sneaky, but she was aware of him now. Other than more creepy attempts to frighten her, there wasn't much else he could do to intimidate her. The firm knew everything about her—all the way back to the unhappy life she'd mostly escaped—having done their due diligence before hiring her. There weren't any skeletons in a forgotten closet to shake loose and use against her.

Her phone hummed with yet another personal email. *Damn it.* She reached to turn off the device and noticed this time the email appeared to be from her bank.

She swore again, her stomach knotted with dread as she opened the email. A screen shot showing a mobile deposit and immediate transfer of nine thousand dollars filled her phone screen. Another email hit her inbox, this one an alert from her credit card showing she'd purchased a twenty-thousand-dollar entertainment system.

"Dear God." She closed her eyes, knowing how that sort of thing would look to her bosses, as well as an outside auditor. As if defense attorneys weren't typically considered corrupt to start with, now her finances actually reflected bad practices.

She picked up her desk phone to report the credit card fraud, determined to keep her cool until she knew why she'd been targeted this way.

A text popped up on her phone screen, the words raising the hair on the back of her neck. Reporting it is useless. I control your accounts now. I control YOU now.

She struggled for a calm breath, to think her way through this choking fear. He had her money? No. *No!* Panic lanced through her with razor-tipped claws. Switching to her bank's website, she discovered he was serious. Even her password recovery email address bounced back as incorrect.

If you want your life back you will cooperate.

Mitch Galway grabbed longneck bottles of beer three at a time from the coolers under the bar. At just past ten, the Escape Club was packed to capacity and the crowd was working up a profit-turning thirst as they danced and screamed and sang along with the bands on tonight's schedule. His next customers ordered the everyday special and Mitch popped open canned beer with one hand while pouring bourbon into shot glasses with the other.

He glanced up at the stage when the last notes of the current song faded away. In the momentary lull, the lead singer introduced the owner of the club as guest drummer for the next set. Grant Sullivan knew drums, the

Philly music scene and how to keep men like Mitch from going stir-crazy when they fell on tough times.

This was Mitch's second week at the Escape and the only thing keeping him sane since the Philadelphia Fire Department had placed him on administrative leave. More than anything he wanted to stay connected with the action at his firehouse on the west side of town, but he didn't dare. Getting impatient would only drag out his case and keep him off the job longer. He owed Grant big-time for giving him all the shifts he could handle between now and whenever the PFD reinstated him.

Another customer served, he moved on to the next. The bustling crowd kept his mind off the troubling thought of how long it might be before he worked a fire. He took an order, admiring the approach of a striking redhead. Chin up, it was as if she dared the whole world to try to take a shot or give her a kiss. He imagined those rosy lips could level a man with a technical knockout.

She squeezed close to the bar. No wedding band. He wondered where her boyfriend was. Maybe it was a girl's night out. "What can I get for you?" He leaned over the bar so she wouldn't have to shout her answer.

"I need to speak with Alexander."

Huh. That phrase meant the lady was in some sort of trouble. "All right." Following Escape Club protocol, Mitch scooped ice into a glass and filled it with water. Anyone who came into the bar and asked for Alexander needed to speak privately with Grant. Usually it was a matter of protection, or an assist getting out of a tough situation. Mitch dropped a straw into the glass and pushed it across the bar toward her. Giving a nod toward the stage, he said, "He's on the drums. I'll take you back as soon as he's done."

She gave a quick nod, her hands closing around the water glass, but she didn't drink.

He continued to work the crowd, keeping an eye on her, noting the way she repeatedly peered over her shoulder and took careful stock of the people ebbing and flowing around her. He interrupted his service rhythm just long enough to send Grant a text message.

Shortly after Grant exited the stage to cheers and applause, Mitch's cell phone hummed.

"Alexander's waiting for you," he said to the redhead.

Her lips compressed to a thin, stern line, she slid off the stool and joined him at the end of the bar. He led her to Grant's office and stepped aside for her to enter. Intending to give them privacy, he didn't follow.

"Join us," Grant said, waving him inside.

With a nod, Mitch entered the office, closed the door and leaned back against it.

His boss extended a hand to the woman for a brisk handshake. "Grant Sullivan. You've met my bartender, Mitch Galway."

"Julia Cooper." She slid a wary glance at Mitch but didn't shake his hand. "Yes."

"Have a seat, please." Grant's chair creaked as he landed in it. The man was built like a boxer, stocky and solid, yet light on his feet with an energy that frequently outlasted his younger employees. "How did you hear about Alexander, Miss Cooper?"

"A woman I work out with had a problem a few months ago. You helped her."

"I'm glad to hear it." Grant maintained a friendly but cautious reserve. With his salt-and-pepper hair and kind brown eyes, he had a way of putting people as ease.

"What sort of trouble are you having?" he queried, his voice full of that patience Mitch admired.

Julia reached into her purse and swiped her cell phone screen before handing it to Grant. "A man sent me threatening text messages during my lunch break and the situation quickly escalated. He followed me back to the law firm where I work. Those pictures arrived in my personal email account shortly after I got back to my desk."

"Quick worker. I'd guess you're probably not his first." Grant looked up, his gaze sharp on the potential client. "You're a lawyer?"

She nodded. "Everything related to my problem is in that file."

A lawyer with an impatient stalker, thought Mitch. An impatient stalker seemed like an oxymoron, but he wasn't the expert.

"You just noticed him today?" Grant peered intently at her phone, swiping through whatever information she'd gathered.

"Yes." She paused while a quiver twitched across her shoulders. "The pictures were taken over the past few days. That's why I'm here."

"I see." Grant continued his study. "Have you spoken to the police?"

"I don't think the police can help me in time. They'd have to catch him stalking me and I have a feeling that won't be easy. Average height, average build, no standout features." She sighed. "And it could take months— if ever—for the FBI to figure out who hacked my credit card and bank account," she said. "On top of that, based on the timing and the wording of those texts, I have to assume he's fixated on me because of a criminal case

I'm working. He could jeopardize my participation in the case, not to mention my career."

Grant's mouth flexed into a frown. "The car-theft ring?"

"Yes."

Mitch stifled an admiring whistle. It was the biggest case in the local news. Every branch of law enforcement had been trying to bust the operation, but witnesses and informants regularly wound up dead. The FBI had snatched one of the key players and managed to keep him alive—so far—and he'd lawyered up with the best defense firm in the area.

Grant scowled at her, his eyes narrowed. "You're with Marburg?"

"Yes." She glanced over her shoulder at Mitch before addressing Grant again. "Will that be a problem?"

"No."

The answer made Grant a better man than Mitch. In his boss's shoes, he wouldn't want to help anyone associated with Marburg. Their legal team had represented the bastard who'd shot and wounded Grant, ending his career with the Philly police department.

"Mitch will help you out," Grant said. "He'll be a buffer between you and the stalker until we can make an ID. He can investigate who might want to target you."

The announcement startled Mitch. Stalkers and investigations sounded like a problem better suited to one of the cops moonlighting at the Escape.

"Buffer? Is that code for bodyguard?" Julia asked. "The partners will know something's up if he's tagging along behind me at the office."

"Tell them he's your boyfriend," Grant suggested.

"That would be worse. No offense," she clarified,

eyeing Mitch. "A new associate with a personal life is frowned upon."

Mitch shrugged a shoulder, holding his ground and taking her measure as she took his. She didn't strike him as the type to scare easy. Not with the deep red hair and sheer defiance in her stormy sea green eyes. He couldn't wait to see what the stalker had done to drive her here. Not that it mattered beyond getting the guy off her. When Grant handed out assignments, it was best not to argue. "Is there a different excuse you'd rather use?"

"No," she replied through gritted teeth.

"I won't create any trouble for you at work," Mitch assured her. "I'll follow your lead and won't even enter the building unless I'm following your stalker." He understood the value of privacy and discretion in the workplace.

Her shoulders relaxed a fraction. "All right. I'll be safe enough at the office and at home. I have a security system in my apartment."

"If you want our help, you'll accept that he'll be with you around the clock," Grant corrected. "At least until we identify the man and his motives."

"I'm not comfortable with that." Her shoulders locked up again. "Surely, Mr. Galway—"

"Mitch."

"—has better things to do than tail me." She glared at his interruption.

"If you're sure you can handle this, why did you ask for my help?" Grant voiced the question even as Mitch thought it.

"I… That is…" She stopped and cleared her throat, those tempestuous eyes skimming over him from head to toe once more before darting back to Grant. "I do need the buffer," she admitted, reluctance dripping from every syllable. "Twenty-four/seven is more than I expected."

"Good!" Grant beamed. "We aim to exceed expectations in every aspect of our operation." He stood, returned her cell phone and brought the meeting to an end. "Send me a copy of that file, Miss Cooper. I added my contact information to your phone. Mitch, I'll cover the rest of your shift at the bar. You take good care of our new client."

"Of course." Mitch opened the door, tipping his head for her to go first. The woman wasn't happy, but she'd stopped protesting. His curiosity about her and the situation revved into high gear and he found a new appreciation for the free time created by his administrative leave.

Maybe this unexpected career detour would prove a little more interesting than he'd thought.

Chapter 2

Knowing it was the smart choice, her only choice, to accept help, Julia wondered why it felt like such an irrevocable mistake. When her friend had enlisted the Escape Club's help, she hadn't mentioned dealing with anyone as tall and imposing and...virile as Mitch.

Virile. Yes, that was the best word to describe him as he stood silently looming over her in the hallway between the raucous club and the office. His brown eyes were intense and curious. He kept his thick blond hair short and burnished gold whiskers shaded his jaw. His bright blue uniform polo shirt with the club logo embroidered on the chest hugged his defined biceps and trim torso that narrowed to trim hips and long legs. She had her doubts that any fat cells would dare to linger on his fit frame.

She'd dated a guy in law school who'd worked his

body into this kind of shape. That guy hadn't been interested in anything that didn't benefit him directly. This man had been assigned to stand between her and the stalker who'd turned her life inside out in the space of an afternoon. She wondered if he had as many doubts about that 24/7 concept as she did. Willing away her immediate reaction to his tall, fit form, she raised her gaze to meet his and caught the spark of amusement.

"Satisfied?" he asked, hooking his thumbs in the belt loops of his khakis.

"How tall are you?" Her cheeks turned warm when she realized she'd voiced the question.

"Six-three most days. Am I taller than your stalker?"

"Yes, I think so. Fortunately, he hasn't been close enough for me to be sure. Yet."

"And I won't let him get that close."

The determined set of his mouth gave her a ridiculous amount of reassurance. Did he practice that expression? He hadn't even done anything truly helpful yet.

"What do you need, Julia? Should we stay for the music so you can unwind or should I take you home?"

"I'd like to go home." What was it about his voice that sliced through her defenses? Home didn't sound scary anymore and yet nothing had changed. Not really. A stranger was still out there somewhere, expecting her to cooperate. What was the protocol for dealing with a temporary bodyguard? "What does twenty-four/seven mean?"

"You're an attorney. I think you're smart enough to figure that out."

"You can't really expect to…to *stay* with me," she protested. She needed more space in her life, more than the average person. Her mother, friends and both former boyfriends were all in agreement on that.

His eyebrows dipped low over his eyes. "Do you believe you were followed here?"

"No." She swallowed, knowing the immediate response might be inaccurate. She couldn't know for sure. She'd just admitted to two strangers that a man had followed her for days and she'd been none the wiser. "At least I don't think so."

"Did you drive here?"

She shook her head, forcing her gaze to remain on his eyes. Steady eye contact conveyed confidence, and she needed him to know she wasn't always frightened of every shadow. "I thought a cab was the safer choice."

"Probably right on that one. Safety in numbers, I guess," he said, echoing her deciding thought.

She folded her arms over her chest. "How many women have you saved from stalkers?"

His eyebrows arched and his lips twitched into a half smile, but his voice was serious. "I've only been on the job here for two weeks. That makes you my first."

She rolled her eyes to the dingy ceiling tiles over his head. "Grant assigned you to me because I'm with Marburg. He's going through the motions for me, that's all." She fisted her hands in her coat pockets. "This was a mistake." She'd find a way to navigate this on her own.

"Hey." Mitch stepped closer, crowding her. "You came here for good reason. We can help. Personally, I think the boss would be within his rights to turn away anyone from your firm. But he didn't. That's not how he operates. Just because I've never done something doesn't mean I can't do it. I happen to know a few things about getting people out of trouble."

"Then show me your skills," she said, spreading her arms wide and then dropping them back to her sides. "What comes next?"

He'd better have some answers, because she was at an absolute loss. Another trickle of icy fear rolled down her spine. If she turned away from Escape's help, the cab fare home would wipe out most of the cash in her wallet. She had more money stashed away at home, but not nearly enough to cover her expenses if the stalker didn't give her access to her accounts. Trying to focus on what she could control, on choosing the best option out of the short and lousy list, she pressed her lips together and waited.

"One step at a time," Mitch began in a soothing voice. "I'll drive you home. I'll walk through your place and make a decision after that."

Him. In her apartment. An image popped into her head, confounding her. The studio space was almost too small for her. "What kind of decision?"

He gave her a pleasant smile she didn't quite trust. "One step at a time," he repeated. "Come on."

"Where?" she asked as he turned his back. Faced with the view of his wide shoulders tapering to lean hips, her feet moved forward of their own volition. Her responses to him embarrassed her, made her feel too much like her mother—the woman who used anyone and everyone in her orbit. "This kind of thing doesn't happen to me."

"Okay." He kept walking.

She followed. "I'm not a drama queen."

"Got it." He pulled open a door at the end of the hall, encouraging her to enter first. "Break room," he said, answering her unspoken question. "I need to grab my coat and keys. Unless you changed your mind about staying for the band?"

"No, thank you." She scolded the voice in her head that encouraged her to forget responsibilities and problems and dance all night with Mitch. "I have to be at the office early tomorrow."

With a nod, he pulled a worn leather bomber jacket from a peg on the near wall and shrugged it over his shoulders. It fell into place as if he'd been born in it.

The burst of attraction zipped through her veins. She blamed it on some unruly, misplaced version of hero worship. He hadn't even done anything but hand her a glass of water and introduce her to Grant. For all she knew this would backfire.

"Mr. Galway—"

"*Mitch*. We're going to be inseparable for a while, Julia."

He made it sound so ominous. *And so tempting*, she thought with a mental sigh. She ignored that hero-worshiping voice. "Right. Mitch." She tested his name as he led her out the back door and into the dark night.

The void of the Delaware River stretching away in both directions startled her and she stopped short. She'd forgotten the club was perched at the end of a pier. On the opposite riverbank, New Jersey sparkled. Little more than the bass of the band was audible once the door closed behind them. She knew thousands of people were nearby, in restaurants and bars, condos and businesses, but right now, she couldn't see any of them. The solitude was blissful.

The cool night air slipped under her coat and she shivered. Mitch stepped up and wrapped an arm over her shoulders, pulling her into his warmth as they walked up the pier to the parking area across the street. Immediately, her body resisted the invasion of her personal space. Just her luck she'd get saddled with a touchy-feely type of buffer. "Do you have to touch me?"

"Relax, play along. If you were followed here, being with me will throw your stalker a curveball."

Followed. One more fear to add to the heap, though the idea of putting the stalker off balance appealed to her. The jerk had demonstrated too much familiarity with her life and habits this afternoon. Giving in, she leaned into Mitch's solid body as if she could truly count on a man she'd just met. No, it wasn't smart, but it wasn't forever. Her entire life had been one lesson after another proving she was better off handling things on her own.

Until now. It had been quite a blow this afternoon to realize she had no idea how to overcome a situation where her opponent operated so swiftly and effectively from the shadows.

"How do you think he found out so much about me in such a short amount of time?"

"That's a tough question. I'll need a look at the file you assembled." Mitch's fingers flexed on her shoulder through her coat. "We'll figure it out."

"How?" She had the impression he was holding back his real opinion of her and her situation. "You think he knows me." Anxiety slid through her belly and she gazed out over the parking lot, expecting to see that orange cap. "Or maybe you believe I'm exaggerating the circumstances."

His sharp inhale was followed by a vapor cloud as he exhaled into the cold night air. "You don't hold back much, do you?" He slipped a key into the door lock of a classic muscle car and opened the door for her. "Slide in," he suggested when she stood there waiting for his reply.

"Answer me," she said. "Please," she added a beat too late to be considered polite.

He laughed. "You'll get answers. In the meantime, let's get warm."

She gave the car a long look. The glossy, midnight-blue finish reflected the nearby lights as if they were stars in the sky. Sinking into the passenger seat, she discovered supple leather upholstery and polished walnut accents on the dashboard, console and gearshift.

"I'm impressed," she said when Mitch settled his tall frame behind the steering wheel.

"It loses points as a classic with the high-end upgrades rather than original features," he said. "But I like it better."

"Must have cost you a fortune."

"You can bet I'll charge someone a fortune when I sell it." He shot her a wink as the engine roared to life.

She pulled her feet away from the vibration as he chuckled again. "You rebuild cars when you're not bartending at Escape?"

"Sometimes." He blew into his cupped hands to warm them. "Where to?"

She gave him her address, relieved her voice didn't catch. When she'd walked to work this morning, her world had been normal and safe. Since the stalker had stormed into her life, any thought of going home—going anywhere she typically went—set off that clawing panic.

"City girl all the way, huh?" he asked.

"It's close to the office." She wasn't inclined to share more about her life than necessary to resolve her problem. In her experience, sharing didn't change how people saw her.

"Some people like to get away and enjoy a change of scenery at the end of the day."

She bristled at the not-so-subtle judgment in his statement. Some people didn't work new-associate hours at the best and largest law firm in the city. "The proximity of my home and office should make keeping track of me easier," she said, hoping her irritation wasn't too obvious.

"Proximity? Fair point," he allowed.

"So, you rebuild cars when you're not tending bar?" She wanted to know what kind of skills he had and how he planned to use them to help her. Details she should have hammered out with Grant rather than simply rolling along because she was scared and well out of her element.

"Among other things. Normally I restore cars when I'm not fighting fires."

"Galway," she said as the name clicked into place. "I read about your case." It had been a big headline a few weeks ago. "The fire department suspended you for punching a victim at a fire scene." She had a sudden vision of Mitch planting a fist into her stalker's face. It was surprisingly satisfying.

Mitch snorted. "Not the best fifteen minutes of fame for the PFD or me." He drummed his fingers on the gearshift while they waited for a red light to change. "*Perp* is a better word for that sorry excuse of a man."

"What happened?"

"What do you really want to know?"

She hesitated. "I'd like to hear your side of it." Her natural curiosity had occasionally proved helpful at work, but on a personal level it usually got her in trouble. "Only if you want to share." Would a man with a quick temper be an asset or a hindrance in her situation? "The news offered up teasers at first, but nothing real ever came out when the PFD went silent and applied the 'ongoing investigation' comment."

"Thank God for small favors."

If he'd been her client, she would agree with him. As her buffer, she wanted to know who he was behind the sculpted biceps and handsome bravado. She cleared her throat. "Well? Do you want to tell me?"

He drove another few blocks in silence. "Look, I've been part of the PFD all my life," he said at last. "First as a fireman's kid and later as a volunteer before I graduated the academy and earned a spot on my own merit." He worked through the gears and then squeezed through a narrow gap in traffic to make the last left turn onto her street.

"Are you trying to scare me?" she demanded, bracing herself against the door.

"No," he said, startled by her outburst. "Sorry. Sorry," he repeated with more sincerity. "The whole mess annoys me."

"Maybe you shouldn't drive when you're annoyed." She reached into her purse for the key to her apartment. "Take the alley behind the building," she said, pointing out the turn.

"Where can I park?"

She swallowed another surge of nerves. "Guest spaces are at the end of the back row. We'll have to give your name and plate number to the doorman." And how many days he planned to stay.

"No problem." He parked in the designated spot and cut the engine.

It felt like a problem to her. She could already hear the teasing remarks from Mr. Capello when he heard the boyfriend excuse. Her doorman was warm and helpful, and forever encouraging her to live a little.

It's temporary. She repeated the words in her mind as she reached for the car door handle.

"Hang on a second," Mitch said, laying a hand gently on her arm. "The guy came at me, all right? At best, the man's negligence nearly killed his little girl. Kitchen fire got out of control. He, the dad…um." He took a deep breath. "We heard her. Still not sure how. Managed to get her out. Saved that whole row of houses, by the way," he added. "Not that he gave a damn about that." Mitch closed his eyes a moment. "She was so thin. No weight to her at all. The paramedics took her out of my arms and started working on her." Opening his eyes, he stared at his hands as if reliving it. "When I asked the father why his kid had been *locked* in a closet, he came at me, fists flying. Trying to shut me up, I guess."

She was almost sorry she'd asked. "The father threw the first punch?"

Mitch lifted his gaze to hers, his jaw tight with the recollection. "Does it matter?"

"Yes." Character made all the difference. With her lousy track record with first impressions and reading people, she preferred to have things spelled out clearly. She preferred the evidence of actions over all the right words.

"He threw the first punch," Mitch confirmed. "My union rep says witness videos support my account that I defended myself until they hauled him off me. He was older—it wouldn't have been right to flatten him. It was a shock to me and everyone on my shift when he filed the complaint."

"Thanks," she said, satisfied. In the awkward silence, she patted his hand. Grabbing her purse, she climbed out of the low-slung car before he could come around and open her door.

She picked up her mail and somehow survived the wink and waggling eyebrows of the doorman while they filled out the information for Mitch's car.

In the elevator, Mitch laughed over the encounter and Julia tried to join him, though she wasn't feeling it. Another shiver of fear or awareness or some troubling combination of the two swept over her as she opened her apartment door and invited Mitch inside. Without a word, he closed the door and secured both dead bolt locks, while she punched in her code on the security system panel.

In this neighborhood, she couldn't afford a big place, and living alone, working long hours, anything more than this tidy efficiency would've been a waste of money. Unfortunately, just as she'd thought, Mitch's presence filled the small space to bursting and he'd barely stepped inside. He couldn't possibly stay here with her—they'd run out of oxygen by morning.

"Go ahead and look around." She forced out the words. No one was here, waiting to spring an attack. "We'd only trip over each other if I gave you a guided tour."

The kitchen to the right and the living area in front of them were self-explanatory anyway. In three strides, he peered around the canvas privacy screen she used to designate her bedroom. Printed with Monet's water lily pond, she suddenly felt overexposed, as if he could see straight through to those last secret soft spots she kept hidden from the rest of the world.

Ignoring what would be a swift orientation, out of habit she dropped her purse and keys on the chair, along with the mail. When she realized that the only space left for them to sit together was the love seat, she changed her mind and moved things to the table snugged under the kitchen pass-through. She'd have to clear that by morning to make room for him to eat breakfast.

The last time she'd had a roommate was during her undergrad years. She'd skimped and scraped through law school without having to share her space. Did he expect her to cook for them? Should she come up with a schedule so they weren't tripping over each other?

A small, square note card envelope dropped to the floor, distracting her. White, no postmark, only her first name typed in all caps as an address, it stood out against the nearly black hardwood floors. "It's nothing bad," she murmured to herself. *Could be any number of happy things*, she thought, willing it to be true as she crouched down to pick up the envelope.

"All clear," Mitch said. "Nice place. Saw your windows are wired into the system, too. Smart."

"Thanks." Julia stood up and faced him, smiling as she hid the envelope behind her back. If he knew what she'd found, he'd stay. If he stayed, she'd never get any rest. Twenty-four/seven or not, she needed him to go, to let her have some peace for what was left of the night.

"What's that?" He raised his chin as if he could see right through her midsection to the envelope fluttering in her shaky hand.

"I'm sure it's nothing."

"And I'm sure that particular 'nothing' has scared

you." He held out his hand, flicked his fingers to encourage her to hand it over. "You're white as a sheet."

Or white as an envelope, she thought with a flash of gallows humor. "You want to open it, go ahead." She held out the envelope but didn't let go when his fingers closed over it. "It's addressed to me." She showed him. "Just my name."

With a shrug, he tucked his hands into his coat pockets. "Any idea who sent it?"

She clamped her lips shut when her teeth wanted to chatter. "Probably a neighbor."

"So open it already and find out."

"Fine." She slid her thumb under the flap and pulled out the enclosure. The paper shook like an autumn leaf in a gale as she read the short list of names followed by another terse message: "Stay on the case, Julia. Cooperate with me or I'll drop these bodies on your doorstep."

Her knees buckled and she pitched forward. Mitch caught her, guiding her to the chair. "Here." She shoved the horrid note into his chest. "Take it."

She couldn't bear to hold it anymore, couldn't bear the implications. She'd only entertained the thought of taking herself off the case for a few brief seconds this afternoon. Why was he doing this? Threatening her career, ruining her credit and credibility was bad enough. Threatening her best friend, her mother and her brother upped the ante.

"It's a bluff," she murmured. It had to be a bluff. "He's making a point that he knows where I live." As if she might be too stupid to put that together from the pictures and messages he'd sent her earlier.

A thick fog of dread blurred everything around her.

She waited for anger to burn through it, waited in vain as her heart raced and tremors racked her body.

Mitch dropped his coat over her shoulders, gave them a brisk rub. Enveloped in his warmth and the spicy scent of his cologne, it was hard to remember she didn't like being touched. Hearing him moving through her kitchen, she couldn't work up the least irritation with him or her paralyzing fear. Where was her fight? Grit and unwavering fortitude had carried her away from home, through college and law school, through pressures far more direct and personal than one bully with a camera and a gift for nasty text messages.

"Drink this," Mitch said, kneeling in front of her.

She focused on his face, on the compassion in his brown eyes. He wrapped her numb hands around a bottle of water. She managed to raise it to her lips, taking one sip, then another. "Don't leave," she said. "Please."

"Not a chance."

Mitch picked up the note and read the brief message, wondering about the significance of each name. He might not have a lot of experience with stalkers, but this note—and her severe reaction to it—meant leaving wasn't an option, regardless of the assignment.

He'd seen plenty of shock victims through the years. Julia, in her current emotional state, needed rest and assurance more than anything else. Still pale, the water bottle wasn't shaking quite so much as she burrowed deeper into his coat.

He read the note again. *Aubrey Wallace, Karen Neal and Justin Carter.* None of the last names matched Julia's. "How are these people connected to the Falk case?"

"They aren't." She pushed her fingers into her hair,

closing her eyes as she tipped her face to the ceiling. "He listed my best friend from college, my mom and my brother. In that order."

No wonder she'd nearly fainted. Mitch gave a low whistle as he tucked the note into his back pocket. He was tempted to drag her into his lap and cuddle her as if she was one of his young nieces fighting off a bad dream. He almost smiled, imagining how poorly that would go over with the prickly attorney. "So the stalker targeted you for personal reasons." He'd be furious if someone threatened his family to force his cooperation. He didn't want to contemplate how fast he'd give in to keep them safe.

"No," she murmured. "No one here knows I have a brother," she murmured. "Other than my mother and whoever did the required background search before Marburg hired me."

Her low, flat voice unnerved him. It seemed as if the note had smothered all that pride and fire she'd shown from the moment she'd walked up to his bar. Then her words hit him like a sucker punch. "Pardon me?"

She burrowed into his coat. "Justin is several years older than me. He joined the Marines when I was in high school. We lost touch while I was in college. Mom called me when he overdosed on painkillers. That was my first year of law school." She rubbed at the frown creasing her forehead. "I did a little digging after that. He'd gone to rehab but didn't complete the program. Checked himself out early. As far as I know, no one's heard from him since. He might already be dead." She leaned forward, her green eyes wild and fierce. "That's actually good news."

"It is?" Mitch didn't believe any threat to family was good news.

"Yes. The creep must be mining old records. He doesn't realize only Aubrey still matters to me." Her gaze dropped to her hands. "Well…that makes me sound like a terrible person."

"Not at all." He used the tone that calmed down panicked victims during a rescue. People had countless definitions of family, not all of them as strong and unified as his. "You're not close to your mom?"

"No."

That one word packed a hefty warning to back off the sore subject. He swallowed his follow-up questions. "Then why were you so upset to read the note?" He could be of more help, be less of an intrusion, if he understood her.

"It's an invasion." Her shoulders shifted under his coat. "Bad enough he's jeopardizing my integrity and twisting up my finances. This? Dredging up old baggage and dumping it here in the place I made for myself?" Her hands fisted on her knees as she emitted an angry growl. "The envelope…he was in my building."

He seized on that point like a lifeline. "Would you rather stay somewhere else for a while?"

She shook her head and shut her eyes tight for a moment. "I won't give in that easy."

"Good." He admired her courage. "Remember, you're not alone."

Her eyes met his again, held. "Okay." She rubbed her palms briskly over her knees and took a deep breath. "We've found a silver lining. I'm home safe and although he got close, the creep isn't lurking in a closet. What next?"

Good question. He was in over his head here. He
fought fires, not stalkers. "We should warn your friend."
That sounded logical. "And your mom."

Julia's features smoothed into an unyielding, emotionless mask. "And say what? They don't live here in
Philly."

"All right." Mitch flared his hands, unwilling to push
her any further tonight. His job was protecting her. Grant
could tackle this issue of warning others if necessary.
"Why don't we get some rest and start fresh in the morning."

She glanced at the small, antique sofa. "You won't
be comfortable there." Her gaze slid toward the privacy
screen hiding her bed.

He wasn't about to make her sleep on this hard sofa.
"Don't worry about me. If you have an extra blanket and
pillow I'll sleep just fine on the floor."

The little furrow between her brows as she examined
the small apartment was endearing. Or it would be under
different circumstances. This wasn't the right time to be
charmed and distracted by the woman he was supposed
to be protecting. One of the hardest lessons of firefight-
ing was doing the job without getting emotionally invested in the people saved.

While he denied it every time it came up, no one
seemed to believe he'd finally grown past the foolish
damsel-in-distress complex he'd had as a kid. Yes, his
last girlfriend had used that specific soft spot against
him and it had taken him too long to see her true colors.
But he'd eventually corrected that mistake. The nature
of the job was to race into danger and bring people out
alive. Without his innate drive to protect those in need,
he wouldn't be a decent firefighter.

"You're really staying over."

He nodded, unable to tell if she was more relieved or frustrated by his protective intrusion. He managed not to remind her she'd asked him to stay only a few minutes ago.

In a flurry of motion, she stood up. Shrugging off his coat, she folded it neatly over the back of the chair. Moving behind the privacy screen that divided the space, he heard her open a closet. A moment later she returned with a pillow in an ivory satin case and the quilt that had been folded neatly on the foot of her bed. "Make yourself comfortable."

"Will do."

"Are you a morning person?" She crossed her arms as if she was cold again.

"I'm a firefighter. I've learned to adapt to the situation and timing, whatever it is."

Her auburn eyebrows arched, then knit into a hard scowl.

"Is that a problem for you?"

"No." The scowl remained, the arms tensed more.

"Something's got your wheels turning." He tapped his temple.

"How can this work?" She spread her arms wide. "You can see my place is too small for you to move in."

"We'll manage."

She wasn't satisfied by his vague confidence. "You're just going to follow me? Everywhere?"

"Sure. Until we identify who's hassling you. Isn't that what you asked for?"

Her shoulders sagged. "Yes. No. I'm just…"

"Tired," he finished for her. "Stressed-out. That's reasonable, Julia."

"I don't like having you here."

"I understand." He could sympathize. Independence radiated off her. He didn't know her well, but it was clear that she was unhappy she'd needed to ask Escape—or anyone—for help.

"This creep might just be a big gasbag trying to embarrass the firm."

"It's possible." Although they both knew that theory didn't explain the stalker sifting through her past for hot buttons of friends and family. Mitch hoped the situation was resolved quickly just by his presence, but her stalker was pushing awful damn hard and fast.

Mitch would have a tough time forgetting the shock and fear on her face when she'd read the note. The facade of the savvy, polished attorney had dissolved, instantly revealing a frightened woman floundering to make sense of things.

The bastard had put a note in her mailbox. Tomorrow, once Julia was safe at work, Mitch would come back and have a chat with the doorman. A building as posh as this one had to have cameras on every entrance. The residents wouldn't tolerate anything less.

"I guess I'll, just, um, head to bed then." She took a step back.

"Could I take a look at your phone, please? It would help if I could review the interactions you've had with him before tomorrow." If he was lucky, he might even find a clue as to why Grant had assigned him to Julia's situation.

"Let me know when you're done. It's my alarm clock." She handed him the phone and excused herself. He tuned out the sounds and the resulting speculative images of her preparing for bed. It required more effort than it should have.

He skimmed the text messages first, then the file with Julia's notes on the encounter, and the pictures and emails that had followed. Despite his limited experience, Mitch recognized this definitely wasn't a typical stalker.

Maybe Grant thought he was dodging that looming threat against the cop by assigning a suspended firefighter. More likely, it was a combination of convenience and intimidation. Mitch made a habit of using his height effectively in any situation and he'd been standing right there while Grant assessed Julia's trouble. On top of that, Grant probably sensed Mitch's restlessness. The man was legendary about reading people.

He glanced back at the closed bathroom door and took advantage of the moment by cruising through Julia's contact list. Only the best friend's name turned up. Interesting. She really wasn't close to her mom, not that he'd doubted her earlier answer.

He heard the bathroom door open and her footsteps approaching. "Are you done yet?"

"Just finished," he said, closing the open files on her phone. Looking up, his jaw dropped at the sight of her. With her makeup gone and her long, red hair tumbling in loose waves over her shoulders, she managed to transform the bulky sweatshirt and sweatpants into the sexiest of lingerie.

His pulse kicked into overdrive. He wanted to feel that hair in his hands and inhale that soft fragrance that seemed just out of reach. What the hell was wrong with him? She'd kick him out in a hot second if she realized where his thoughts had gone.

He kept his feet rooted in place, holding the phone at arm's length. "Here you go."

She didn't go to bed. She came around to sit in the chair again, inadvertently teasing him with that warm fragrance as she passed by. She tucked her feet up by her hip and studied him. "Did it help? Do you have a plan?"

"A starting point," he said, resuming his seat on the sofa. The apartment was truly too small. "Once you're safe at the office, I'll see what I can dig up. If we're lucky he'll show up wearing that orange hat again."

Her lip curled. "I hope not."

The admission startled him. "Why?"

"Because if the hat is his habit or signature or whatever, it means I've been oblivious to him for days."

"Stop." Mitch reached for her and thought better of it. "You can't do that to yourself." He waited until she lifted those lovely green eyes to meet his gaze. "It's a very popular hat around here."

It took a second, but when she finally laughed her entire body relaxed. And his tensed up as the sound rolled through him. He stretched his arms across the back of the sofa and changed the subject. "What's with the furniture?" She didn't strike him as the sort of woman who preferred fragile antiques to modern, sturdy furniture.

"You don't like it?"

"I didn't say that. I just pegged you for something more current."

Her mouth twisted in a wry smile. "You wouldn't be wrong. These are my inheritance from my grandmother." She traced the carved wood accent on the arm of her chair. "The pieces fit the space and saved me money."

Sensing more to that story, he waited for her to elaborate. She didn't, leaving him wondering how to politely nudge her out of the way so he could stretch out on the floor.

"You'll never be comfortable on that."

"I'll manage," he replied.

With a heavy sigh, she pushed to her feet. "Hang on." Her footsteps were quiet on the hardwood as she padded to a closet and rummaged around. "I've got a sleeping bag and mat I use for camping." She leaned both items against the chair. "There. You'll be more comfortable and I won't feel like a total bitch."

He smiled at her candor. "I never would have known the difference."

"I would have." She shrugged. "I set out clean towels and a travel toothbrush for you in the bathroom. Sleep well, Mitch, and thanks for staying."

"You're welcome." The woman was full of surprises behind that thick wall of lawyer, he thought as he unrolled the mat and sleeping bag. It was hard to imagine her roughing it in the woods, but he was grateful.

He studiously kept his gaze averted as he passed her bed on the way to and from the bathroom. When he slid into the sleeping bag, he found himself surrounded by the elusive scent that was uniquely her.

With a sigh, he folded his hands behind his head. The few hours left between now and morning were going to make for one long night.

Chapter 3

By some miracle, Mitch did get some sleep and upon waking, he managed not to interfere with Julia's morning routine too much. After a quick argument against walking her to work, he drove her over and, when he dropped her off at the curb, he made her promise to stay put in her building until they met for lunch. Not only that, but she'd given him her word she'd forward any communication from the stalker. After last night's emotional roller coaster, he believed she'd cooperate. In the short term, anyway.

Leaving her office, he drove to the west side of town and the house he shared with his oldest brother, Stephen. Braced for an interrogation, Mitch was relieved to find the place empty. He really wanted to avoid a discussion about where he'd spent the night and why. After a fast shower, he pulled on dark jeans, a T-shirt and a blue button-down. His typical off-day wardrobe of concert shirts was fine for the garage but wouldn't translate well if he needed to blend in at her office. With that in mind, he packed a bag for a few days and grabbed his laptop. On his way out, he left a note to head off any unnecessary and uncomfortable questions from his family.

The extended Galway family could turn the big city into a small town whenever they got the urge. He'd been fending off concerned texts and calls from his parents and siblings since his suspension, as if they were afraid he'd go stir-crazy if he couldn't fight fires. They weren't exactly wrong—he missed the sense of purpose at the firehouse—but at just shy of thirty, he'd grown out of his youthful restlessness.

His irritation eased as he thought of Julia's brother. He'd rather be surrounded by too much caring than none at all. He couldn't imagine any of his siblings or cousins going missing for years. It just wouldn't be tolerated.

With his gear in the trunk, he drove back to Julia's building for a chat with her doorman before he reported in to Grant. The results after an hour of conversation were disturbing. Whoever had slipped that note into Julia's mailbox had hidden their tracks well. Either the stalker lived in her building or he'd convinced someone in her building to drop the note in her mailbox. Worse, the security video didn't show anyone other than the mailman near Julia's box yesterday.

Frustrated, Mitch made notes and sent them on to Grant. The technical expertise involved to erase or alter surveillance was beyond him. Julia would expect better results than Mitch's fumbling attempts to track down the man who matched her description of an average man wearing a popular hat.

Since he had her spare key, he took his belongings upstairs to her apartment and stowed his bag out of sight behind the privacy screen. Setting up his laptop at her table, again he reviewed the file she'd created, searching for a lead among the pictures and messages the stalker had sent. Not one similar angle, not even in the park. It was as if the creep had tagged along through her daily routine, completely invisible. He read and reread the line that Julia's assignment to the Falk case wasn't yet public knowledge.

Mitch got up to pace, but her apartment wasn't big enough to make it worthwhile. He made a cup of coffee and drank it down as he studied the one picture she'd captured yesterday. It wasn't any more enlightening today than it had been last night.

Every time he looked through the information, he came up with more questions than potential answers. Who was close enough to Julia and the car-theft ring? Searching for those connections meant digging into her life, which he suspected would go over like a lead balloon if he did that without her. There had to be something he could do.

He sent her a text message to check in and got an immediate positive reply, which eased the tension building in his neck and shoulders. With two hours until her lunch break, Mitch headed out for a walk. Her stalker knew the area and Mitch needed to get equally familiar with her typical routes and favorite places in the neighborhood. He needed to mitigate the stalker's advantage. Mentally he crossed his fingers her stalker would be bold enough to wear the same orange hockey team cap today.

He left her building and walked the route she took every day to her office, passing her gym and her bank.

With the pictures on his phone, he took in the various sight lines and angles. Where had the bastard been hiding?

By the time he'd walked the circumference of the park where she normally ate lunch, he realized just how easy it would be to target her or anyone else. The foot traffic and tourists that made her feel safe gave her stalker similar cover.

Taking a seat on a bench where he guessed the stalker had been watching for her, he used his phone to poke into the key players and time line on Marburg's current big-ticket case. At first glance, it seemed obvious the stalker was all about the case, with his demands for names and cooperation. But what if Julia was the real goal? Maybe the creep had a fixation with sexy female defense attorneys on high-profile cases.

Mitch wasn't a cop, but he felt the theory deserved an examination. As he put the text messages and pictures up against the case time line and growing pile of dead witnesses against the perps at the center of the criminal activity, he wound up agreeing with Grant and Julia.

Her stalker was dialed in to the legal issues, determined to have an inside informant on the Falk case. Why?

The criminals organizing the car-theft ring had plagued the city for nearly three years. More than stealing prime cars, it was generally believed that newer recruits committed robberies, arson, battery and even murder against competitors or hapless citizens to move up the ranks.

Only the recent bust at the docks three months ago had restored a measure of peace. The cops had wrangled a number of wannabes and hit the jackpot when they caught a man they were sure was one of the masterminds of the system.

Naturally, Mitch was more familiar with the suspected arsons linked to the operation. They'd been nasty and, in addition to a terrible fatality, at least two fires had been used to divert emergency resources from a bigger crime discovered later. He reviewed pictures of those scenes on news websites, searching for anyone who could be a match to the guy she had spotted yesterday, but there was no distinguishing feature to make a legitimate connection.

Marburg, with all their clout, must have been on retainer, considering how quickly they negotiated the deal for Falk to await trial in a safe house rather than a jail cell. As grumpy as the Philadelphia PD had been about relinquishing jurisdiction, Mitch thought it was a good thing the FBI was in charge of keeping Falk alive to testify against his partners.

How had the stalker learned Julia had been added to the case before it hit public record? It couldn't have been a lucky guess. As she'd said, Marburg was full of eager associates eligible for the choice opportunity extended to Julia. Was her office really as safe as she thought? Could the stalker have an informant inside the firm who hadn't gotten on the case as expected?

Mitch pushed to his feet and started up the block, doing his best to walk when everything inside him wanted to run. He had to get to her. Right now. Pulling out his phone, he sent her another text as he rounded the corner. She'd appreciate the fair warning.

When she entered the lobby, those high heels snapping against the marble with every stride, he gave himself a moment to soak up the gorgeous view before she got close enough to be offended. Her suit jacket was gone, and the sleek short-sleeved dress skimmed over her curves. Chin up, she projected an unshakable confidence as she advanced. Knowing what she'd endured in the past twenty-four hours, he was more impressed with her than ever.

Her closed expression, those auburn eyebrows raised in an arrogant arch, didn't give off the appreciation he was expecting. "This is a surprise," she said.

Her voice, pleasant enough, contrasted with the chilly reception in her green gaze. "A nice one, I hope," he replied, listing only his first initial and last name in the register. "Can you get away for a quick lunch?"

The older man at the desk waggled bushy white eyebrows at Julia. "How about an introduction, young lady?"

"Of course," she said. Her mouth lifted into a patently false smile. "Arthur, this is Mitch. He's a—" she paused as Arthur's eyebrows bobbed up and down again "—potential client."

"Nice to meet you." Arthur stuck out his hand and Mitch gave it a firm shake. "You couldn't ask for a better attorney to have on your side. You two stay out of trouble."

Too late for that, Mitch thought. "Yes, sir."

"Come on up," Julia urged him, backing toward the elevators. "I'll give you a tour before we go."

"Great. Thanks." Still concerned about her safety here, he needed to learn the building layout and the places she frequented. The building wasn't as stuffy as expected, thanks to the soaring three-story galleries above. They passed a coffee stand, what appeared to be a cafeteria in one corner, and two smaller business offices.

When they were alone in the elevator, heading up to

her floor, she turned to him, her face pale. "Is he here? You said you wouldn't come inside unless—"

"Oh. No." Crap. Afraid of letting her down, he'd allowed his nerves to get the better of him. "That's not it. I'm sorry." He took her hands and gave them a squeeze, just as the doors parted on her floor. No chance the receptionist missed it. Her eyes were dancing with curiosity on the other side of the glass doors as they approached.

"I'm heading to lunch, Bethany," Julia said, breezing by the reception desk, with a tip of her head in his direction. "Potential client."

"I'll make a note," the receptionist replied.

"You lie as easy as breathing," Mitch murmured, impressed.

"I'll take that as a compliment," she replied, an edge to her voice. She unlocked the bin over her desk and pulled out her purse. "Let's go." She led him down the stairs and out a side door, apparently determined to avoid any further introductions or encounters.

He took her hand in his the moment they reached the street.

She looked down, trying to tug it free. "What are you doing?"

"Playing my part." He gave her an encouraging smile.

"Boyfriend?" Her green eyes turned sharp. "This wasn't our agreement." She stopped talking as they waited at the corner for the crossing signal. "I just introduced you as a client."

When they were moving again, she launched into all the reasons his showing up made things worse. He followed most of the lingo she tossed out in place of any solid reasons against his approach.

When they turned the corner, he raised their joined

hands to his lips for a quick kiss. "Relax, Julia. It's temporary." They strolled on toward her favorite lunch spot and he led her to the line for a food truck. "I won't be around long enough for the partners to bark at you about having a social life."

His promise didn't seem to ease any of the tension simmering in her body, but she stopped fighting against their joined hands. He studied her as the line advanced. "I came to the office for two reasons."

"Yes?"

He started with the easier reason. "I'd like to look a little deeper into your background. I didn't want to start without your permission."

She leaned back, peering up at him with laser-focused intensity. "My background is irrelevant. This is connected to work."

So much for easy. "Hardly irrelevant. What sounds good to you?" he asked, his attention on the menu.

She made her selection and he placed the order when it was their turn, handing over cash before she could pull her wallet out of her purse.

"What do you think you're doing?"

"Picking up lunch? Your accounts are still frozen, right?"

She gave him a brusque nod. "I'll pay you back as soon as this is sorted out."

"You're welcome," he teased.

Her eyes went wide as they stepped aside to wait for the food. "This isn't a game. And thank you." She smoothed a hand over her hair. She'd gathered all that gorgeous hair up in a glossy clip, exposing the long column of her neck, but the breeze was teasing a few strands free. "Why are you really here?"

"I'm creating a buffer for you," he replied, sticking closer than a polite client would. He hovered enough to give the impression he was enamored with the new woman in his life, while trying not to irritate her with too much physical contact. He wondered if she held everyone at arm's length or just him. His money was on everyone.

"Oh." Her lips made a perfect, rosy circle. "The camera at my building. Did you see who left me that note?"

He wished he could give her a better answer. "No," he admitted, regretting it as the little surge of hope drained from her face. Worse, she started scanning the people milling about the park. "Searching for a certain orange cap?"

"Aren't you?"

"No. I'm not useless to you. I know you wanted a different answer, but we'll get there." That brought the full force of her attention back to him. He liked it a little too much. "Your doorman and I didn't make much progress on that front *yet*," he emphasized. "But I spent the rest of the morning reviewing Falk's arrest and events leading to it. Which is why I surprised you at the office. Again, I apologize."

She waved it off. "I'm over it. Do you have a lead?"

His explanation was delayed by the food pickup and their brief search for a spot to eat. He could tell she felt exposed, but he figured his presence as an unexpected boyfriend would be enough to have her stalker reassessing the situation if he was out there watching.

When they were settled on a bench under a tree, he waited until she'd eaten some of her sandwich before he began. "Falk's gang or followers or whatever you'd call them are suspected of a few arsons around the city in recent years."

She nodded, her gaze sweeping across the people moving around them.

"None of those left enough evidence to prosecute a particular individual."

"Which is related to my stalker how?"

"I'm a curious guy," he replied. "After the *momentary* dead end in the mail room, I went looking for a better lead." He decided not to mention his trek home for his clothes and his computer.

She blotted the sauce from her lips with a napkin, bringing his attention to her very kissable mouth. "Start making the connections. Please."

Stay on point. It was his turn to scan the park. He didn't spot anyone with an orange cap, but he felt as if they were being watched. A small measure of paranoia was to be expected, he supposed. "People take pictures at fires. Arson investigators gather them up when they can, hoping to find the firebug. That was my approach, comparing the media shots of fires suspected of being connected to Falk's organization with the picture you caught yesterday, but it didn't pan out."

"I know it's a lousy picture." She shifted on the bench, crossed her ankles and tugged the rising hem of her skirt over her knees. "None of this explains why you barged into the office."

Her unrelenting green gaze made him sympathize with any witness or client who landed on her bad side. She must be hell in a courtroom. Mitch swallowed, bracing for the worst. "Who did you share the news with when you were added to the case?"

She froze, her sandwich halfway to her mouth. Slowly she lowered the food to her lap and pulled the wrapper around what was left. "N-no one."

"Come on, being assigned to the Falk case is a big deal. Your mom?"

Her teeth sank into that rosy lower lip for a split second. "No. We're not close."

"What about your friend Aubrey?"

She shook her head. "It's not the kind of thing you share," she said.

That startled him. Clearly he didn't understand lawyers at all. She'd said it was a career-making assignment—wouldn't she celebrate it? "Why not? Some confidentiality thing?"

"Sometimes," she allowed. "In this situation, I was thrilled, but it's a very public case and most people don't want to see Falk get acquitted. Plenty of my peers in the office would rather take my place than pat me on the back."

"Okay." He obviously didn't know how to think like a defense attorney. "Does it bug you that your stalker knew you had the assignment even though it's not public knowledge?"

"Of course."

"Me too. I think it's an important clue."

"You think the stalker works at Marburg?" She pressed her fingers to her lips. "Am I safe at the office?" she asked behind her hand.

Hearing her voice, thin and frightened, pissed him off and his self-control started to unravel. When he found her stalker, he'd wring the bastard's neck. His free hand flexed and fisted. Bullying a woman was a coward's game. Mitch put his arm around her shoulder, wishing he could make this go away with a snap of his fingers. "That very concern is what had me barging in and scaring you. Let's do hourly check-in texts. I want you to let me know the minute anything makes you nervous."

"All right. Though now I'll probably be jumping at every shadow."

"No problem since I'll be close by. My earlier over-reaction aside, I think you are safe there," he said. Un-wrapping the cookie that came with his meal, he offered half to her. "None of the pictures were from inside. I think if he had that card to play, he would have done it."

"That's something, I guess."

"Eat up and I'll walk you back."

He downed his half of the cookie while she nibbled around the edges, watching people go by. He could al-most see the wheels turning in her head. "Do you think your stalker holds the kind of clout to pull strings and get you specifically assigned to the case?" He felt ter-rible that the question made her tremble just as she'd started to relax.

"Choosing me makes no sense." She jerked back, put-ting a little more distance between them. "Anyone with real clout would ask for someone more important or more informed. All I know about Falk came from media re-ports and the case files I've been allowed to see."

"Anything sensitive?"

She glared at him, refusing to answer. "Why would anyone believe I'd cave to this kind of intimidation?"

He preferred the defiance in her eyes. "Every con-tact so far implies the stalker intends to use you as an inside source."

"Yeah, I got that loud and clear." She pursed her lips. "We both know I can't do what he wants. What hap-pens then?"

"We'll burn that bridge *if* we get there." Somehow

he'd make sure the stalker didn't push things that far. "You won't have to face that dilemma."

"*Hmm.* Your confidence is impressive, Mr. Galway."

He shot her a grin. "Hopefully it's contagious, too, Miss Cooper. Take all you want."

She smiled, genuinely amused despite the lingering worry shadowing her green eyes. "Thanks."

As they walked back, she slid her hand into his. That expression of budding trust slipped over him, made him feel ten feet tall and invincible. This wasn't the first time he'd made a promise with no foolproof plan for how to back it up.

He wouldn't let this be the first time he let someone down.

With his hockey team ball cap turned backward today, Leo Falk watched Miss Cooper exit the Marburg offices with a man he didn't recognize. They looked cozy heading down the same route she'd used on every clear day for her lunch break. In another deviation from her regimented schedule, today they stopped at a food truck. Watching the new guy pay the bill, he gave her credit for finding someone to ease the bite of the cash flow crisis he'd created.

He'd followed her for two weeks straight before deciding the young associate could expedite his plans and assist in his brother's acquittal. She'd proved to be more work than play, keeping her nose to the grindstone at Marburg except for short jaunts to the park for lunch and three visits each week to her health club. She lived alone, didn't have regular contact with family by mail, phone or email, and, until now, her social life had been limited to only two obvious friends, both from the law office.

He'd assumed the trek to the nightclub last night had been an effort to blow off steam after he'd seized control of her finances and convinced her to cooperate. The idea that his careful investigation of her life had missed a detail as big as a boyfriend troubled him. He preferred to view this as some demonstration of her resourcefulness.

How unfortunate for her if this new man turned out to be someone significant, someone she cared for. He'd chosen Julia because her loner tendencies and lack of a support network worked to his advantage. His plans to help his brother beat the multitude of criminal charges could work regardless, but her isolation had been a distinct benefit to their unified cause.

Now, when he was ready to advance, he had to pause and reassess the angles and potential pitfalls of his plan.

He used his phone to snap a few pictures of them in the park before moving along to find a better vantage point for their return to Marburg. When they walked into his view, he used his camera and telephoto lens to get better close-ups for his investigator's benefit. They needed to know everything about this man as soon as possible.

Who is your new friend, Miss Cooper? Leo's thumb hovered over the send button for a long moment. Rethinking his approach, he deleted the text.

No sense wasting a move too early in this game. He'd wait until he understood what sort of player she'd added to the board.

Chapter 4

The conversation with Mitch prickled at the back of Julia's neck throughout the afternoon. The notion that she'd been chosen because of something other than her skill and dedication to the law rocked her confidence. The stalker might not be in the building, but why did he believe she was weak enough to be manipulated?

It worried her that she was missing a critical connection. She reviewed every name associated with the case from petty thieves all the way up to Falk himself, including the missing and dead witnesses. She couldn't find a point where she'd crossed paths with any of them. What did the stalker expect her to share?

To and from lunch she'd seen flashes of orange everywhere and yet no one she could point to as her stalker. It felt as if the whole world had decided to support the hockey team today and the season hadn't started yet.

Though she knew it was a symptom of her fear, the feeling that she was being watched followed her through the building. As much as she wanted to, she couldn't shake the image of someone lurking in the shadows, right here in the firm, ready to spring a trap. Her solution to any vulnerability was to face it head-on and power through, but this time there wasn't a target.

The stalker's silence continued throughout the day. Contrary to all logic, the lack of more threats or direct demands put her on edge. The only alerts on her phone were the check-in messages from Mitch and teasing inquiries about her new "client" from Bethany, the receptionist on her floor.

When summoned by a call from her boss, she sent Mitch a text message and then silenced her phone as she headed upstairs to join the rest of the defense team in the conference room for a status update. Being new to the case, she only had to sit and listen.

And pray no names were mentioned.

Every minute of the meeting was an ordeal. Two days ago, this glass-enclosed space had felt like a pinnacle of achievement. Today it felt as if she were in a fishbowl, exposed and vulnerable to anyone who cared to look in this direction.

After an exhausting hour hiding her personal distress, a wave of relief left her shaky when her prayers were answered. The team had discussed strategy rather than plea deals or the names of people Falk might turn on to gain favor with the prosecutor.

Moving along with the others as they left the meeting, Julia felt a heavy hand land on her shoulder. Panicked, she spun around, raising her elbow. The reflexive strike landed on the chest of her boss, Eddie Haywood.

Recognizing him and realizing there was no danger, her hands came up in surrender this time.

Stalker or not, this was inexcusable. "Sorry," she murmured into the stunned hush.

"Easy there, Cooper," Haywood said. "You okay?"

"Yes. My apologies." She was a mess. "I was distracted." The rumors about why she'd strike her boss were probably flying through the firm already. At least she'd have something to talk about with Mitch tonight. They could debate whether today had turned out worse than yesterday.

"Distracted?" He stared down the severe angle of his nose at her. His lips spread into a cold, toothy smile. "My office, please."

Miserable, she trailed after him, silently cursing the stalker who'd made her too jumpy to function normally. Getting kicked off the case or suspended wouldn't fix anything. Julia didn't believe the stalker could really hurt Aubrey or her mother, but she couldn't imagine any explanation that would convince the man who'd upended her life.

When she saw Mitch again, she'd be sure to tell him confidence was *not* contagious. She trusted Haywood and had learned a great deal from him, including his zero-tolerance policy for weak links on big cases.

"Close the door," Haywood instructed, rounding his desk. He dropped the thick file he'd carried from the meeting onto the glossy desktop. Hands on his hips, he gave her a long study. "I'd say the gym membership is paying off." He rubbed the spot where she'd planted her elbow. "What's going on with you?"

"I'm not sure what you mean." She wouldn't volunteer anything. Though he'd added her to the case, he couldn't be her stalker. He had full access to the case and more access than she did to Falk.

One dark eyebrow arched as the other dipped low. "You were quiet in the meeting. I recommended you for this case because you aren't afraid to speak up like the rest of our chicken-liver new hires."

"Thank you?" As compliments went, she'd received better.

"Sit down." He settled his lanky frame into his over-size executive chair after she sat. The proof of his power and her debt to him was stamped all over his body language.

"Well?" he demanded. "Have you made any progress on the research I gave you?"

"I've been working on it."

"No excuses, Cooper. We need to get some of this evidence tossed out."

"Yes, sir." She nodded. Her hands in her lap, she forced herself to keep her gaze on his. She might not have the results he wanted yet, but she couldn't let him cow her. Although she'd sought help from Escape, she had to draw the line and stand on her own two feet at every opportunity.

She would *not* let this stalker change her entire way of interacting with the world. Who was she kidding? She'd just thrown an elbow at her boss in the hallway. Such a blatant mistake, fueled by ridiculous paranoia, could undermine everything she'd done to land on her feet at Marburg. She needed to keep her head on straight until they identified the man behind the threats.

"You're feeling restless?" Haywood queried. "Having second thoughts representing a man like Falk?"

"I'm fine," she lied. "I believe Mr. Falk deserves the

best possible defense and he has it with us." It was the only truth she could offer convincingly.

"I don't think so." He leaned back, those sharp eyes raking over her, waiting for her to crack. "I've watched you, Julia. From the first day you joined us as an intern. I know you."

What? She pressed her knees together to hide the fear surging through her and waited him out.

"You've never left work behind in favor of clubbing." Haywood reached for his cell phone.

"I beg your pardon?"

"Consider this a warning about your erratic behavior. A case like this is the worst time to pick up a 'distraction'—" he put the word in air quotes "—like a boyfriend."

A dozen protests came to mind, along with a few demands as to how he knew where she'd gone and with whom last night. "You're having me followed?" Had the stalker stunt been a test or hazing tradition? She didn't know whether to feel relieved or appalled. Should she file a formal complaint or laugh it off as paying her dues?

Haywood sneered at her suggestion. "God, no. I have better things to do with my time and resources, Cooper." He pushed his cell phone across the desk toward her. "Take a look. A friend sent me this just before the meeting."

There she was, sitting at the bar at Escape, moments before Mitch put the glass of water in front of her. She couldn't recall a single friend she and Haywood had in common. Either her boss was lying about the source or the stalker was somehow dragging him into this mess. Nothing on the picture showed the sender's information. Asking for details would make her sound defensive and lend weight to his accusation that she was slacking off.

"I was verifying a witness statement," she improvised. "On another case."

"That's the Cooper I know. Always overachieving." Haywood's smile warmed a fraction. "One of your best traits," he added, retrieving his phone. "Drop the other case. Push it off on someone else. The Falk case is your only priority until I say otherwise. Am I clear?"

"Yes, sir."

"Good. There are no small jobs on this one. It's going to take every last one of us to get Falk acquitted." He jerked his chin to the door. "Get to it."

"Yes, sir." She could practically hear the whiz of the bullet she'd just dodged passing by her head. "Thank you for—"

"Thank me by doing the job."

Dismissed, she retreated to the relative safety of her cubicle. As furious with herself as she was with the stalker who'd made her so jumpy, she sent a text message to Mitch.

Working late. Dig up whatever you need, just find the jerk.

If she was going to be stuck at the office for most of the night, there was no reason to hold Mitch back from his own research. There had to be a reason, some connection she'd overlooked, that made her a target. Although she didn't want a decent guy like Mitch uprooting her grimy past, it couldn't be helped. The sooner they identified the man hassling her, the sooner they'd know how to deal with it.

She wasn't going to sit back and let a stranger wreck her career.

Okay. Check in hourly.

She smiled at Mitch's reply. Seemed she was taking orders on all fronts today. She set a timer on her phone so she wouldn't forget and then applied her substantial focus to the Falk case.

Marburg attorneys were famous for putting the client above all else. The firm's core philosophy had been exactly what she'd wanted, what she'd needed after graduating law school. Career was the best, most acceptable reason to put the skeletons of her personal life to the back burner.

The hours flashed by, afternoon giving way to evening and then a late night, marked by the exchange of all-is-well text messages with Mitch. At ten thirty, Mitch's response changed.

Bring the work with you, but I'm picking you up in fifteen minutes at the front door. Wait inside until you see me at the curb.

She dug her fingers into the dull ache in her neck and decided he had a point. Haywood wanted Falk to be her sole focus. The stalker was connected to the case, so she could work on both fronts in good conscience. Gathering up what she needed, she packed her purse and laptop bag to bursting before she powered off her desktop computer.

She didn't have long to wait for Mitch to arrive. The beefy engine purred as the restored beauty glided to a stop, and she felt a happy zing in her pulse. Probably not a smart reaction, but after the past two days, she needed the boost of cheer.

He came around and opened the passenger door for her. "Your chariot."

She laughed, giving him style points for the light-hearted theatrics. "Thanks." Her stomach rumbled loud enough for him to hear when he slid behind the steering wheel and buckled his seat belt.

"You didn't eat?"

"Crackers and a cup of coffee around seven," she admitted.

His brow wrinkled in concern. "The Escape will have food."

"No." She thought of the picture on her boss's phone. "Thanks, but no. Just drop me at the apartment. I got reprimanded for going clubbing last night."

"You didn't go clubbing," he countered, driving farther away from her building. "Who reprimanded you? What are you talking about?"

Reluctantly, she filled him in on the elbow strike and the meeting that followed.

"You should have told me."

She laced her fingers, keeping her gaze on the view through the windshield. "It was a bit much for a text message and I could hardly discuss this on the phone."

"Fine." He flexed his hand around the gearshift, knuckles white. "All the more reason to check in with Grant," Mitch said. "I've bumped into a couple of things outside my expertise."

"Fires and cars, by your own admission, are your expertise."

"And you now." His smile flashed. "Thanks for letting me pull back that veil."

"Was that meant to be comforting?" She shifted in the seat, wishing she could ditch the suit and heels and crawl into her sweats to relax. "If so, it failed." The comment left an icy ball of dread in her stomach. It didn't matter that he had valid reasons. She didn't want a stranger poking at the past she'd worked hard to leave behind. The law firm was different. Being her dream job, Marburg had a right to make sure she wouldn't be an embarrassment by accident or design. Would the stalker ruin that before she had a chance to show her real value?

"Hang on." He reached over and gave her hand a quick squeeze. "I'm here to help, not judge you. This guy is intent on the case. I think you're just a pawn."

"Stop. Just stop talking." She choked back a bitter laugh. "You're making me feel worse."

"Well, in your shoes I wouldn't like a stranger poking through my life."

"Or sleeping on your floor?"

"Probably not that, either," he admitted with another grin. He found a space in Escape's employee lot and parked the car. Swiveling to face her, the sincerity in his brown eyes was unmistakable. "I want you to know I searched from law school forward, not backward, Julia. No sense digging up crap that's irrelevant."

She nodded. "Thanks," she said, gratitude clogging her throat. There were mistakes in law school, but none quite as grim as her childhood. She wanted to avoid stirring up the old pain of cutting herself free of her dysfunctional past. Although her mother never believed it, Julia did care. "Why are we here?"

He leaned against the car door, concern evident in his eyes. "Let me just say it once, okay?"

She didn't like the sound of that, but he exited the car before she could say so. Like last night, he draped his arm around her shoulders, giving her shelter from the colder air out here near the river. "I'm wearing a perfectly good coat," she reminded him.

"And my arm is even better." He gave her an unrepentant wink as he opened the back door to the club. "We have time to grab something hearty while we wait for Grant."

The late hour and the savory scents smothered any further argument she might have mustered. After a quick exchange with one of the cooks, Mitch had her seated out of the way at a prep counter, a steaming bowl of French onion soup in front of her. It smelled divine.

"Dig in. Leftover from lunch service. Want a salad?"

"No, thanks." A sudden wave of shyness chased through her. "This is great." The man was a force of nature and she either she was too weary or too foolish to put up any appropriate resistance.

It had been years since anyone had cared enough to feed her. She'd dated since coming to Philly, or rather she'd gone out with groups occasionally. None of those experiences made her feel as if her welfare mattered. It must be something in Mitch's community values as a firefighter, some innate gene for compassion and kindness.

She slid a look at him and gave him a bright smile to cover her sudden sadness. In her world, cold and ruthless were the right strengths to cultivate for success. They were people at absolute opposite ends of the spectrum.

Mitch kept an eye on Julia while she ate the soup. The lack of color in her cheeks and the worry in her green eyes made the situation more challenging. He had no experience as a private investigator and had only pulled a

few shifts as extra security when his cousin, in charge
of staffing big events like concerts and hockey games,
needed the manpower.

Being a buffer for Julia was completely different and
it made him uncomfortable that he didn't really know
what he was doing. True, it kept his mind off his problems, but that wouldn't help her if he screwed up. As he
ate, he reviewed the best options for delivering the update to Grant. It would be a hell of a lot easier if he had
a real lead to share with them.

The back door slammed open with a bang and Julia
practically leaped off the stool.

"Easy," he said. Under the counter, he bumped her
knee with his. He must not be doing a very good job if
her anxiety was increasing with him around. "Would you
rather listen to the band while I fill in Grant?"

"No. I should be there."

"Should be there—or shouldn't be seen out partying?"

"Both," she said, her voice firm and her eyes clear as
she met his gaze. "Don't try and shut me out."

"Wouldn't dream of it," he replied.

"Please." She rolled her eyes. "You're a guy."

"No kidding?" He didn't take the bait. His sisters had
taught him not to argue about the general faults of being
a guy. "You could wait back here and have more to eat."

"That picture sent to Haywood was no coincidence,"
she said, eyeing the people moving through the kitchen.
"He told me it came in just before the meeting."

Not long after they'd had lunch together in the park.
Mitch suppressed an ugly oath.

"It has to be from the stalker."

"I agree." The bastard was making her afraid of everything. He didn't dare speculate how things might

change now that Mitch was in the picture. He was about to suggest they shake things up even more when Grant caught his attention from the kitchen doorway and motioned for them to come to the office.

Mitch gave her an encouraging smile, hoping it hid the worry he felt. "Come on. Grant might have some better suggestions."

Julia kicked things off, explaining the note and the significance of the names listed. While Grant mulled that over, Mitch told him about meeting with the doorman and the complete lack of any helpful video from the building security system. Julia and Mitch both confirmed they had yet to find so much as a frayed thread tying her to anyone involved with the Falk operation.

"Last but not least," Julia added at Mitch's encouragement, "after lunch today, someone sent my boss a picture of me here, shortly after I arrived last night."

Grant fixed his perceptive brown gaze on her, his bushy eyebrows flexing into a frown. "How can you be so sure of the timing?"

"The picture shows I didn't have the glass of water yet."

"Not good," Grant allowed. "You didn't mention your plans to a friend?"

"I wish I had," she replied. "Somehow intercepting a communication is easier to swallow than the concept of some stranger correctly guessing my decisions."

Her weary expression pissed off Mitch more and he swore under his breath. "The guy must have a network at his disposal."

"Considering the swift responses, I'd say you're right," Grant said. "I'll ask around about any loose ends from

Falk's organization." He turned to Julia. "What would you like to do? What's your ideal outcome?"

"Expose him," she replied. "Ideally, we protect the case and I keep my job." She linked her hands in her lap until her knuckles turned white. "He didn't make any contact with me today."

"No, today was an indirect hit," Grant said.

"Yes. I assume that picture was supposed to make me feel like a trapped mouse. As if all his other tactics haven't been annoying enough."

"Did those annoyances make you want to help him?"

"No." Those auburn eyebrows arched high. "They make me want to rip him to shreds," she said. "I want my life back."

"We'll get there," Grant assured her. "It may take some time. I'll have my team scour our security feeds for any clues."

Mitch stood up, antsy with his lack of progress. "I'm at a loss." Mitch hated admitting it in front of Julia, but she deserved to know. "Tracking down who left the note or who snapped that picture last night won't get us anywhere. We need to know who's calling the shots. I've done some digging." He caught Julia's wince. "I can't figure out why she's the target."

"We'll get there," Grant repeated in that steady, deep way he had.

The knot in Mitch's stomach loosened. It was far too soon to worry that his inadequacies would let her down.

"Who might have been selected to the defense team other than you?" Grant asked. "Maybe the clue to the stalker rests with who wasn't chosen."

"A number of new associates were eligible." Closing her eyes a moment, she rubbed at her temples. "I do know one of the associates was passed over because his brother was part of the squad that arrested Falk. Other than that…" Her voice trailed off and she spread her hands in a helpless gesture. "Your guess is as good as mine."

"Then we wait and see," Grant said. "Is there a trial date set?"

"Not yet."

"Any talk of a plea deal?"

She shook her head, and for a moment Mitch was distracted by the soft wisps of hair that had escaped her clip swaying against her neck.

Grant frowned. "I sent the picture you took to a friend and there weren't enough markers to make it worthwhile for facial recognition."

"I'll get a better picture when he shows his face again," Mitch vowed. The stalker had taken an indirect shot today, but he still had the advantage.

"Stick to your routine, Julia," Grant suggested. "And you—" he pointed at Mitch "—become a very obvious part of that routine."

"You okay with that?" Mitch asked Julia.

She shrugged a shoulder. "I have to be."

Hardly a glowing affirmation, though he didn't blame her. He should tell her he admired that spark of determination in her eyes, that fortitude that kept her going despite the fear plaguing her.

"Keep me informed," Grant said, interrupting Mitch's thoughts. "I'm here for both of you."

When they were back in his car, he started it and kicked the heater up a notch. The autumn night had turned chilly, offering a preview of the winter to come.

"Can you drive for a bit, please?" she asked when he pulled out of the lot.

"Sure. Any particular destination?"

"No. I'm just not ready to go home."

He couldn't blame her. Not only did she have him as an unwelcome houseguest, but it had to be tough knowing the jerk stalking her had been so close.

While he took the expressway across town, he weighed his options. He'd grown up here and, learning that she'd only moved here to attend law school at Temple, he wanted to show her something special. At nearly midnight, he left the expressway and headed for Boathouse Row.

She smiled when he pulled over, parking in a space that overlooked the Schuylkill River. On the other side of the river Boathouse Row shimmered with white lights edging each architectural detail.

"How beautiful," she said, a hitch in her breath. "Thank you."

"You've never been here?"

"No."

Feeling a ridiculous amount of pride, he climbed out and came around to open her car door. "You need the full experience," he said. He zipped up his jacket and pulled her coat snug around her, turning up the collar against the night air. "Wait here."

He pulled the blanket out of the emergency kit in the trunk and spread it across the hood of the car. "Up you go."

"Won't it dent the hood?"

He shrugged. "I can always pop it out again." He gave her a boost and then wrapped the blanket around her legs before he took a seat beside her, leaning back against the windshield.

"It's lovely, Mitch." She tipped her face up to the dark sky, a smile teasing her lips.

He savored the peacefulness of the view and the woman for several long minutes. "I come out here when I need to clear my head."

She reached over and patted his hand. "Thank you."

"You're welcome." He'd come here for her, but also for himself. Out here he was able to confirm his instincts that they had been watched today in the park. Grant had told them to stick with the routine, but Mitch instinctively wanted to get her away from the danger zone.

"How many lawyers will Marburg add to the team?" he asked.

"As many as they need," she replied absently. "I'm not being intentionally vague, that's just how it goes. Marburg is involved personally, of course, but his focus is managing media and publicity." She sighed. "The rest of the team will do research and develop arguments that improve Falk's chance of being acquitted."

"And you're okay with that?" Why would she eagerly defend one of the biggest criminals in the city?

She turned her head, gazing down the river toward the city center. "That's how our legal system works. Everyone deserves a solid defense."

He'd been through her transcripts, picked apart her life in law school and couldn't see what had pushed her toward criminal defense. "But—"

"Can you judge me another night?"

"I'm not judging you," he countered. He didn't want

to ruin a pleasant moment. "I'm trying to understand your stalker."

"Right. You're trying to understand my motives."

Mitch bit back the urge to argue with her. He didn't expect her to believe him. This wasn't easy on either one of them, though she wouldn't believe that either. "I've got a union rep defending me," he blurted. Once the words were out, he decided maybe his problem would be a distraction for her, like her situation was for him.

"According to your explanation of the incident, you won't need a strong-arm firm like Marburg."

He chuckled. "Not even if I could afford it."

She shifted a few inches closer, her covered legs bumping his, and faced him. "So what's bugging you about your situation?"

"It leaves a mark, official or not."

"You're worried about how others will look at you when you're back on the job."

He'd assumed, tough as she was, that she wouldn't understand. "It's a small world, y'know?" He laced his fingers behind his head to keep his hands from reaching for her. They barely knew each other and she'd been clear she liked her personal space. "Eventually, I want to move up through the ranks, and this kind of thing is something they can point to as an excuse to turn me down for promotions."

"Even if you're cleared?" She sat up a little straighter. "That's not fair."

"That's life."

Her eyes narrowed. "Are you playing me?"

He gave her a long look. "Hell, no." The flood of honesty might be the dumbest thing he'd done since they'd met. "What good would that do?"

"I don't know, that's the problem. Are you taking this 'infiltrate my life' thing too personally and trying to create a bond or something?"

Would that be so bad? "I wasn't. I was talking about me." He stared out across the river. "It does bring up a valid question."

"What's that?"

"Why don't you want to like me?" He'd noticed her utter lack of a social life and he thought it had more to do with her past than her present career. It wasn't really his business and fewer people in her life meant fewer people who would ask about him hanging around.

"Take me home," she replied. "We're not friends. We're basically client and expert. Two people stuck in a new and apparently difficult situation."

Interesting. She resorted to the attorney lingo and unflappable courtroom voice when she got rattled. "We could be friends." He heard the words and knew that's what he wanted. To start with. He could list a dozen reasons why being friends was a good idea and probably a dozen more why distance was the wiser choice.

She slid off the hood to her feet, keeping the blanket wrapped around her. "I don't play well with others, Mitch. I'm a better person when I'm alone," she said.

The quiet words hung in the air, choking out what could have become a decent conversation. He wasn't buying it, but he wouldn't argue. Not yet. He'd been raised in a big noisy family that boasted the opposite philosophy. Mitch decided whatever the stalker's motives were, he wanted to learn what the hell had turned her into such a loner.

As they drove back to her place in silence, he told himself to let it go. Except she wasn't half the hard-nosed terror she thought she was or pretended to be. Under that tough-attorney exterior was a woman he wanted to get to know better.

A lot better.

Chapter 5

In the Marburg library, Julia rocked back in the task chair and stretched her arms over her head. She was exhausted. The words printed on the pages kept getting smaller and blurring into nonsense. A glance at the clock on the wall showed she'd been at it for over two hours since the last five-minute break she'd allowed herself. *Two full days in the library and only the rest of my life to go*, she thought bitterly. Precedents abounded for potential pretrial motions for the Falk case and her bosses expected her to present every possibility.

Seeking a respite, her thoughts drifted to Mitch. The way he'd infiltrated every corner of her personal space, it was tough not to think about him. He'd been camped out on her floor since that first night. Over the past days, she'd learned he could be awake and on full alert at the merest provocation, that he preferred free weights to machines at the gym and that he was itching to get back to the firehouse.

Mitch could cook, his coffee was better than hers, he rarely complained, he spoke fondly of his family and he maintained a solid, steady presence she often wanted to lean on. Having him around was simultaneously comforting and unsettling. She had to constantly remind herself it was temporary. Sticking with Grant's orders, they followed her pre-stalker routine to the letter, even through the weekend. They'd worked out a method of sorts and a division of space that almost kept them from tripping over each other in her small apartment. In short, he was an exemplary roommate.

Why don't you want to like me? His question echoed in her head, all these days later. She was far too willing to like him. What didn't make sense to her was his determination to like her. Most people didn't like her unless she could help them somehow.

If she could put a stop to her hot, needy dreams about him, she might feel less edgy and more willing to count him as a potential long-term friend. Certain parts of her body protested the friend concept, but Mitch was a great guy who deserved better than to be saddled with a troubled defense attorney. The more time they spent together and the more he revealed about his life and values made her increasingly aware that their only common ground was their determination to advance within their respective careers.

Since Mitch had entered her life last week, she hadn't heard a single demand out of her stalker. It would be easy, and naive, to think her personal bodyguard had scared him off, since the creep continued to block her attempts to regain control of her money. Her rent was due in a few days and she didn't have enough cash on hand to cover it. She'd gone into the bank branch to make a withdrawal only to find her accounts depleted. Embarrassed and infuriated, if Mitch hadn't been there she would have reached out to bargain with the stalker just to get it over with.

Her phone hummed in her pocket and she grinned at the midmorning check-in text from Mitch. She sent the all-clear reply and returned to the case work. While the computer databases set her in the right direction for her research, she always preferred to read directly from the source whenever possible. A habit from law school she hadn't broken yet.

After making another page of notes, she pushed away from the big table to go find another cup of coffee. She'd nearly pitched her phone through the window when the alarm sounded this morning, having spent the night tossing and turning in her bed, wishing she was bold enough to invite the handsome fireman to join her under the covers.

The outrageous and inappropriate attraction was taking its toll. Day after day she tried to chalk it up to proximity and failed. He was in her life to protect her and she didn't want to cross a line and make things uncomfortable…but then she'd catch him looking at her in a way that made her want to ask if she could climb all over that sculpted body.

Down, girl, she scolded herself as she filled her coffee mug. Her mother used men, discarding them when she finished, and Julia had vowed not to follow that poor example.

If they made it through the rest of this week without any new threats or demands, she would assume this had all been an elaborate robbery and the stalker had succeeded. The financial blow was harsh but not impossible to overcome. Bolstered by the fresh jolt of caffeine, she returned to her research.

Her concentration was terrible today, flipping between the case, her unresolved predicament and Mitch. Why had she been targeted as a potential informant? No one in town really knew her. She enjoyed the ability to be her best self, without the clouds of her past hanging over her. The first time her personal and professional lives had intersected had been the day Mitch had shown up to take her to lunch and everyone assumed he was more than a new client.

Whatever had put this in motion, however it ended, she wanted to find a meaningful way to thank Mitch for his help. With a guilty glance around the library, she changed the target of her searches again. When her next alarm went off, Julia gathered her personal belongings, bookmarking her research to resume after lunch with Mitch in the park.

She stepped outside to find the day had turned cloudy. Mitch saw her and jogged up the sidewalk, a smile on his face that seemed to brighten the entire street. A woman could get used to the focus and attention Mitch applied to every task. That sexy smile haunted her dreams, creating delusions that a man as good and decent as Mitch would truly want her for more than a little temporary fun. His button-down shirt was open over a dark T-shirt tucked into his jeans, and her palms tingled at the thought of sliding her hands under that soft fabric.

"Any contact?" he asked, greeting her with his habitual warm hug. He'd overruled her protests, claiming a hug was the bare minimum affection allowed for a new couple.

"No." She resisted the urge to cling as the masculine scent of his cologne surrounded her. Linking her hand with his as they strolled down the block, she refused to dwell on how natural it felt. She'd miss that when they went their separate ways. "I'm starting to think you scared him off."

"Not a chance," Mitch countered with a sly smile and a feisty glint in his brown eyes.

Her footsteps faltered, and he steadied her. "Did something happen?"

He shook his head. "I've got a feeling," he said, pressing his free hand over his stomach. "I think he's biding his time. Probably poking into me and why I've appeared in your life now."

The idea made her queasy. "That's ridiculous." Bravado would have to carry her until they had hard evidence on a real lead. "He must have found someone more malleable."

"Oh? Has he fixed the trouble he made with your finances?"

"No." And she had no idea how she'd pay her rent on time. She could hardly ask for an advance on her salary without causing more problems. The embarrassment of asking her landlord for an extension would be torture, but it might be the best option. "If he doesn't give me access to my money I won't be able to pay my rent," she confessed quietly. "I'm not sure what I'm going to do," she murmured.

"Keep going through the motions," Mitch replied.

She waited with him at the food truck and they walked together to their favorite bench. She pulled out the salad she'd packed at home while he doused the burrito he'd ordered with hot sauce. Normally she soaked up sunshine right here, refueling for the long afternoon and evening hours ahead. Today, low-hanging clouds gathered, underscoring the downturn her mood had taken.

"Does your lease allow you to sublet?"

"If I could, how would I find anyone in time?" She frowned at the salad in her bowl, poking through the greens. The conversation was ruining her appetite. "And why would I want to?"

"You're worried about your credit and keeping up appearances, right?"

"Mmm-hmm." She had enough to overcome at the firm, after throwing her reputation under the bus with the sudden appearance of a serious man in her life.

"You don't want to take this to your bosses."

"You know I *can't* do that." She glared at him. "Even without the now-silent stalker, I refuse to give them a reason to toss me off a career-boosting case or fire me. Either result is more likely than any show of compassion."

"I've been giving this some thought. What if you sublet your apartment to my brother and move in at my place. He can cover the rent, my house gives us both more space to work, and—bonus—throws your stalker pal a serious curveball."

The idea had merit. "You mean the stalker who's gone silent?"

He shrugged, his hands tucked into the pockets of his jacket.

"Playing house at your place?"

"We've been doing it at your place," he said. "Mine's bigger." His unrepentant grin put a flutter in her pulse. "Think about it."

Oh, she was thinking about it, reveling for a moment in the sweetness of the offer. She'd never lived in a house, only run-down apartments and dorm rooms. Making that move would be using Mitch to test an experience she didn't know she'd longed for. "Let's give it to the end of the week? Maybe he's been caught or really did give up on me when you showed up." It was a weak argument and they both knew it.

He nodded thoughtfully while he finished chewing a bite of his sandwich. "You're defeating your own argument," he said once he'd swallowed.

"How so?"

"By definition stalkers are patient and thorough, even if your creep came out of the gate too fast. If you kick me to the curb he wins just by waiting you out. It sends the message that my presence was just a stunt."

"It is," she said, reminding herself as much as him. She didn't like admitting it, didn't like thinking of them as performers, but that's what it came down to. She stabbed her fork through her salad. "You were assigned to be my buffer and all evidence proves you've been effective. I'd think you'd be happy to get your life back."

His shoulders hitched as he laughed. "Spare me the legalese." He balled up the burrito wrapper and stuffed it back into the paper bag. "Do you have your life back?"

"Not entirely." She'd give that to the end of the week, as well. If the stalker hadn't made another move, she'd file the fraud charges and a police report on the theft. It probably wouldn't get her money back, but she'd feel better. She'd worked her tail off to create a career and financial stability and here she was, scraping by on the generosity of strangers, just like her mom always did.

"Then it is way too soon to back off now." He leaned forward, elbows on his knees.

"Why are you so determined to keep this up? To stick

with me?" She'd been told all her life how difficult she was to live with. How regimented, unwilling to cut anyone slack. Her mother had said it, her brother too before he'd moved out. Even her first two roommates in college complained about living with her.

He faced her, a wistful half smile on his lips. "You need me."

Before she could respond, her phone screen lit up with a text message alert. Dread built in her throat when she recognized the number as her stalker's. When he told her to save his number, she'd thought he was being cocky, yet so far he had successfully dodged the efforts to trace the phone. "It's him." Her voice cracked. Guess she wasn't going to get a break and slip free of this jerk after all.

Mitch sat up casually, bumping her knee with his. "I'm scanning the park for any sign of him. You check the message."

She could barely manage a nod of agreement as she swiped the screen.

Noticed you found yourself a boyfriend with money. Seems decent enough. Which means he can't stop me.

A chill ran through her, raising the hair on the back of her neck. Keeping her voice low, she read the message to Mitch. "Should I reply?"

"Try asking for your money."

She typed in the words before she lost her nerve. Nice to hear from you. I want my money back today or I call the police.

No police, Julia. Your money is safe, even earning interest. Give me the names I need and it's all yours.

"I can't do that," she whispered as she typed the same in reply. Money first. If I'm evicted they'll fire me.

Then you'll have to cooperate with me. Remember who is in charge.

She showed the messages to Mitch. "I'm sorely tempted, but I don't have what he wants. How is it this creep knows everything but that?"

"What are you doing?" Mitch asked when she started keying in a new message.

"Suggesting he torment someone in the prosecutor's office. They know more about any plea deals Falk is planning than I ever will."

Mitch watched Julia hit Send on the message before he could advise her to stop and think about it. He swallowed back the worry, scanning the crowd for anyone showing signs of aggravation. Preferably some aggravated person wearing a hockey team ball cap. He spotted more than one man with eyes on his phone fitting the general description. No way to round up all of them. What would it take to make the stalker flinch? "Let's get you back to the office," he said to Julia as he stood up.

He wanted her back behind the safety of Marburg's granite walls and security systems.

Did her stalker have any idea how miserable Julia would be if anything happened to someone at the prosecutor's office? He prayed the jerk hadn't dug that deep into her past.

Over the past several days every conversation between them had shed a little more light on the real woman hiding behind the lawyer's stoic face, classy wardrobe and mile-high defenses keeping the world far from her tender, battered heart. She'd be furious if she knew he'd decided to go back further, searching for any clue to her present trouble.

Her childhood had been less than ideal—a vast understatement—the things she must have seen and survived made his heart ache for that little girl with no control or guidance. She'd grown up in the Midwest and been between foster homes when her mom wasn't considered a fit parent. He had yet to find any sign of her father. Despite the pile of disadvantages, Julia had single-handedly broken free and made her way through college and law school, landing at the top of the heap at Marburg.

For days he'd wanted to tell her how much her courage and grit impressed him. He wanted to hold her and make up for all the affection she'd missed growing up. Not yet. If he moved too soon, she'd boot him out of her life. Every day he told himself to wait a little longer, to wait until she made the first move.

"I'll pick you up at seven," he said when they reached her building.

"Why don't I call you when I'm ready?"

Because every moment she was out of his sight was more unbearable than the last. With the stalker in play again he refused to take chances. "Are you going in there to get names and cooperate with him?"

She leaned back as if he'd sprouted a second head. "Of course not."

"Then I'll pick you up at seven. I have a shift at Escape tonight."

"And I have a career on the line," she shot back. "I'll order delivery and work through. You can pick me up after your shift."

He shook his head. "We can't keep going on this way."

"What?" She tilted her head and opened her mouth, then clamped her lips shut. "I'm edgy," she admitted with obvious reluctance. "What have I missed?"

She'd missed the part where he was caring about her as far more than a client. He was into every part of her routine and it should've been weird. Instead, he was increasingly content with the situation, despite the risky reasons behind their association.

Association? He almost laughed. Her world, her scent, her patterns were seeping into his clothing, his skin, going deeper into his heart. "You can work your caseload from Grant's office," he suggested. "Or just take a night off."

"I can't get caught partying at the club again."

"You didn't last time. Trust me."

"I do trust you." She stepped closer and lowered her voice. "I do, or you wouldn't be living with me."

He ran a hand over his hair to keep from touching hers. His extended stay at her small place was wearing on her. On him, too, though the reasons probably differed. The more time he spent in her orbit, the more time he wanted. He'd had crushes and a serious relationship or two. What he felt for her was light-years from any previous experience. *Too soon*, he reminded himself.

"Julia, please." His gaze roamed the people streaming by them. "After days of silence and searching, we're no closer to guessing who this jerk is."

Her lips parted on a frustrated sigh that mirrored his assessment.

"We owe Grant an update, in person." He pushed the point.

"And?" Her eyebrows pulled together as she studied

him closely. "You have something else on your mind. Just spit it out, Mitch."

She was on his mind. Her safety, her happiness and her future monopolized his thoughts. He should tell her. *Not yet.* He gripped the lapels of her coat and tugged her in for a brisk kiss. Basic. Chaste. Yet his lips sizzled and her eyes were huge when he eased her back. "Seven," he said, angling her toward the revolving door and giving her a nudge in that direction.

He sent Arthur a wave as Julia entered the lobby. Turning away, he headed up the block. Scanning the street, he sought out the one man he'd thought had been paying too much attention to them in the park. Mitch had until seven to make some serious progress on her behalf.

Patience had never been his thing, and the situation was testing him like nothing else. He had to figure out who would be so intent on using Julia's access to the Falk case. Either everyone from the FBI on down the line had missed something—someone—obvious, or the stalker was protecting bigger interests than the car-theft ring.

Except all of the statements and arrest records pointed to Falk as the head of the operation. If he was, what could he offer the prosecution? Mitch swore. He had to get off this mental gerbil wheel. They had this conversation every damn night. Theories wouldn't save Julia or restore the stable life and control she'd worked so hard to achieve.

Mitch put his head down and shoved his hands into his pockets, lengthening his stride to pass a man wearing a blue coat and a hockey team ball cap. This guy had been near the food truck when Mitch and Julia approached today, though he hadn't had any food. He wore sunglasses despite the gray skies and had circled the park twice while Mitch and Julia were eating. And Mitch had seen him use his phone while Julia had been messaging the stalker.

All circumstantial pieces, and yet all worthy of a closer look in Mitch's opinion.

He ducked into a coffee shop and waited for the man in the cap to pass by, hoping the move didn't backfire. If he could get his hands on the man's cell phone it would go a long way to confirming he was Julia's stalker. With no experience as a pickpocket, Mitch had to take a different route. He pulled out his phone to dial the stalker's number from memory. The man Mitch had in sight answered the call.

"Ah, Mr. Galway. To what do I owe the pleasure?" He turned a slow circle, forcing others on the sidewalk to move around him.

"Let Julia Cooper out of your wild-goose chase."

"She's free as a goose or any other bird as soon as she gives me what I need."

So far, it didn't appear that the bastard had spotted Mitch. He gave thanks for small favors. If he could keep the man on the line, maybe he could make him slip up. "She's stronger than any of your threats."

"Are you sure? I own her, Mr. Galway, and she knows it. Her career, her money, her life are all in my hands."

"She has help now. She's not alone."

"You?" The man smirked. "You'll be out of the picture soon enough." He stared hard at the coffee shop.

Mitch angled back farther from the window. "Come after me," Mitch dared him. "A real man would pick on someone his own size."

The jerk's short bark of laughter shot through the phone. "Julia is proving a worth adversary, I admit."

"So quit while you're ahead." Mitch disconnected the call and joined the short line at the counter.

Closing his eyes, he committed every detail to memory. Maybe it was enough for a sketch artist to work with. Grant would know someone willing to draw it up, off the record. He sent him a text message. With any luck, a more comprehensive description of the stalker would match someone tied to the Falk case. Mitch eyed the distance between the line and the back door.

He glanced over his shoulder to see the jerk cross to this side of the street. Mitch pulled a dark knit cap out of his pocket and tugged it over his head. He shrugged out of his jacket, folding it over his arm as the bell over the shop door jingled.

It seemed the stalker had accepted the dare. Mitch placed his order and stepped aside, keeping his gaze away from the door. His blood ran high, eager for a fight. He wanted the jerk to storm in and throw the first punch. A public fight would cause problems with the PFD review board, but Julia was worth any speed bump on that road.

The waiting grated on his nerves. He took out his phone, pretending to be absorbed by the device as much as the customers around him. The tension snapped when the barista called out, "Cooper!" as he set a cup on the counter. Mitch didn't move from his place near the back counter. He pressed the button on his camera app that would take a burst of pictures while he watched the room for reactions.

The stalker, hovering near the door, zeroed in on the pickup counter. To Mitch's surprise, two other men went on alert, as well, looking to the stalker for a cue.

Progress at last. Mitch stepped into the rear hallway,

passed the restrooms and slipped out the back door. A cold drizzle hit his face as strolled away from the shop, prepared to run.

The lack of a chase didn't improve his mood. He wanted to draw focus away from Julia. He'd feel better if she'd agree to sublet her place to his brother until this was over. It wasn't about accommodations. He wanted her out of the stalker's reach, away from the area he knew too well. Any unexpected move would buy them time to figure out how he factored into the case.

He hadn't dismissed the idea of the reporter as easily as Julia had done. Experience within the fire department had taught him how sneaky reporters could be. After the coffee shop, seeing the stalker and the men with him, Mitch had all the confirmation he needed that they were dealing with a criminal.

Pleased with himself, he sent the pictures from the coffee shop on to Grant, along with a warning that Julia would be hanging out in the owner's office at the club tonight. After his shift, hopefully she'd agree to move in with him until this was over.

If they were at his place... He paused to savor the idea, imagining her there, her scent lingering in the air, on his sheets. *Take it slow.*

Grant's terse reply interrupted his fantasy. He ordered Mitch to lay low, that he'd tempted the stalker enough for one day.

Mitch deferred to the older man's expertise. He decided that tonight, in the safety of Grant's office, was soon enough to bother Julia with the pictures of the man who'd turned her life upside down. He didn't want to upset her at work any more than necessary. Just because she was holding up valiantly didn't mean he had to pile on.

Julia wanted to hold on to her job. More than that, she wanted to advance. Mitch was determined to find a way to eliminate her stalker so she could get her life back on track.

With her best interests in mind, he picked up his car and headed to his house. He had arrangements to make before he picked up Julia on the way to his shift at Escape. Whether or not she got any work done, they needed a change of venue.

Chapter 6

The afternoon raced away from Julia at twice the speed of the morning. She pulled together the research Haywood needed and drafted a report while her mind put Mitch's offer on a never-ending replay loop.

Sublet to my brother. Move in with me.

Absurd or brilliant, her opinion of the idea changed on the hour. More space would be a definite bonus. Probably. What if more time in his environment unraveled the last of her resolve and she gave in to that sexy grin? The chemistry between them wasn't the point. Her entire system and schedule would have to be adjusted if she moved.

Temporarily, she reminded herself. It was all temporary so what did it matter where they stayed while trying to drop a net over the stalker? Mitch had a fair point about shaking things up on that front. Her apartment was close to the office as well as her gym and she knew most of the faces in her neighborhood, but Mitch didn't. In his place, she'd be the one on edge, thinking everyone was the stalker ready to close in on her.

His brother couldn't possibly have any use for her antique furniture, her only link to her father's side of the family. Taking the time to put those items in storage wouldn't go unnoticed and that would defeat any advantage.

Absurd or brilliant? She just could not decide.

Logic reared its ugly head again. With the black marks the stalker had put on her financial record, she couldn't afford to be late with her rent, too. Somehow Mitch understood she wouldn't ask for or accept assistance from work, friends. More likely he'd discovered her lack of personal connections during his nightly research sessions.

A chill raised the hair at the back of her neck. If he'd found the wreckage in her past, surely he would've asked. He was too direct not to. Hopefully, their swift determination that her stalker was only interested in the Falk case meant she'd dodged that embarrassing bullet. Bad enough she had to explain her brother's trouble. If he found out the whole story about her mom…if his eyes ever filled with the same scorn and disgust she'd endured those last months at home…it would break her. She couldn't risk it, couldn't let her mind slip into that abyss.

Frustrated with herself and her persistent fear of how much she liked Mitch despite all common sense, she gathered up her notes and laptop and headed out of the library.

As she walked along the gallery that overlooked the stately marble lobby two stories below, she caught sight of a ball cap in that unmistakable bright orange. She stutter-stepped, torn between moving forward for a chance to snap a picture or backing into the dubious protection of the next available door.

Phone in hand, she inched closer to the railing and scanned the lobby for any sign of Mitch. He'd promised if her stalker entered Marburg, he'd be there to protect her. Mitch wasn't anywhere to be seen. A check of her phone confirmed she hadn't missed a warning text.

Deep breath, she told herself. The man in the hat down there wasn't her problem. She told herself she'd been silly and self-absorbed, willing herself to believe it. Tourists frequently came into the Marburg building and, while the bright orange cap stood out, plenty of people on any given block in Philly at any time of day, displayed their favorite sports team pride.

She shook off the residual anxiety and chose the stairs to get back upstairs to her desk. Her stalker would win by default if she let him interrupt the portions of her life within her control. Despite his current control of her finances, there were actions she could take if he didn't relent.

One thing she could do right now was stop the direct deposits. Taking that first proactive step meant Mitch wouldn't have to worry about her living with him indefinitely. Decided, she called Human Resources from her desk and put her request into action. She went a step further, arranging to pick up a paper check personally on paydays until further notice.

She waited, an eye on her cell phone, half-expecting something dreadful in response. When nothing happened, no nasty text messages or email, she felt a genuine smile tugging at her mouth. The modest act of defiance settled her, making a dent in the gray clouds of uncertainty.

Shortly after five, Julia pushed her chair back from the desk and headed for the break room at the end of her floor.

A moment later Bethany walked in. "Staying late again?"

"It's that obvious?" Julia tried to smile. Her temper simmered, knowing her regimented lifestyle made the stalker's job easier.

"You always brew a cup of coffee about this time when you're working late," Bethany explained.

"Creature of habit, that's me," Julia agreed. Mitch's idea to move into his place sounded brilliant once more. "Only a couple more hours for me tonight," she said, setting the machine to brew a single cup.

"Oh? Tell me you have plans with your new guy." Bethany fluttered her eyelashes dramatically. "He is gorgeous. Any chance he has a single brother?"

Julia laughed. A picture flashed in her head of Bethany and Mitch as a couple. The receptionist was a much better fit for him. She was pretty, girl-next-door nice, and she worked steady hours in a respectable role.

"He's a client," she reminded Bethany with a mental disclaimer. She couldn't help poking into the charges against him, just in case he needed legal advice. It was the least she could do in light of everything he was doing for her. "We're not involved that way." *Yet*, a wistful little voice in her head added.

"Please." Bethany winked. "He kisses you hello and goodbye. Kudos for trying to keep it professional." She paused at the doorway, a big smile on her face. "Everyone in the firm is sure you're dating."

Mitch would be so happy to hear it, she thought, picking up her full coffee mug. "See you in the morning, Bethany."

With a muffled pop, the lights went out, plunging the windowless break room into darkness. Bethany squeaked in surprise. Startled, Julia spilled coffee over her hand. She muttered a curse.

"Are you okay?" Bethany asked. She stood at the doorway, under the weak glow of the emergency exit sign.

"Just mildly scalded," Julia replied. "You?"

"Fine. Must be a power outage," Bethany said. "Guess you're leaving on time after all."

"Don't we have a generator or something?" The silence was eerie. No computers or appliances humming, no ringing phones, no air rushing through the vents. In all her late nights, she'd never heard Marburg this quiet.

"It should be on by now," Bethany replied. She rummaged through her purse for her phone and turned on the flashlight. The bright light cut a swath through the break room, illuminating the splash of coffee at Julia's feet. "Let me clean this—"

An emergency siren interrupted her, followed by an annoyingly calm computerized voice that issued a situation number and ordered an immediate evacuation. The cycle repeated.

"We have to get out of here." Bethany rushed forward and grabbed Julia's arm, hauling her out of the break room. "We'll take the stairs."

"Let me grab my purse and coat." Julia leaned in the opposite direction. "It'll only take me a second."

"No time," Bethany insisted. "That's the code for a bomb threat."

"What?" She froze in disbelief.

"Come on!" Panic tightened Bethany's grip.

A bright flash blazed near the lobby door. Glass splintered and smoke poured into the office space. Julia stopped arguing, rushing for the stairs with Bethany. Other employees flooded the stairwell, all of them wondering what was going as they rushed for the exit.

Sirens sounded from every angle, and flashing emergency lights disoriented her as they poured into the side street. Police and firefighters guided everyone across the street. In the fading evening light Julia searched for Mitch, but she couldn't spot him amid the growing crowds of onlookers.

She shivered, wrapping her arms around her middle as the brisk air seeped through her blouse and dread crept into her heart. From the moment the lights went out she'd told herself it was coincidence. Not about her. Not about Falk. This was the result of a glitch in the building's wiring, a damaged transformer down the block or something equally innocuous. She couldn't make herself believe it, recalling the damned orange ball cap she'd spotted and the shattered glass doors. How could one man wreak this much havoc?

Her teeth chattered, nerves getting the better of her as she asked to borrow Bethany's phone. She clamped her lips together and sent a quick text to Mitch, willing him to stride down the street and escort her out of this chaos. He had to be close. *Had to be.*

She dialed his number, waited through the unanswered ringing and left a terse message at the voice mail prompt. Should she walk home or call her building and ask Mr. Capello to check her apartment? Neither. She returned the phone to Bethany before she did something so paranoid and clingy. She could manage a minor crisis. It wasn't as if she was out here alone with the stalker bearing down on her.

"Do you want me to take you home?"

Yes! Julia shook her head. "No, thank you." She forced her lips into a tight smile. "I'll wait until they let us back in. I need my purse." She couldn't leave without the last of her cash. Her keys, phone and identification were up there along with her laptop. Her stomach rolled. The locked doors were shattered. Anyone who'd stayed in the building could be going through her things right now.

"I'm sure this is all just a drill," Bethany said. "Or a false alarm."

Julia blew into her chilled hands. The receptionist hadn't been so confident when they were upstairs. And the flash and smoke? "They'll sort it out," she said, hoping they'd do it quickly. She checked her watch. Mitch would be here by seven at the latest. She just had to stay with the crowd and keep thinking positive thoughts.

Apparently, she wasn't up to the challenge. Chilled and increasingly edgy with every minute Mitch wasn't there, Julia struggled against a tidal wave of imaginative and outrageous scenarios. His car had broken down, he was hurt, the stalker had kidnapped him after lunch. It didn't matter that none of those were likely explanations for his absence. The crucial point was that he wasn't *here.*

Frustrated, she milled about with the rest of the firm's employees, keeping an eye out for an orange ball cap. The bomb squad arrived in tactical black, complete with two trained dogs. Her head started to spin. The files were backed up regularly to secure cloud servers, but Marburg could hardly manage Falk's acquittal in a timely manner if the building blew up.

The thought brought her up short. She and Mitch had assumed the man wanted to be sure Marburg would get Falk acquitted without jeopardizing the rest of the car-theft operation, but what if that wasn't what the stalker wanted? Julia glanced at her watch again. The next scheduled check-in time with Mitch was only fifteen minutes away. When she didn't answer, he'd come racing up the block.

Wouldn't he?

With an effort, she thought good thoughts, imagined him striding onto the scene. He'd have that baffled expression he wore whenever she expressed the simplest concern for him. She let it roll like a classic, romantic movie in her mind. He'd walk up, she'd throw her arms around him, and he'd lead her away to a sweet and happy ending after a moment's terror.

She was losing it. Clearly she'd grown too dependent on a man who'd only be with her until the danger was over. All she had to do was stay with the group until the building was cleared.

Catching a flash of orange in her peripheral, she noticed a man wearing his ball cap backward, loitering at the west end of the block. He raised his phone, presumably taking pictures of the scene. Her comforting delusion of happy-ever-after dissolved.

Was his phone aimed at her? She moved closer to the center of the crowd, nudging Bethany along with her, grateful her friend hadn't left the scene. Julia didn't care if Bethany stayed out of concern or curiosity or admiration for the first responders assessing the scene across the street, she just needed a friend.

"What do you think happened to the doors?" Julia asked quietly, her mind kicking into solution-and-survival mode.

"Probably just a malfunction with the electronic lock or something," Bethany replied. "Do you think I should tell them what we saw?"

Julia nodded. She couldn't imagine a lock malfunction would have shattered the glass. "It might give them a better starting point." She suppressed a shudder. "I'll go with you."

While Bethany explained what they'd seen, Julia watched the emergency teams swarming around them. It was so easy to envision Mitch working among them, focused and calm despite the questions and anxious bystanders. Just as he'd behaved with her from the moment she'd walked up to the bar. He kept moving forward, intent on his assigned task of protecting her, levelheaded and kind at every turn.

Thinking about Mitch as a firefighter, working among those who'd responded, stemmed another surge of distress. She hadn't known him long, but it was easy to see this was exactly where he was meant to be. His suspension, as she'd told him, was cut-and-dried and should be reversed without any trouble. Although she wasn't familiar with the fire department's internal policies or politics, it troubled her that they were taking so long to schedule the hearing to reinstate him.

They'd been guided back across the street. Julia's mind was so absorbed with Mitch that the next officer to approach them startled her.

"Pardon me, ladies," he said, and smiled. "We'd like to take you to the station for a few more questions." He gestured toward the west end of the block, well away from the crowd of temporarily displaced employees.

"Anything to help," Bethany replied.

Julia hesitated. "We can answer questions right here. Please," she added belatedly.

"Station is warmer." The cop's smile disappeared. "This way." He reached for Julia's elbow.

She sidestepped out of his reach, pulling Bethany back, as well. "Why don't you send someone down tomorrow? We're overwhelmed right now."

The officer muttered an insult to lawyers everywhere. "Come on, lady." He glanced toward the corner. "I'm just trying to do my job."

Bethany yelped as another officer came up behind her. "Julia, what is this?"

"Stop that!" Julia tried to help her friend. "We'll answer your questions right here." Neither she nor Bethany was going anywhere without someone she trusted and, right now, the only name on that short list was Mitch Galway.

"Cool it." The unyielding barrel of a gun dug into her ribs. "Cooperate or I shoot your friend," the officer said.

At the now-familiar order to cooperate, Julia stopped fighting. No doubt in her mind that the stalker was behind this. He'd probably managed to keep Mitch from intervening, as well. She was on her own with no ideas. All she could do was pray for an opportunity to let Bethany escape whatever fate the stalker had in mind.

After an hour of prowling around the Marburg office building, watching for the stalker's return, Mitch had gone out to his brother's auto shop. He'd spent the afternoon convincing Stephen to take the sublet. He even gave Stephen the spare key, letting him know they'd be cleared out later tonight. At this point it was better to go back to Julia on this issue as a fait accompli. She had enough on her plate with the case. Though he respected her preference for familiar surroundings and routine, they needed to force the stalker to make a mistake.

His thoughts about the apartment vaporized when he found Walnut Street blocked off by police. It was hard to tell as he turned the corner, but it seemed as if a convention of emergency vehicles, flashers swirling, were gathered near the Marburg building.

Stopped at the next traffic light, he checked his phone for any communication from her. Only one text had come through since his last check-in with Julia, and it was from her stalker.

You'll need more than this phone number to stop me.

Mitch's pulse slammed into overdrive. He drove to her apartment building and parked in the space Mr. Capello had assigned him. He'd get there faster on foot anyway. He sent Julia a text message and then leaped from the car and ran to the Marburg building.

Fire department and police vehicles had cordoned off the entire block. Wincing against the glare of emergency and media lights, Mitch sought out Julia, praying she was with the cluster of people behind the tape the police had stretched between barricades.

He chided himself for not having a plan for this type of emergency. How arrogant he'd been assuming the only threat to her would be direct and personal. He could almost hear the lecture Grant would level on him when they reached the club.

And they would reach the club. He had to think positively.

He searched for her red hair. She'd pulled it up again today and worn a charcoal blouse under another sexy, feminine power suit in dark blue. He swore. She might as well be in camouflage in this crowd. It was clear the building had evacuated quickly—very few people had coats or belongings with them. He stopped at the corner, looking up and down the route she normally would walk to and from work. She wouldn't have gone to her apartment, not alone. Why hadn't she contacted him?

Where the hell was she? Spotting a few familiar faces among the firefighters on scene, he resisted the temptation to stop and ask about the situation. Julia would fill him and they could search for answers later—together.

Mitch waded into the milling onlookers, asking for Julia by name, but no one seemed to know her whereabouts. He was ready to call Grant for help when he heard a woman shouting. Ignoring the protest of the nearest cop, Mitch ducked under the tape and into the slightly clearer space of the roped-off scene. He needed a better view of the bystanders on the street.

Hearing another shout, closer to a scream this time, he turned toward the sound. Julia and a woman with dark hair were being led away from the scene by two cops. They were nearly to Washington Park. Mitch sprinted down to block them.

"Hang on a second," he called out. "You've got my girl there."

The closest cop turned. "This isn't your business." He rested his free hand on his service weapon at his hip, his other hand gripping the arm of the woman who worked as a receptionist on Julia's floor. She had tears in her eyes. "You can pick her up at the station in an hour."

Mitch held his hands out at his sides. "I don't want

any trouble." His gaze raked over Julia. She appeared fine, no tears, just fury in her green gaze.

He studied the men, recognizing them as the team who'd been with the stalker in the coffee shop earlier. What the hell was going on? He couldn't get into a brawl with two armed cops, yet he couldn't let them lead the women away. "Can't you do witness interviews or whatever over there?" he asked, jerking his thumb back toward the scene.

"Go on and let us do our jobs." Cop Two urged the party forward.

Having been to the gym with Julia twice, he knew she was grittier, tougher than the skirt and heels implied. Keeping his gaze on the man closest to him, he addressed Julia. "Do you believe these men are cops?"

"No."

"Shut up." Cop One gave Julia's arm a hard jerk and shoved her along. Cop Two and the receptionist followed.

Julia protested with a flurry of legal terms Mitch had only heard in movies.

"Hey." Mitch hurried forward, putting himself between the fake cops and the quieter end of the block. "Are they under arrest?"

"Persons of interest," Cop One claimed. "Out of the way."

Mitch shook his head. "What a line. You don't even have a cruiser down here," he said. He advanced a step, halting when Cop Two drew his gun out of the holster. "Easy," Mitch said. "I don't know who gave you your orders, but these women are needed back there at the scene."

"Just kneecap him," the cop holding Julia muttered.

That put an end to his attempt at diplomacy. "Run!"

Mitch lunged at the nearest man, driving his shoulder into the rib cage. The force carried them into the shadows of the trees lining the sidewalk.

He caught a glimpse of legs flying as the receptionist raced back toward the Marburg building screaming for help. With his hands full of fake cop, he could only hope Julia was right behind her.

Mitch hooked his foot around the other man's ankle, causing him to stumble backward. Any second now, the second cop would leap into the fray to help his friend. Mitch pressed his momentary advantage, throwing a right hook into the man's jaw, pleased when the man's body slumped lifelessly.

Swiftly disarming the unconscious man, he rolled him over and dragged him a few feet until he could handcuff the man's wrists around a tree. Then he turned, simultaneously relieved and alarmed to see why the second man hadn't attacked. Julia held him frozen at her feet, his gun aimed at his chest.

"You okay there?" Mitch asked.

"Fine," she snapped, her gaze locked on the fake cop. "What now?"

"Nicely done," he admitted in the tone he reserved for keeping victims calm during a crisis. "You'll have to tell me how you did that." He walked over and took the impostor's handcuffs off his belt. "Over here."

The second impostor sat down as directed by Mitch, his eyes wide and wary as he tried to keep his distance from Julia. "We had our orders."

"You're not cops."

"No," the man admitted, his gaze darting toward the end of the block.

Mitch couldn't see anything in that direction worth

investigating. Right now his priority was getting Julia away from here and somewhere safe.

"Give me the gun," he said to her when he had the second man handcuffed. She handed it to him and he breathed a little easier as he stepped between her and the impostors. With her eyes fierce and her stance strong, he would have believed anything about her murky past.

Hearing footsteps and labored breathing, Mitch put the guns down and turned with Julia to see another man in uniform jogging toward them with the receptionist in tow. "What the hell is this?" he asked.

"Good evening," Mitch began, hands open and visible. "My friends were—"

"Galway?" The officer squinted, eyeing Mitch and then the guns. "You're Samuel Galway's boy, right?"

"Yes, sir." Mitch extended his hand. "Call me Mitch."

"Conway," the officer said as they shook. "You sure do have the look of him." Officer Conway slanted a glance at each of the women and winked. "His knack for admirers and trouble, too, apparently."

Mitch laughed it off, hiding how deep that particular barb hurt. "No trouble. Just helping out a couple friends."

Officer Conway eyed the weapons on the ground and the men cuffed to the tree before he radioed for backup. "Bethany gave me her version. Why don't you tell me yours?"

A chill slid down his spine as Julia explained how they'd been separated from their coworkers shortly after telling the police what they'd seen upstairs.

Officer Conway took notes and contact information while another officer bagged the guns and hauled the impostors into a squad car. "The ladies are lucky you came along," he said with a sigh. "We'll find out what they were planning to do." He handed each of them a business card. "Call me if anything else comes to mind." He stuck out his hand to Mitch once more and gave it a firm shake. "I'm glad you were here to put a stop to this kind of nonsense. We have a hard enough time as it is."

Mitch walked with Julia and Bethany back toward the growing cluster of bystanders. Her hand felt cool and small in his, as if the chill of the autumn night had taken root under her skin. He released her long enough to shrug out of his jacket and wrap it around her. He kept expecting her to go into shock or break down into adrenaline-infused tears. She did neither. If he didn't get her out of here, away from so many factors he couldn't control, he might be the one to break down. "We're leaving," he said at her ear.

"I need my purse and coat. My laptop," she added, her gaze drifting over his shoulder to the stately limestone building behind him.

"You can get whatever you need at home. We're leaving."

"Mitch." Her voice cracked on his name and she clamped her lips together.

"Are you hurt?" The paramedics should check her out. He looked around for the nearest ambulance. "This way."

"St-stop. I'm fine." Her hands fisted in the fabric of his shirt.

He pulled her into his arms, drew her head to his shoulder. As much as he wanted to be strong for her, his knees were shaking. "That was too close." If the stalker's fake cops had succeeded...if he'd lost her to that bastard... He couldn't let his thoughts drift far or he'd lose it and be of no help whatsoever.

Either the stalker and his pals had orchestrated all of

this or he'd moved like lightning to capitalize on a golden opportunity. Mitch couldn't stomach the grim thoughts of Julia's fate if he'd been only five minutes later. Although the fake cops made it obvious, he should tell her what happened at the coffee shop, that the stalker wasn't working alone. He couldn't do it, not while the jerk was surely watching them. "We're sitting ducks out here," he said, struggling to regain his composure. "Let me protect you, Julia."

She nodded, her chin bumping his shoulder. "Yes," she whispered.

He zipped up his jacket and tucked her hands into the pockets. She didn't resist. With his arm around her waist, she leaned into him as they walk the two blocks to her apartment building. At the elevator, he punched the call button with his free hand. "We'll pack up what you need and you'll move in with me. My brother will cover your rent." He wasn't taking no for an answer anymore.

"Okay," she whispered with a tight nod.

Her complete lack of argument floored him, worried him more than any other response she might have given. "Take a breath. You're not alone." He kept her close as they rode the elevator to her floor.

In her apartment, she turned a slow circle, her eyes glazing over. The events of the past hour were swiftly catching up with her. She turned that green gaze on him and it took all his strength to hold his ground when he wanted to scoop her into his arms and tell her it would all work out. He could hold her, but he couldn't lie to her.

"You think the stalker was trying to kidnap me," she said, her voice thin. "You think he set all this up tonight."

"That's just one possible explanation." He shoved his

hands into his pockets. If she didn't start packing, he would.

"I've had time to think of a few others." She shrugged out of his jacket and returned it to him.

"Let's save the theories until we talk to Grant. By the time we get over there, he'll have some idea if the bomb threat was a hoax or not."

"He hasn't heard about the fake officers?"

"We'll fill him in on every detail, I promise," Mitch replied. "Now tell me how I can help you pack."

She arched one auburn eyebrow with such incredulity he wanted to laugh. "I'll manage," she said. At the closet she pulled out a suitcase and a tote bag. "Where will I be sleeping?"

With me. He nearly blurted out the inappropriate answer. Oh, he wanted her body with an intensity that left his heart racing. Those chaste kisses and hugs for the sake of playing her new boyfriend were becoming far too tempting. Spending the nights on her floor, listening to her sleep, had him longing to hold her when she tossed and turned. He wanted to rub the tension out of her neck and shoulders after a long day. The woman wasn't at all his type, with those perfectly tailored suits and her lofty career. Except when her guard was down at the gym, or when they shared lunch in the park and her eyes lit with fire to debate or agree with something he said. Then she seemed perfect.

The kicker was Julia didn't seem to be affected by him at all. Oh, her eyes would flash with interest occasionally, then fade too quickly. His job was to protect her, to buffer her from the jerk pushing her to capitulate to his demands. She was in a tough situation, one wrong move away from needing to be rescued. Mitch had learned the hard way a rescue didn't create the best foundation for a relationship.

"You'll stay in my brother's room," he said at last. "He'll pay the rent here and keep an eye on things."

"That's—" She cleared her throat and stepped away from the closet, stumbling back into the bed. She pushed her hands through her hair. "That's great," she said. "I know arguing is useless, especially after this fiasco." Her hands fell to her lap and her shoulders drooped. "Can we just make sure I get a chance to thank your brother personally for uprooting himself on my behalf?"

"Sure." Mitch suppressed the chuckle. The woman appreciated a good routine. He could respect it, since repeated training and drills kept a firefighter sharp.

She packed up in record time while he straightened the area where he'd been sleeping and stuffed the belongings he'd brought over back into his duffel. Still, she hesitated at the door. "I want to argue," she admitted. "I feel like moving is admitting defeat."

"Nothing of the kind," Mitch replied. "We're changing the rules midgame to work in our favor. It's time your stalker learned he doesn't have all the control."

She gazed up at him, her chin angled and her eyes sparking with more of the familiar fight. "That's an excellent assessment. Thanks."

"You're welcome." He meant to reach for her bags and found his hands sliding around her waist. She'd changed into trim jeans and a silky cream-colored sweater his callused hands would probably ruin.

He gave her time to turn away, to stop him as he lowered his lips to hers. She didn't. All those chaste, brief kisses evaporated in a flash of heat. He sank into the textures and flavor of her generous mouth as his tongue curled around hers. She pressed her lush curves to his body, her hands digging into his shoulders, and her eager response stole his breath.

The kiss surpassed every fantasy he'd woven around her in recent days. His heart pounded against his rib cage, confirmation this hot and tender contact was absolutely real. Pushing a hand into that amazing hair, he angled her head and took them deeper still.

Every need he hadn't known was essential to his life was right here in his arms. The new awareness rocked him back and he stared down into her dazzled face. Her lips, fuller after the kiss, drew him in for one more swift taste. Her cheeks were flushed, her breath coming in sexy, shallow pants. *Good. That made two of them.*

"We should, um…" Her gaze darted to the bed, then quickly back to the door. "Grant is expecting us, right?"

"Right." He gathered the bags and ushered her out into the hallway. "We'll grab dinner there, too."

"Okay."

She sounded dazed again, and he felt better, knowing that kiss had given her a much better reason than fear.

Kissing her hadn't been a planned tactic, but it had been an effective restorative for both of them. Whenever he looked her way at the club tonight, he'd know that rosy color in her cheeks was because of him. He felt strong once more, capable of sheltering her from any harm.

Chapter 7

For more than four hours, Julia hadn't been able to stop thinking about that kiss. The happy flutter in her pulse was new. The soft, wistful sigh that occurred when she pressed her lips together annoyed her. There were far more important things to think about, yet she couldn't quite push Mitch—and that stunning kiss—out of her mind.

She'd caught herself wandering out to the bar to check on him, just to know he was here, in one piece. He'd caught her peeking around the corner more than once. She'd seen the evidence in the cocky tilt of his lips. Lips she wanted to kiss again.

Analyzing that moment, comparing that kiss to the others in her experience hadn't helped a bit. The exercise had sent her pulse into overdrive, repeatedly. She knew she couldn't keep her balance or perspective around

Mitch if they detoured into intimate behavior, but she had yet to effectively convince herself to tell him they couldn't have an encore.

She wanted that encore far more than she should. Reaching back, she pulled the tie from her hair and shook it out, massaging her scalp. She had to remember she was all wrong for him, despite the unbelievable chemistry between them.

"Knock, knock," Grant said, pausing in the office doorway. "Making any progress?"

"I wish," she confessed. "Without my laptop or phone, there isn't much for me to do."

"But without your laptop or phone, the stalker can't bother you," Grant pointed out.

"He can't tell me he's bothering me anyway," she corrected him.

Upon arriving at the club, they'd walked Grant through every step of the evening from the power outage to Officer Conway's arrest of the stalker's friends. They suspected the stalker managed to interfere with the messages she'd tried to leave Mitch as the situation unfolded. "I wish we knew a name so we could call in an anonymous tip," she said. "We know he's responsible for the bomb threat at Marburg."

"We assume he's responsible," Grant corrected. "Jumping to conclusions could make things worse." He shifted to lean the other shoulder on the opposite side of the door frame, still not coming into the office. "Mitch caught a good look at him this afternoon. Had a conversation, too."

Julia sat up straighter in her chair. "He didn't mention that to me."

"I expect he was more than a little distracted when he found you."

"True. Do we have a lead?"

"I'm working on it. Mitch will meet with a sketch artist tomorrow."

"Great." Even small steps forward were reassuring. Had everything been a ruse to kidnap her or to get into the building? She could make a case for either theory. The mounting, unanswered questions plagued her. Why was she a target? "I need to *do* something," she said.

"I'll find something to keep you busy," Grant replied. "First, walk me through it once more."

She raised her eyebrows. "Have you heard something new?"

Grant shrugged. "Not yet. Being retired means the information flows a little slower than it used to. Go on."

Although she didn't see how it helped anything, she relayed the story one more time, answering Grant's more detailed questions about the fake policemen. Hopefully, his instincts would lead to something that helped identify or catch the stalker making her life miserable. When she finished, Grant walked over to the desk and handed her a tablet. "Do me a favor and page through these arrays. Tag anyone who looks familiar."

"All right." It wasn't the distracting task she'd anticipated, but it would suffice. With the fake cops in custody, she had to assume she was looking at their known associates, one of whom might be her stalker.

"How did you disarm the man holding you?" Grant asked.

She rubbed a hand gently over her sore arm. There would be bruises from those horrid, hard fingers by morning. "Self-defense and martial arts classes in college," she explained. "I'm pretty good with my elbows and the element of surprise."

"Good to know," Grant said. "Why don't you come out to the bar and enjoy the music while you page through those arrays," he suggested with a fatherly smile. "You'll be the perfect decoration."

"Decoration?" She gave him a hard look, pretending to be offended while she weighed the offer in the friendly spirit he'd intended. Still, going out there was an invitation to trouble. She couldn't afford for her boss to get another picture and accuse her of having a personal life again. "I'm safer back here."

Grant shook his head slowly, staring at her with the wisdom of a man who understood the complexities of human nature all too well. "Nowhere is safe, Julia. Not entirely. There's less risk with our help, but there's still risk."

"I'm aware." Too aware. This club existed primarily because Grant had been forced into retirement after being shot in the line of duty.

"Then multitask. No one wants to look at scumbag mug shots on a Friday night. It'll be easier to take if you're surrounded by music and upbeat energy. We've got quite a crowd tonight."

"You don't have any receipts I can sort? Supply orders to place? When I'm done with the photo arrays, I mean."

"Julia." He shook his head. "Next you'll ask to wash dishes. I can't afford the cleaning bill if your clothes get ruined," he added when she perked up at the idea.

She laughed. Her position at Marburg required her to dress the part, and her past had trained her how to manage that requirement without blowing the budget. "I picked up this outfit on clearance."

"In that case…"

"Nope." She stood up and scooped her hair back from her face, pocketing the hair tie. "First choice was being a decoration and I'm taking that one."

Tablet in hand, she followed Grant out of the office and into the club. She caught the curious expression on Mitch's face when she was settled on a bar stool with a frosty bottle of beer at her fingertips.

He worked his way down the bar, serving customers until he was right in front of her. "Does the most beautiful woman in the place need anything?"

Her heart did a little pirouette at his words and the heat in his eyes sent her temperature climbing. She moistened her lips and his eyes tracked the motion. "I'm good, thanks," she managed.

"I'm surprised to see you sitting out here," he said. "I like it."

"Me, too." She leaned a little closer to the warm affection in Mitch's face. "Better than playing scared and peeking around corners."

"Don't sell yourself short," he teased. "That move had its charm."

"It did not," she countered, unable to stop grinning and blushing like a crushing teenager faced with her favorite idol. She wanted to kiss him again, until neither could have a single thought outside of each other.

Mitch reached out and curled a lock of her hair around his finger, laying it over her shoulder. "What changed your mind?"

Her entire body sighed into that movement. "Grant had a valid argument." Thank goodness the music was loud enough that she had to shout rather than dissolve into a breathless puddle at Mitch's feet.

"Which was?"

"He said cruising through the perp version of online dating would be more fun out here with you." The little voice in her head insisted countless things in life would be more fun with Mitch.

"Hmm." His brown eyes twinkled. "You're not the sort to dismiss a valid argument."

"That's true." She also wasn't the sort to boldly flirt with a bartender, a fireman or anyone else. He made her forget everyone in the club and their cell phone cameras. "Maybe I should go make a case for getting you out of here early." What was she saying?

He leaned back and shook his head, a hungry grin tilting his mouth. "No. I'll finish out the shift." He applied his bar towel to the gleaming wood in front of her and then flipped it over his shoulder. "Then when we go home there won't be any second thoughts."

As he turned back to the customers vying for his attention, she admired the view and the easy way he had with them. Men or women, he managed each order with a friendly smile and economy of movement.

She'd never been that easy with anyone, not even growing up. That sense of belonging, of having a safe place, had always eluded her until she'd landed at Marburg. Even as an intern, she'd been comfortable there and somehow found her rightful place within those elegant and stately offices, so far from where she'd started. Studying each face in the various arrays, she worried about the stalker robbing her of the one place where she felt she belonged. She could *not* let him win.

"That's a serious expression for a pretty girl."

Julia glanced up at the strange voice, to find a man leering down at the scoop neck of her sweater. His sharp features might be considered handsome, but his calculating gaze ruined the overall effect for her. She pegged him as the type who believed the undivided attention of any woman he deigned to approach was merely his due.

She'd had enough trouble for one night. Ignoring him in favor of her beer, she hoped he'd take the subtle hint. After the past few hours, it wouldn't take much for her to deck him rather than find the right words to send him packing.

He tapped her shoulder. "Come dance with me. I'll make you forget whatever his name is."

Julia recoiled at the touch. "No, thanks. I'm not your type."

"You're just the girl I'm—"

She stopped listening to his nonsense. At the other end of the bar, Mitch caught her eye. She could see the protective streak from here and gave a little shake of her head. Between the two of them, edgy as they were from the near miss earlier, she decided to get rid of this idiot on her own. She couldn't ask Mitch to fight every battle or rescue her from every arrogant man who crossed her path.

Twisting in her seat, she aimed her best and brightest smile at the stranger. "I'm not your girl." She showed more teeth. "I'm an attorney here on business. If you don't want that business to be you, I suggest you leave me alone. *Now.*"

The stranger's eyes went wide and he backed away quickly, squeezing into the safer anonymity of the crowd.

"Who was that?" Mitch asked when he reached her.

"An idiot, not another problem," she explained calmly.

His gaze scanned the crowd behind her. "You're sure?"

She nodded, infused with a fresh surge of independence. "I like watching you work," she blurted out, bringing those intense brown eyes back to her.

His expression softened. "You're joking."

She leaned across the bar and kissed him. "Not a bit." Hopefully, he wouldn't ask for any specific examples.

He glanced at the bottle in front of her, his brow creasing. "Did the idiot drop something in your beer?"

"No." She tucked her hair behind her ear, pleased to see him track the small movement. "Go do your job so I can enjoy the view again."

His grin was absolutely wicked. "There's a suggestion I won't ignore."

For the remainder of his shift, Julia could almost believe she was here under purely social circumstances. The music pounded from the band onstage to the swell of cheers from a raucous, appreciative crowd. Only the photo arrays reminded her she had more serious problems.

By the time Grant retrieved his tablet and cut Mitch loose, she was a messy blend of exhaustion and excitement. She wanted to fall into bed, and knowing it would be a bed in Mitch's house had filled her brain with tantalizing, unwise scenarios.

It didn't help that his hand was at her back, making her want to snuggle into the shelter he offered as they headed down the hallway. Someone called Mitch's name as they passed by the kitchen. He tensed, doing that thing where he put himself between her and the unknown as he turned. He was so close she felt his body relax in one fluid rush.

"Carson Lane!" Mitch reached out to give the other

man half a hug and then introduced Julia. "What are you doing here?"

"Marking time," he replied.

Julia noticed the pervasive sadness lingering in the man's eyes and she felt an unexpected urge to comfort him.

"I heard about what happened. I'm sorry, man."

"We're in a risky business." Carson's shoulders hitched in a valiant effort to shrug off the sympathy. "Grant threw me a line. You know how it is."

"Yeah, I do," Mitch agreed, his hand flexing on Julia's waist.

"Hey, Grant said you need a sketch artist."

"Crap." Mitch tensed again, shooting her a contrite look. "I meant to tell you."

She waved off his unnecessary worry. "We've been busy."

He turned back to Carson. "He meant you? You're a sketch artist, too?"

"I prefer driving the ambulance, but I have some other skills." A hint of a smile tugged up one side of his mouth. "You want to do this now?"

Julia was relieved to hear Mitch ask for a rain check. "We've had a long, tough day," he said. "Will tomorrow work?"

"Sure." With a swift exchange of phone numbers, Mitch and Julia made a hasty exit.

"What happened to Carson?" she asked quietly when they reached Mitch's car.

"His partner on the ambulance was killed while they were out on a call. He's had some trouble overcoming it and getting back on the job."

She couldn't imagine that kind of struggle. "I hope spending time with Grant helps."

"Grant won't let him slip through the cracks," Mitch said, reaching over and patting her hand. "Carson will find his feet again."

"Grant is a good man."

"Definitely."

They let the rest of the short drive to the west side go in silence until he took a quick detour and pointed out the garage where Mitch and his brother restored cars. She twisted in her seat, craning to get a better look. "Will you take me by in the daylight sometime?"

"Are you telling me you're into classic cars?"

She was into *him*, a fact that worried her a bit more without the diversions of the club as a buffer. "It sounds interesting. And I'd like to meet the man who's taken over my apartment."

"Ah. That makes more sense," he said, turning the corner and immediately pulling into a narrow carport tucked back between two houses. He stopped in front of a detached garage and turned off the car. "Home sweet home," he said, pushing open his car door.

Once they were inside, he gave her a tour of the house. "We inherited it from our uncle," he explained. "My mom's brother got sick of winters. He wanted to head to Phoenix, but my mom badgered him into staying on the East Coast. They live in Orlando now."

She couldn't imagine adjusting her plans to keep family happy. "That's nice, I guess."

Mitch shrugged a shoulder as he hauled her bags down the narrow hallway. "I can't complain. Living here beats paying rent for something half as nice, even if we deal with more maintenance on this place."

She didn't know the difference. "I've been an apartment dweller all my life."

"Bedrooms are this way." He set her bags down on the floor near the hallway and stared at her, his eyes wide. "You're kidding. No backyard, no neighborhood bike races?"

She shook her head, surprised at the foreign sensation that she'd missed an important life experience. "There was a park a block down." At one place. "And a pool," she added, as if that would erase the stigma of being different. That had been a different year, and one of her favorite summers.

"Did you go swimming a lot?"

She nodded, wishing she'd never brought it up. That summer had been one bright spot in a childhood lacking so many typical happy memories she'd heard about from friends over the years.

"This is Stephen's room. Yours now," Mitch said, changing the subject abruptly. He plucked a note off the pillow and gave her a half smile. "Stephen says he changed the sheets for you."

"Thanks." This felt so awkward. She didn't want to leave any room for him to doubt her, to believe she was using him for protection or to scratch a lusty itch. "I really appreciate you, Mitch. For all your help tonight. Thanks," she repeated lamely.

"To hell with that." He crowded her, bracing one powerful arm on the wall just over her shoulder.

Her pulse skipped, eager for another kiss and more than a little afraid to make the next move. Warmth radiated from him and she wanted to burrow in, soaking up that heat and life until she felt complete again. Normal. It was probably too much pressure to set on his broad shoulders. "Hell with what?" she asked, her mind racing with the possible answers.

"I was assigned to protect you, sure. But you matter. You matter to me, Julia."

His words, the intensity in his gaze, had the air backing up in her lungs. She swallowed, trying to remember how to breathe. "I... Oh, Mitch..." Words failed her. No one had ever said anything so profound to her in her life.

"Don't worry about it." His lips tilted up at one corner. His palms caressed her shoulders, but the touch was gone too soon as he pulled back and tucked his hands into his pockets. "You're exhausted. Get some rest and we can start fresh in the morning."

"All right." Rest was the last thing on her mind, though it was the smart choice. She supposed one of them should be responsible. Desire and yearning were mucking up her attempts at rational thought. "Do you have an alarm system?"

"Relax. We're safe here. The jerk stalking you doesn't know anything about me."

She wished she could believe that. From the phone to her banking, the stalker had proven remarkably informed and tech savvy. And now, thanks to her, the creep might have more to work with. "My phone and laptop were left behind at the office. Someone broke into my floor." She cleared her throat. She'd spent time researching the circumstances of his suspension. That information was fair game if the stalker had used the bomb threat to disguise a theft. "I know he has your cell number, too, now. Grant told me you talked with him," she added when he winced. "He's dangerous."

"Easy, Julia," Mitch crooned. He rocked back on his heels, his hands balled up in his pockets as if he was afraid what would happen if those hands got near her again. "We can tackle those questions tomorrow when we have more facts."

"Grant reminded me. I know we can't assume the stalker organized the whole mess. And we know he has help now." She pulled a hair tie from her pocket and gathered her hair up off her neck into a messy bun. It gave her something to do besides reach for him. "It's not a wild bet, all things considered."

"No, it's not," Mitch agreed reluctantly. "Will you have trouble sleeping?"

With him in the next room, where she probably couldn't even hear him breathing, while she relived memories of fake cops who'd nearly kidnapped her? Of course she'd have trouble sleeping. "I'll be fine," she lied. "It helps knowing you're here." She stopped before she could ask to sleep in his room. "Helps that I'm not alone."

"Good. The bathroom is at the end of the hall," Mitch said. "If you need or want anything before morning, speak up. I'm in the bedroom across the hall."

She bit back more of the gratitude that had annoyed him. "Okay."

In the bathroom, she stripped away her clothes and indulged in a fast, hot shower just to wash away the lingering anxiety and remnants of the bomb threat trouble. In the gray cotton tank top and boxers she wore as pajamas, she saw the bruises from the impostor's grip already blooming on her arm. As she passed Mitch's bedroom door, she recalled he still owed her an explanation about his encounter with the stalker.

She hated to bother him at this hour when they both had to be up early, but she wanted to know what he'd seen. What had been said. In the hallway, she nibbled on her lip as she raised her hand to knock on his door. "Mitch?"

"Come in."

She turned the knob and opened the door a crack. He was sitting up in bed, his chest bare and the sheet bunched at his waist. Her mouth watered.

"Is something wrong?"

"No." She felt foolish bothering him now. "This can wait until morning."

"Talk to me, Julia."

"Grant told me you saw the stalker. That you spoke with him." She could tell by the way his expression clouded that this wasn't the topic he expected. "We can discuss it in the morning."

"Hang on." He started to rise and changed his mind. "I wasn't cutting you out of the loop," he said. "We just had more immediate issues. When we got to the club, you'd settled and I didn't want to get into it."

"No problem. I just wanted to know if you recognized him. Do you have any idea who he is?"

"No." He shook his head. "I walked right by him on the sidewalk and got a better sense of his build."

She gasped at that.

"I got a good profile first, then a better look when he came after me. He wasn't familiar at all, though I plan on going back through every report on the Falk case in the morning."

"Okay." She stepped back into the hallway. "Good night."

"Julia."

She froze at the command in his voice.

"I wasn't hiding anything."

"I didn't imply that at all." She hesitated in the doorway, sensing he wanted to say something else, then his expression clouded.

"What is that?" He tossed back the covers and prowled across the room, loose flannel pants riding low on his lean hips. "On your arm," he said, pointing to the marks.

His ripped torso mesmerized her momentarily. She followed his hard glare to the bruises on her arm. "Temporary souvenir," she replied. "It looks worse than it feels."

Gingerly, he raised her arm up and to the side, letting the brighter hall light show him each detail. "Do you need ice?"

"It's nothing, Mitch, really." This had been a terrible idea. Here they were, more undressed than they should be. He was being kind again and all she could think about was the big empty bed behind him. She backed up another step before she embarrassed them both. "Good night."

"I don't want you looking over your shoulder forever, second-guessing every conversation and glance. We made progress today. I got a good look at him. His two cronies are in custody. We'll get him, Julia."

She nodded, wanting so badly to believe him. "Good night, Mitch." She ducked into her room and closed the door. Pretending she still had hope was as exhausting as outrunning a bomb threat. Sliding under the cool, fresh linens, she reminded herself tomorrow was another day, another chance for the stalker to screw up or succeed.

She closed her eyes, letting the images of the day stream by in a tension-relieving meditation. Grant and Mitch were right to move her here. There was a peace to the house, a quiet calm her apartment had lost in recent days.

In the morning, they would take what they'd learned today and turn it into a fresh lead—either from the sketch of the stalker, or maybe one of his cronies would flip. There would be a lead that would put an end to this tenuous situation and allow her to reclaim her life.

Leo Falk paced the width of the hotel suite in Society Hill, waiting for K-Chase, his so-called computer genius, to wrap up the work on Julia's cell phone and computer. Planning the audacious, fast-strike invasion of the Marburg building had been fun, despite the obvious risks. He'd kept himself from the high-octane action on the front lines for too long. The strike had been effective, if costly. Two men were in custody and the man currently tailing Julia reported she hadn't returned to her building. She wouldn't go far and if she had, he knew just how to reel her back in.

Soon K-Chase's tricks would give Leo full access to Julia's computer and phone. Seizing her finances, keeping them out of her control, had been easy for his genius, coming at it through the institutions. Staying a step ahead of her was crucial to making her dependent on his generosity and giving her good reason to say yes when he offered her a retainer and a beachside villa. He smiled, imagining how the lovely Julia would enhance the view at his compound in the Caribbean.

It would have been a sweet bonus if the men had been able to draw Julia away for a quick face-to-face chat. Leo had high hopes for the intelligent, savvy redhead. She continued to surprise him with where she chose to apply her loyalty.

As much as he enjoyed the change of pace, Leo couldn't stay in Philly much longer, not if he wanted the system to keep believing he was dead. Being a ghost, out of sight and out of mind of law enforcement agencies, had allowed him to build an operation no one could take down. Unless his brother rolled.

Leo hadn't completely set aside his anger about the careless mistakes Danny had made leading up his arrest. He'd trusted his brother, the only man with access to both the management and labor sides of the operation. Now, rumblings from the defense team and rumors in the prosecutor's office suggested Danny was impatiently looking to make a deal. Didn't he realize Leo would never let him rot in jail?

"All right," K-Chase said. "You have her hard drives to use at will and I can get in and out undetected if necessary."

"No trace at all?"

"Let's just say a crack forensics team would need years to find a lead."

Leo rolled his eyes at the cockiness of youth. They all thought they were immortal. Irreplaceable. It didn't matter. Leo needed only another few days at best. He tossed a stack of money at the boy.

K-Chase caught it, hefted it and stared up at Leo. "This is only half."

Leo grinned. "If you want the other half, you'll run an errand for me."

"That wasn't our deal."

Leo merely clasped his hands behind his back, waiting for the boy to come to his senses.

Chapter 8

Mitch woke up early, having slept poorly knowing Julia had gone to bed bruised and unhappy. His jaw tightened. Those bruises would stand out on her pale skin even more today. Given an opportunity, he'd dish out equal treatment to the man who'd put those marks on her.

His fault.

He turned his face under the hot spray and scrubbed away another rush of guilt. He'd taunted her stalker and Julia had suffered in the retaliation. Whether or not the jerk had orchestrated the evacuation, it had been his thugs who'd tried to take her. Aggravated, Mitch recalled Grant's warning about patience—a virtue he'd never quite mastered.

Once he'd dressed, Mitch went to the kitchen to start coffee and breakfast in a belated attempt to make up for his many mistakes last night. He should have kept his lips to himself, should have warned her about the coffee shop and should have done a dozen other things to make her more comfortable with this change. He should have said something about *her*, not just her case, while they'd been standing in the hallway. The only words that had filtered through the flood of desire had been mushy declarations no sane woman would be ready to hear within hours of a first kiss.

He understood their differences. He was quick and decisive. She was deliberate and enjoyed a debate. He had supportive family and she did not. Huh. Had he truly appreciated his big, noisy, meddlesome family before now? There were parts of Julia that were seriously messed up though she hid them well behind those tough-lawyer layers. He'd gained a few messy scars, too, but he was willing to share the story behind them. With her.

He heard her bedroom door open and close, followed by her soft footsteps in the hallway. Knowing her typical routine, he figured it wouldn't vary too much now that they were at his place.

After filling a mug with fresh coffee, he drank deeply and skimmed through the updates on his phone. The safe bet was he'd be taking her to the office, same as last weekend. Regardless of her status as a new associate or the intricacies of a case, he figured taking a day off wasn't her style. Beyond the ingrained work ethic, he knew she wouldn't wait until Monday to retrieve the items she'd left at her desk. He pulled out a package of bacon and gathered ingredients for French toast and then set the griddle on the stove to heat.

As a firefighter, he was no stranger to rigorous work schedules. He wondered if she realized how much they had in common or if she focused on how different they were. He didn't generally populate the circles she ran in. She didn't have much of a social life and he didn't have much cause to visit any law firm.

Without the trouble of this case they might never have met. While he didn't wish her harm after the past few days, he couldn't imagine his life without her in it. His hand flexed at the thought and he accidentally crushed the egg he'd been holding. Better to find other things to think about. Like how to keep her safe and out of the stalker's reach. Moving here, they had a small advantage over her stalker and he didn't want to squander it. Could he get her to agree?

He cleaned up the mess and started over, cracking fresh eggs into a bowl. Whisking them lightly, he added milk, a dash of cinnamon and a splash of vanilla until the mixture smelled right. When he heard the squeaky hinge on her bedroom door again, he checked the clock and turned up the heat under the griddle. He had a plate of crispy bacon ready to go and had just started dipping slices of bread in the egg mixture when she walked into the kitchen.

She wore trim black slacks and a chocolate sweater that showed off her curves. As she came around the counter, he noticed her slender, bare feet. The deep purple polish on her toes sent his imagination into overdrive. Not for the first time. He tamped down the lust factor and gave her a warm, friendly smile. It was a sorry excuse when he wanted to kiss her until her cheeks were pink and she couldn't quite catch her breath. "You're dressed as if you want to go in to the office today." No surprise.

"I'm an incorrigible workaholic." She wrapped her hands around the mug of coffee he poured for her. "You don't have to wait on me," she said after the first slow sip.

A man could get used to watching the caffeine slide through her system, perking her up from the inside out. "First morning in my place, I thought it deserved a little fanfare."

Her wide mouth tipped up at one corner. "I'm not complaining. Is that French toast?"

He grinned at her over his shoulder, inordinately pleased by her eager curiosity. "My mother's secret recipe."

"I'm honored."

He flipped the slices on the griddle and set out butter and syrup for her. "Is there any chance I can talk you into staying here today?"

"Not without my phone and laptop."

"You could use my gear," he offered. He was curious if the items she'd left behind were still in her cubicle. He'd checked the news reports, as well as the email Grant had sent this morning. "Grant heard there are no leads on the tipster who called in the bomb threat. Apparently, the damage is limited to your floor and the side door." There was more, but he didn't want to dump all of it on her at once. She hadn't even had one full cup of coffee.

"That's weird. There are cameras on the side door and the stairwells, and throughout the building."

Mitch shrugged. Her stalker had likely beaten the cameras at her apartment. "Seems to me the direct attack is too obvious," he said. He stacked hot slices of French toast on a plate for her, ignoring her protest about serving sizes, and then made a similar plate for himself. At the table, he watched her eat, taking her silence as confirmation that she enjoyed his mother's recipe as much as he did. It pleased him to relax and enjoy such a normal moment.

It felt too right having her here like this. He hadn't done more than kiss her, though he wouldn't hesitate if she gave him a chance to take her in his arms and explore that stunning body. He couldn't quite think of her as a client anymore. Hell, despite all his training, he'd been too attached even before the kiss. This attraction between them had a potential that went beyond her circumstances.

Maybe the overwhelming rightness came from being so close. He'd certainly never felt it with any of his previous girlfriends. Mitch made a concerted effort to put his thoughts on the case rather than the way her lips closed over each bite of her breakfast.

"Back to the office for your laptop and phone," he said. "Then what?"

"Same story, new verse. You watch, I work, I suppose."

"I could get behind that. To a point." He pushed his last bite of French toast through the syrup on his plate. "We could throw the jerk another curveball."

She paused, her coffee mug suspended just below her lips. She placed it back on the table with great care. "What are you thinking?"

"He knows your cell phone number and he's been following you far too easily. I know you want your stuff back, and we'll do that, but do you think we could stop using your phone?"

She bit her lower lip as she considered. "It's not a bad idea."

Mitch pressed the idea. "The fake cops who tried to lead you and Bethany away are low-level thugs with a flimsy connection to Falk's organization."

"Connected by known associates?"

"Exactly," Mitch replied. "Makes Falk the natural suspect, but they don't know how he's issuing orders from the safe house."

"That would be an interesting trick." She raised her coffee mug again, sipping this time. "The FBI has him isolated from everyone but Marburg."

"And Marburg wouldn't authorize an attack on his own building." Mitch watched her face, intrigued as she examined the situation from all angles. "Which circles back to the stalker."

"Whose side is he on?" She rubbed her forehead.

Mitch reached for his coffee rather than her hand. "Did you sleep at all last night?"

"Yes," she replied absently, her thoughts clearly on the problem. "The stalker planned this out. He wanted that building evacuated. Getting a hold of me was just a bonus."

"You're basing this on…?"

"My gut," she replied. "Nothing as helpful as evidence, unfortunately."

"That doesn't bother me, since I'm not trying to build a case. My goal is to keep you safe."

"My goal is to stay employed. And safe." She reached out and rested her hand lightly on his forearm. "I know you don't want me to say it again, but thank you for everything you've done. I know this isn't convenient for anyone."

There it was, another moment to tell her his encounter yesterday had probably baited the stalker into the attack and he left it unsaid, too selfish to ruin the sweetness of the contact. She'd reached for him. That little touch gave him a boost of optimism that she wouldn't ditch him as soon as they caught her stalker. "Do you hear me complaining? You're far better company than my grumbling brother."

Her expression brightened at the vague compliment. "He's not a morning person?"

"Not a bit," Mitch said, laughing. "He wakes up early just so he can get in two cups of coffee before the rest of the world. That makes him human enough to carry on a brief conversation. He's not the least bit friendly until he's had at least an hour alone under the hood of a car."

"Tough roommate."

Mitch nodded. "I had years of experience staying out of his way before we moved in here." He waited, hoping she'd share something of life with her brother before the Marines.

"Thanks for breakfast," she said, clearing the table. "I'll take care of cleanup and then we can go to the office."

Mitch followed her to the counter and poured another cup of coffee. "I don't want you bringing your phone here. We should make sure your laptop doesn't have any kind of tracking on it, either."

She shut off the water and turned around, leaning back against the counter. Her green eyes were full of irritation, her mouth set in a hard line. "He knows who you are, right? I mean, you called him from your phone. He managed to divert messages I sent to you from Bethany's phone."

True. "That doesn't mean he knows where I live. This place isn't in my name. My permanent address is still listed as my parents' place."

That irritation shifted immediately to concern. "*Mitch*. This was a mistake. Having me here puts all of you at risk. It was a dumb move."

"Gee, thanks." He watched his sarcasm cut through her distress. "You need help. You're the target, not me or my family. Trust me, the Galways can hold our own."

"I hope you're right. Let's get to the office." She flicked her hand, urging him out of her way, but he held his ground, blocking the only exit from the galley kitchen. "Move, Mitch."

"Why did you become a lawyer?"

Her auburn eyebrows furrowed. "That's irrelevant."

"Not to me." He folded his arms over his chest. The longer they stayed in the safety of the house, the happier he was. He silently dared her to draw this out.

She tilted her head. "Is this about the kiss last night?"

"Absolutely," he admitted, gauging her reactions. "Now give me an answer."

"I became a lawyer for the money. There. You kissed a shark." Her sharp chin came up in defiance. "Happy now?"

"Not even close." He stepped in and stole a kiss. He lingered over it, until the hard edge of her temper drained away. As she relaxed, he eased back, keeping his hands on her waist. "Why did you really become a lawyer?"

She raised her gaze to the ceiling as if an escape from his questions could be found up there. "Why does it matter?"

He smiled at her exasperation and brought her hands to his lips. "Whatever your reasons, you're well suited to it the way you answer so many questions with another question."

His observation brought out a self-deprecating smile that lit her face and seemed to brighten the room. "How about I tell you the story while you drive me to the office?"

Resigned, he shifted to the side so she could scoot by. He hadn't missed her lack of complaint about him kissing her again. When her stalker was out of the picture, he'd ask her out on a real date. It would be a crime to ignore the potential and promise under the mutual attraction.

Julia slid into the passenger seat, feeling a bit lost without the things she normally carried with her to and from the office. She owed Mitch a real answer about why she'd become a lawyer. He'd been so open with her, even about his flaws, that it pricked her sense of justice.

He was either too nice or too polite to accept her raw reply at face value. Money had been a big motivator for her career choices and she was okay about that. Her entire childhood had been balanced on a precipice with disaster encroaching on all sides. Her mother had made life a misery with bad habits that exacerbated the drawbacks of her paycheck-to-paycheck lifestyle.

"It *was* money," she blurted out as Mitch turned at the end of his block. He needed to know who he was protecting—and kissing—so he could ditch any altruistic delusions he might have about her. "There wasn't much when I was growing up and I refused to stay in that trap."

"Money is a good reason," he said easily. "You mentioned a story," he prompted.

"You'll notice I'm not in the public defender's office," she countered.

"Money is a good reason," he repeated. "Being a firefighter isn't a get-rich-quick scheme. My brother and I restore cars for the money."

"You love it," she said.

"Do I?" A grin tugged at his lips.

"Yes," she said. The care he'd taken with this restoration was obvious. "I'd argue restoring cars is more than money for you."

"You'd argue most anything," he said with a smile. "But you're not wrong." He smoothed a palm over the steering wheel while they waited for a traffic light to change. "I'll tell you about it. Another time. Right now I want you to tell me the nonmoney reason you became a defense attorney at the biggest firm in town."

"I think you have me confused with a nice girl."

He laughed, raising his chin in the direction of the Marburg building. "Better start talking. I'm not letting you out of the car until I have an answer."

"Funny."

"If only I were joking."

She gave a put-upon sigh in a lousy attempt to stifle her own laughter at his strategy. "Marburg is the best at criminal defense, not only the best in the state, but the region. They're consistently a top-five law firm in the country. Not all of their clients are innocent, but they're not all guilty, either."

She swallowed. Would she ever be able to think about those last weeks at home without the dull ache of regret in her chest? "I needed to be part of the best. Needed to prove myself." She'd never admitted that to anyone. There was no rational explanation for sharing such a personal detail. Wiping her suddenly damp palms on her slacks, she wished she'd held her ground and kept him out of her past. "You can drop me at the side door."

"I'll find a spot and walk you in," he said. "You're not leaving my sight until I'm satisfied about what happened on your floor last night."

"You think I'm all lawyer-ego," she said when they

were parked a block down and around the corner from the building.

Mitch's mouth twitched into the sexy grin that made her knees weak. "You're wrong. I think it takes serious drive and grit to get through college and law school, and land a job in that marble castle back there. I admire drive and grit. I admire *you*."

"You didn't at first," she accused. "I noticed you were less than thrilled when Grant told you to protect a Marburg attorney."

"A man's entitled to a mistake or two. As long as he owns it. I don't mind admitting I was wrong about you."

She didn't know what to say to that. "We'd better go in."

"One more thing." Mitch caught her hand. "Why such a drive to be with the best?"

She caught herself before she proved his earlier statement by asking him a question. "Call it negative motivation." At his frown, she explained. "My mother isn't the best. Not the best mom, provider or anything else," Julia said quietly. Although her mother was damned good at scamming people. "When I showed an interest in practicing law, she discouraged me. Laughed in my face." The memory still left a bitter taste in her mouth. "After that, I refused to be an average lawyer. I needed to be at the top of the heap."

"Does your mother know where you landed?" he asked quietly.

Julia smothered her disappointment. Mitch had integrity and ethics. Hot kisses would never overcome this much brutal honesty. "Yes. She appreciates my success enough to ask me for money periodically." Most of the time, Julia successfully ignored where her life had started. Not today, not with Mitch staring at her with that baffled expression on his face. "Let's go in." She opened her door and let the cool autumn breeze blow away the cobwebs of her past. Having broken free of the cycle of dysfunction, she had no intention of falling into the sticky trap disguised as family again.

Everything seemed normal as they walked through Marburg's front door. Quiet and calm, less bustle on a Saturday morning, there was no obvious sign of last night's uproar. She chose the stairs rather than the elevator, grateful Mitch followed her without voicing any more tough questions.

At her floor the shattered glass had been cleaned up. The only sign of damage were the workmen taking measurements to replace the oversize doors. She stutter-stepped at the sight of Mr. Marburg, founder of the firm, standing by in a royal blue golf sweater with the law firm's crest on the chest pocket.

"Do you need to say hello?" Mitch murmured at her shoulder.

With a quick shake of her head, she aimed for the aisle behind her desk. She preferred to avoid any interaction with Marburg. Meeting him at the new-associate orientation had been intimidating enough. The man was a legend and, while she had plenty of confidence in her education and abilities, she knew Marburg had forgotten more about legal defense than she might ever know.

Nearing her cubicle, she did a double take. Her doorway was blocked with yellow police tape and fingerprint dust marred most of the surfaces. Her desk had been torn apart, files and papers scattered, her personal belongings nowhere in sight. The bin where she locked her purse was open. The key remained in the lock and her purse was gone. She clapped a hand over her mouth, smothering the blast of fear and fury before it exploded out of her.

"Not how you left it?"

She shook her head, not trusting her voice.

"May I?" He peered into the cubicle and reached past her, taking a few pictures with his cell phone camera. "Take a breath, Julia. It'll be okay."

"How?" she demanded. She tried to breathe, just one slow and easy inhale, but the air rattled in and out of her lungs.

Mitch turned in a circle, taking in the surrounding work spaces. "Whoever did this went straight for your desk," he observed.

"Hell of an effort to steal a laptop," she muttered. She rubbed her hands over her arms, suddenly chilled to think that the stalker might be going through her belongings right now.

"Who else is working the Falk case?"

"About a dozen of us, I guess, plus the partners and Marburg." Wasn't it enough that the jerk had intruded on her life, threated people she cared about and jacked up her finances? Did the man really need to pull a stunt like this? He wouldn't gain anything useful poking through her scarce personal contacts, social media, or the movies and games she used occasionally as a distraction.

"We can replace your things."

She groaned. Replacements cost money, money the stalker had tied up. A headache pierced her temples when she thought of the inevitable maze of getting her driver's license reissued. None of that mattered, not compared to the trouble in store here at the office. The sensitive case details she had backed up to the firm's cloud storage, so her work wasn't a complete loss. No, the worst would be reporting this new fiasco to Haywood. Whatever the police might have told him, a problem of this magnitude required more than an email from a new cell phone. A breach like this could get her kicked off the case. "So much for the stalker originating the bomb threat," she whispered to Mitch.

"Why change your theory now?"

"I have to report the potential security breach to Haywood. There were case files on my personal laptop. That's reason enough for Haywood to take me off the Falk case."

"Which means he'd have to find a new source of insider information."

"Exactly."

"He seems pretty invested in you," Mitch said. "Specifically."

"I'm not taking that as a compliment." The last thing any new associate wanted was to bring down negative attention on the firm.

"Not meant that way," he replied. "Give me a second to update Grant." Mitch used his phone to report the problem, then he tucked the device back into his pocket. "Where to?"

"Upstairs. If there's any mercy in the world, Haywood's working this morning and I can get this over with."

She didn't consider asking him to wait for her while she took the stairs up to Haywood's office. Last night had amped up her paranoia about being alone. If Mitch hadn't shown up, who knows where she and Bethany would be right now. As they rounded the next landing, Julia reached for his hand, grateful for the gentle reassurance when he laced his fingers through hers.

This floor didn't show any signs of trouble, as quiet and serene as the lobby on a weekend morning. Julia should've been comforted. Instead, goose bumps raced over her arms, under the long sleeves of her sweater and up the nape of her neck. If the bomb threat was a ruse to steal the Falk files, Haywood's office should've been targeted, as well. Having Mitch close kept her facade of courage in place.

"You can wait here," she said when they reached the deserted reception area in front of Haywood's office. "It won't be very interesting."

"I'll stick around," Mitch replied, giving her fingers a gentle squeeze, before releasing her hand.

Her heels sank into the thick carpet of the hallway. She rapped on the open door of Haywood's office and peered inside. The office was empty. Disappointed, she debated her next move.

Her boss would know by now that she hadn't returned when the building had been cleared, and if he'd tried to reach her directly last night, he'd be more than a little irritated that she wasn't answering his calls.

"No sense at all," she muttered to herself, wondering again about the stalker's motives and methods. As she prepared to leave Haywood a note, she heard voices near the conference room at the far end of the hallway.

She stood tall, shoulders back, and remembered to apply her modest courtroom smile.

Seeing her, Haywood immediately dismissed the men he'd been speaking with. "Nice of you to show up," he said. "I've been calling you since last night." His sharp gaze slid to Mitch. "Why is your boyfriend here?"

Julia felt her smile slip. "Mitch Galway—my boss, Eddie Haywood."

"A pleasure," Mitch said, stepping forward and giving Haywood a friendly greeting.

Haywood scowled, focused once more on Julia. "My office." When the door was closed, he went on the attack. "This isn't the time for a personal life, Cooper. And *that* man is about the worst choice you could make. Do you even know who he is?"

"Mitch is a friend. An *innocent* friend who will be vindicated soon, I'm sure."

"Why do I bother?" Haywood groused, dropping into his big desk chair. "You're supposed to be on research. What the hell did you dig up that has our firm under attack?"

She opened her mouth, but her boss barreled on.

"We get a call that the building is about to be reduced to rubble, not the first time, of course. When the all clear sounds, the only obvious problem is at *your* desk. I've had security reviewing footage since last night. What haven't you told me?"

Julia did her best to match her boss's cool and calm tone as she gave him her account of the evening. She'd called herself a shark, but Haywood had years of experience to perfect the persona and hone his instincts. If she showed the first sign of fear, he'd be on her in a heartbeat.

"Why didn't you answer my calls?"

So much for hoping her belongings had been seized by police. "As I said, I was in the break room when the power went out. My phone, laptop and purse were left behind at my desk when I evacuated. They aren't there anymore."

"What?" Haywood roared, rising from chair.

The office door slammed open and Mitch filled the

doorway. "You okay?" he asked her, his gaze riveted on her boss.

"I'm fine." It was almost true now that he was here.

"Private conversation." Haywood sneered at him. "Wait outside."

"No, thanks." Mitch closed the door and planted himself in front of it, the move reminiscent of the night she'd sought help from Escape.

Haywood glared at her. "They told me about the destroyed door on your floor and the preliminary report said your desk had been searched. Because we couldn't reach you—" he aimed his chin at Mitch "—we didn't know anything had been stolen. Tell me what kind of breach we're dealing with."

Julia explained the precautions she employed with passwords and backing up her files. Her boss seemed mollified, though she harbored more doubts. Haywood picked up the phone and barked at the person on the other end. It took her a moment to follow his questions, but she realized he was verifying that the police hadn't confiscated any employee belongings last night.

"Well, at least we know your work on the Falk case isn't half a step closer to the prosecutor's office. Get yourself a new phone and laptop and charge it to the firm. HR will give you the authorizations. I need to be able to reach you. Day or night," he added with a sneer for Mitch.

Julia felt as if someone had lifted the weight of the world off her shoulders. "You're not tossing me off the case?"

Haywood drummed his fingers on the edge of his desk, his gaze going to Mitch once more. "I should." He shook his head. "I damn well should," he repeated.

"But I read through your reports. The work you've done is exceptional." He didn't sound all that pleased about it.

She debated telling him about the stalker and threats and managed to keep her mouth shut. Mitch and Grant were working that angle. While she'd been grossly inconvenienced and unnerved, she hadn't been asked to give up anything confidential. *Yet.*

"Thank you," she said, making a hasty exit with Mitch.

"He's a pleasant guy," Mitch said when they were in the elevator.

"Most of the time he is," she stated. "The Falk case has everyone more stressed than usual. At the last strategy meeting there was an argument about plea deals."

Though he didn't say a word, she sensed judgment in Mitch's silence as they made their way to the Human Resources department. Soon, armed with a corporate credit card and the contact name at the electronics store, Julia and Mitch left to fulfill Haywood's orders.

"Well, this isn't how I thought today would go. I'm sorry to make you drive me around town on these errands."

"Keeping you in sight, remember?" He took her hand as they walked to his car. "You should probably report your credit cards as stolen."

She stopped short, forcing people on the sidewalk to move around them. "I can't." She bit back an ugly oath. "Oh. I'm an idiot. He threatened to retaliate if I tried to get into my accounts." Sick to her stomach, she covered her mouth with her hands as she looked back at the building. "It's my fault."

"What are you talking about?" At the corner, he crossed the street and boosted her up on a brick wall so

she was closer to eye level with him. Caging her or sheltering her, he placed his hands on either side of her hips.

"Last night." Her chest hurt. "My fault. I changed my
pay so I could pick up a physical check and open a new
account. Then...then the evacuation and the c-cops. Fake
cops."

"Shh." Mitch smoothed a hand over her hair. "You
can't blame yourself."

"It's my fault," she insisted. "Enough games. I'll just
leave town or something before he endangers someone
else." She didn't want to contemplate what sort of move
came after a bomb threat orchestrated to hide a theft.

"By that logic you should blame me." Mitch rubbed
the chill out of her hands. "I've been wondering if bait-
ing him yesterday caused the evacuation and put you in
danger. I got a look at his face and a couple of lackeys,
too, remember?"

She shook her head. Mitch was only trying to help,
to do his job. "I was already in danger."

"The blame belongs on the jerk stalking you. Not either of us."

"What if—"

Mitch interrupted her. "You have to trust the rest of
us to take care of ourselves, Julia. He's focused on making your life miserable."

"Well, he's doing an excellent job of that. I can't believe I let Bethany drag me out of there without my
stuff."

"She did the right thing." Mitch helped her down and
slid his arm around her waist, drawing her close. "The
way you explained it, that would've put you far too close
to the person who tossed your cubicle."

She stared up into his warm eyes, momentarily

speechless. The desire in his gaze was unmistakable and her body responded with a delighted shiver.

"You're cold. Let's get to the car."

Hardly. "I'm thinking," she replied.

"You normally just scowl a little right here when you're thinking." He tapped the space just above the bridge of his nose.

He knew that about her?

"I'm all kinds of observant," he said with a wicked grin, making her wonder if she'd voiced her question. "Let's take the day one step at a time. Your boss made new technology your first priority."

She tried to find a bright spot. "At least the creep won't have the phone number."

"A definite plus," Mitch agreed.

"He has your number, though." It felt as if the stalker had managed to put a pothole or speed bump in every possible path. "I don't like how this is shaping up," she admitted when they were in the privacy of Mitch's car.

"We'll figure it out," Mitch said with persistent confidence as he pulled out of the parking space.

Julia withheld judgment. Although Mitch's protection offset the distraction he presented, her job was still hanging precariously in the balance. "We need to figure out who he is. You need to meet with the sketch artist. There has to be a reason he's operating so erratically."

"Maybe the jerk is just crazy and confused."

"No." She watched the city go by, developing her reasoning. "A crazy person would have slipped up by now." She sighed. "I can't make up my mind if he created the bomb threat. It just won't fit into the bigger picture. Why take the risk that his inside source would be denied further access?"

"Unless you haven't mentioned it, you haven't shared anything anyway."

"He hasn't asked for anything I'm privy to," she said. "Although there's dissension about a plea bargain tactic, no names have been mentioned around me, and none have been logged into the records I can access."

"A protective measure?"

"Yes." Her mind wandered through every encounter with her stalker. How had he known to strike at the very root of her independence? He held her finances hostage in exchange for cooperation. He wanted names she couldn't access and seemed to know or anticipate her every move. Why had he chosen her?

They were missing a critical piece of the puzzle, and she could only hope no one would get seriously hurt before they found it.

Chapter 9

Mitch didn't push her to talk about whatever was going on in her head. There were shadows under her eyes and her typical bravado was cracking around the edges after the encounter with her boss.

They'd known from the start they weren't dealing with a typical stalker. This jerk wanted access to the Falk case and with her laptop, he had it. So why attempt a kidnapping? He sympathized with Julia's frustration and confusion. If he believed walking away from the case would work, he'd do everything possible to talk her into that.

Whoever was behind this definitely understood Julia's hot buttons. That bothered him as much as all the other details combined. She wasn't an "open book" kind of woman. Yes, she was clearly independent and living alone, but that wasn't a complete reason to target her.

What confidence did the stalker have that Julia would cave to the pressure?

In the stalker's shoes, he would've gone after someone with real secrets, someone who'd proved susceptible to greed. All of his digging into Julia's past had only turned up adversity and problems that held many people back. Not her. She might not be proud of where she came from, and it seemed she'd cut most of her family ties, but she'd never done anything unethical.

They'd parked and were nearly to the storefront doors when Mitch's cell phone sounded. He saw his brother's name and answered immediately.

"Hey, Stephen. Everything okay?" He stopped outside the store and Julia stopped with him.

"Not even close," Stephen replied. "I'm at the garage and I found your new roomie's purse and laptop in the bin out back."

"You're kidding. Is the computer intact?" Mitch didn't want to give Julia any false hope.

"How the hell would I know? The wallet's here with ID, credit cards and some cash. There's a cell phone, too. Get down here and check it yourself."

"Did you see anyone toss it?"

Stephen snorted. "I'm hanging up now."

"We're on the way." Mitch shook his head, uncertain if his brother had heard him.

"On the way where?" Julia's eyebrows arched.

"Good news." Mitch smiled at her, but it only put a wary glint in that stormy green gaze. He slid the phone back in his pocket and turned her away from the door. "My brother found the things that were stolen from your cubicle last night."

"Pardon me?"

Mitch cleared his throat, considered a white lie and discarded the idea immediately. The truth would worry her, but it wouldn't erode the fragile trust she'd placed in him. "At the garage where we restore cars."

She gasped.

He didn't understand the shock. "Is that such a terrible problem?"

"Yes!" She pushed her hands through her hair. "He's out to cause trouble for you. You don't need more problems before the review board lifts your suspension. Grant needs to get you away from me."

"Hey, relax." He wanted to hug her for that burst of confidence and offer some comfort as much as he wanted to growl at her for suggesting he be replaced. "Let's get over there and see what's what before we panic about anything." He put a hand at her back and urged her toward the car. "I want to know what kind of game we've been sucked into as much as you do." He started the car and aimed for the west side of town. "Keep in mind I haven't done anything wrong."

"Except help me," she said through clenched teeth. "Your brother wasn't hurt? His property wasn't damaged?"

"No, and no," Mitch answered. "Stephen would've griped about damages." He weaved through traffic, seeking the shortest route. "He doesn't know anything about the state of your laptop."

"He shouldn't touch it. I'll have someone from Marburg's IT department examine it for any issues."

"That'll be the next stop. I thought you'd be doing backflips that you don't have to get a new driver's license."

She did a double take and then laughed at the joke.

"Good point, though I'm sure he didn't leave it out of any kindness."

Probably not. He fished his phone from his pocket and handed it to her. "Send Grant a text message and let him know what's going on."

"Sure." She balanced his phone on her thigh when she finished. "He took my things for a reason," she said quietly. "The computer, in particular."

"Go on." He was curious if her opinions would line up with his.

"He cracked my finances and he had every reason to believe I'd give in to his demands for info on the Falk case."

"Bull."

"Pardon?"

"You've never done an unethical thing in your life," he stated simply.

"How would you know?"

He cleared his throat, resisting the urge to squirm like a worm on the hook. "You told me I could poke into your past. You know I've been digging. There's nothing there to be ashamed of."

"Then you didn't dig deep enough," she said, her fingers laced tight in her lap.

"Fine." Mitch pulled into the gravel drive and paused at the gate that protected the garage property. Rolling down the window, he entered the code into the security panel. "Tell me why he had any cause to think you'd cave."

"Well, I'm the new kid on the case trying to prove my value."

A bogus argument and they both knew it. "The jerk

didn't offer to help you prove yourself, did he? Next?" he asked.

He glanced over when she didn't answer. His chest swelled with pride when he realized she was soaking up every detail of the business he and his brothers had built. "That ploy wouldn't have been effective," he said, eager to make his point. She was a rare breed among attorneys, if she didn't shatter the mold completely. Not all lawyers were corrupt, but Marburg had a particular reputation in town. In Mitch's opinion, nothing shy of threatening the people she cared about would break Julia's iron will or integrity. And the jerk had chosen the wrong people the first time around.

"How can you be so sure?"

"Of what?" He parked the car and released his seat belt.

"That I won't cave despite the risks to my livelihood and reputation."

"You came to the Escape Club for help." He started ticking off the points in her favor on his fingertips. "You could have given in and begged or bartered to get back control of your money. You could've run to your bosses and hoped for the best. You held your ground and against every expectation, forcing the stalker to take serious risks to gain what he wants."

Her lips slanted into an aggravated frown. "Do you have cameras with this security system?"

"Always on point." Mitch swallowed a laugh. "Yes. We'll go through it together, once you're sure the thief didn't take anything."

She scrambled out of the car, clearly reenergized by the discovery of her belongings.

Mitch didn't hear any swearing or tools going in the

garage, so he led her toward the office. It wasn't big, but it was neat as a pin, per Stephen's extreme need for order. Mitch made quick work of the introductions.

"Is everything all right with the apartment?"

"Are you asking if I trashed your place?" Stephen raised an eyebrow.

Mitch bristled at his brother's attitude, but Julia spoke first.

"No," Julia replied with far more patience than his brother deserved. "I wanted to be sure the creep hassling me didn't give you trouble."

"He didn't."

She smiled weakly. "My place is really small. Are you sure you'll be comfortable there?"

Stephen visibly relaxed. "It's a great address and a nice place despite the size. Mitch said switching for a while helps you out, but it helps me, too. Thanks."

Mitch gawked at him. That had to be the longest speech unrelated to cars that he'd heard his brother deliver in over a year.

While they continued reviewing the pros and cons of her apartment, Mitch glanced around for Julia's purse and laptop. "Where did you stow her things?" he asked.

His brother tilted his head toward the bottom drawer of a filing cabinet. "Didn't know how long you'd be. Seemed better not to leave them out."

Mitch bent down and opened the drawer for Julia. She withdrew the items and went through everything. "It's all here," she said with a relieved smile. "Let me call my boss and—"

"Leave it off a bit," Mitch said. "The guy knows where he dumped your things. Let's keep him guessing as to exactly when you found them."

Her relief dimmed. "Okay."

"Want to tell me what the hell is going on?" Stephen's jaw was set as he glared at Mitch. He wasn't going to be put off any longer. "How did her purse and computer land here?"

"They were stolen last night from her office during a bomb threat evacuation."

Stephen sputtered, shifting that hard glare to Julia. "You're with Marburg?" His fury made Mitch cringe. "A little warning might've been nice."

"It's irrelevant," Mitch replied evenly.

"Like hell." Stephen swore again. He pushed back from the desk and stomped out of the office.

"I'm starting to understand why associates work eighty hours a week," Julia said. "It keeps us sheltered from our adoring public."

Mitch leaned back against the old metal desk. "My brother's an ass." He wouldn't coddle her, but this wasn't her fault. "We lost two completed cars to Falk's organization last year." That wasn't nearly the whole of Stephen's issue with Marburg lawyers, but he wasn't about to burden Julia with the story of how her law firm had successfully defended the man who'd killed his brother's fiancée. Although Stephen had good reason to detest Marburg, Mitch wouldn't allow his brother to dump that grief on Julia.

"The cars were stolen from here?"

"No. Stolen from clients." Mitch tapped his fist over his heart. "Still hurt. All that work, vanished."

She gazed up at him, her eyes wide and curious. "You weren't going to say anything."

"Like I told my brother, it's irrelevant. You didn't steal those cars."

Her eyes moved to the wide window that overlooked

the yard where several cars were in various stages of repair. "No, I just represent the man who did."

"You're working a job you love." Mitch bent forward. "I get that. Hell, I think that's the only way to live."

She dipped her chin, but not before he caught a glimmer of tears in her eyes. "Everything's here," she repeated. "As for the computer…" Her voice trailed off.

"Do you want to take that back to the office?" he asked after a long moment of silence.

"I don't know." She gave a little growl of exasperation, her hands fisting around her purse strap. "I just don't know. He's toying with me, Mitch, and I'm tired of it."

"I understand that, too. Let's take a look at the cameras." He gently tugged her to her feet and pulled the chair around to the working side of the desk. "Have a seat," he said as he logged in to the garage computer system. "We put this in a few years ago when Stephen decided to turn our hobby into a profession."

"This is the cleanest garage I've seen."

The warm scent of her hair drifted toward him as she leaned closer to peer at the four views on the monitor. Mitch cleared his throat. "Have you spent a lot of time with mechanics?"

"Enough. My mother could only afford beat-up cars and she dated mechanics whenever she needed repairs."

Mitch refused to comment. She'd spoken without any emotion, as if that part of her life belonged to another Julia Cooper.

"Wow, your brother works late," she said, extending a finger toward the time showing on the video record.

"It's a habit by now." One he didn't expect his brother to shake anytime soon. He kept pushing the video feed faster, past the midnight mark, as the motion-sensor lights stayed dark on the camera aimed at the front gate. "Well, he didn't come in the front."

"Ugh. The idea of someone going through my things makes my skin crawl."

"Are you talking about my brother or the stalker?"

She bumped her fist lightly on his shoulder. "You know I'm talking about the stalker. I want to string this guy up by his toenails when we catch him."

"I agree with the sentiment, but I'm not sure that's a legit tactic for the police department."

"Oh!" She pointed to the screen. "Is that him?"

Mitch enlarged the picture as a man in dark clothing and gloves climbed halfway up the chain-link fence and tossed Julia's computer and purse into the open garbage bin early that morning. "Being pretty careful about it. Almost six thirty. If he'd waited another twenty minutes, he would have run into Stephen," Mitch observed. "No way that's the guy who wears the orange ball cap." The man on the fence was skinny enough to be called bony. The stalker's voice and face had shown more age, his body older. "Does he resemble the man who broke into your floor?"

"Hard to tell," Julia said. "He seems smaller through the shoulders, but I didn't get much of a look at him last night."

Mitch swiped his cell phone screen and dialed Grant's number again. "He's probably working on setup for tonight's band, but I want to get his take on this." He wasn't pleased about leaving a second message. He could keep her out of the stalker's reach, but he was far less confident about how to proceed with any sort of investigation. Her purse and laptop were probably considered evidence—or they would be if she'd reported them stolen.

"My boss expected to be able to reach me by now. If you don't want me using my cell phone, we'd better get back to the store and pick one up."

"What about your laptop?"

She sighed. "I'll have the store take a look, then get Haywood's opinion. I'm sure he'll want our own tech department to look it over."

Mitch didn't trust anyone else at Marburg. Not because they were defending Falk, but because someone on the inside had to be helping the stalker follow Julia. There hadn't been any direct pictures of her inside the building, but an inside ally was the only logical explanation for the swift responses from the stalker.

Mitch put everything in the office back in place and they thanked Stephen on their way out. Stephen replied with his typical grunt, but the half wave was positive progress.

"He's a charmer," Julia said as they drove away. "It's hard to imagine you two living together."

"He's always been serious," Mitch said quietly. "But he wasn't always miserable. Hopefully, he'll remember how to be happy again one day."

When they'd purchased the phone and had her accounts synced up so she could use it, she called her boss and let him know she was having the laptop screened for any viruses or problems. Haywood then confirmed her suspicions and ordered her to bring the laptop into the office for the Marburg team to double-check it.

Mitch managed not to voice his opinion on that idea. The stalker had repeatedly proved his willingness to cause havoc. He didn't think it was a coincidence that Julia's things had wound up at the garage—a place where he'd spent most of his off hours, before his suspension.

"I'm sorry about all of this," she said as they walked up and down the store aisles while they waited. "We're going to be here all day. I should've just bought new stuff and not mentioned we recovered the old."

"It doesn't matter." He picked up a display model of headphones, turning them side to side. "My job is spending time with you." He smiled. "It's a good job."

"Your job is being a firefighter." She stuffed her hands into her pockets. "This is maddening, being caught up in something that I can't fix or see a way out of."

He set down the headphones. "We'll get out of it, I promise."

"You should be with the sketch artist by now." She perked up. "Why don't you go on ahead? I'm safe enough here."

"Not a chance." He started making up outrageous, danger-filled stories about the other customers and a few of the employees until she was nearly doubled over with laughter.

While he admired her intelligence and her serious determination, he thought he might become addicted to the bright sound of her laughter. A stunning woman in all circumstances—when she relaxed and smiled with genuine pleasure, he lost his breath.

How could he feel so much for a woman he hardly knew? Tomorrow was Sunday and he'd be expected at home for dinner. Last week he'd dodged it because of his responsibility to Julia. His mother wouldn't put up with him missing two weeks in a row without a better explanation than a closing shift at the club.

It didn't matter that her children were all adults now, Myra Galway kept a sharp eye on each of them. Even in the worst of his grief, Stephen hadn't been granted two consecutive weeks away from Sunday dinner.

As they started yet another circuit of the store, Mitch debated which path offered the least resistance. He could take Julia with him and face the endless ribbing and blatant speculation about her significance in his life. Or he could face the inevitable and relentless guilt trip his mother would heap on him for missing two straight family dinners. He had opened his mouth to invite her and explain why they had to go when his phone rang.

"It's Grant," he told her as he answered. "Did you get my messages?"

"Yes," Grant replied. "The purse and laptop aren't evidence and even if I could call in a favor, I'm sure her stalker was careful not to leave anything helpful behind. Keep her boss happy, or you'll give the stalker more cause to escalate," he added.

Mitch watched Julia wander farther down the aisle. "Learned that the hard way last night," he said under his breath. He'd been reckless pushing at the stalker that way. The only thing he'd gained was a profile that wouldn't do them much good.

"That bomb threat wasn't your fault. Your job is keeping her safe," Grant said, echoing his earlier words to Julia. "I know this isn't the work you're used to, and not the work you anticipated when you signed on at Escape, but she's alive and well, right?"

"Right." Mitch smiled as she poked at a display of jump drives in various themes.

"So keep up the great work," Grant said. "The stalker is hell-bent on a purpose we haven't identified. All we know is that he has resources and personnel."

"True." He thought about the impostor cops and the

man tossing Julia's laptop into the garbage. "Keeping her boss happy might get tricky. I'm not letting her out of my sight until the sneaky bastard is in custody."

"I'm confident you two can figure it out. Everyone I know is clammed up about the bomb threat and the impostors. I can't tell if it's because they're afraid of making a misstep with Marburg or if there's more to it."

Mitch caught Julia's signal that her computer was ready. "Looks like they just finished the evaluation of her computer," Mitch said to Grant. "If anyone tampered with it, I'll let you know. Next stop for me is meeting Carson for the sketch."

"Good," Grant replied. "Stay alert."

With nothing more to discuss, Grant ended the call and Mitch joined Julia at the service counter. On the seat beside him, Julia folded her arms over her chest, as if trying to warm up or protect herself from bad news. He hated that she was caught in this trap, with no hint of how to break free. They needed an identification or at least enough new information to make a logical guess as to the man's next move.

He wasn't sure if he hoped for an all clear or obvious signs of tampering on her computer. Surely, the stalker hadn't gone to such extreme lengths just to annoy her. No matter how Mitch reviewed it, he agreed with her that the jerk's actions weren't adding up.

Let him try, Mitch thought. If the jerk wanted a run at Julia, he'd have to find a way through Mitch first.

Julia had her fingers crossed there would be good news on the technology front. She wanted to know her laptop wasn't just clean, but that the information hadn't been stolen or tampered with. Had the stalker found what he wanted and then "returned" her things just to delay the inevitable identification?

She'd watched the clouds pass over Mitch's expression during his conversation with Grant. Mitch couldn't possibly be a good poker player. His emotions were too easy to read. She'd recognized relief and frustration in alternating turns. It was hard to hold on to any hope that they were making significant progress at uncovering the stalker's name or motives.

This had to be more than he'd signed on for. Maybe the sketch artist would help them—if they could ever meet up with him. That seemed like a stretch the way the day was going.

"Good news and bad news," the technician said, setting her computer down gently on the counter.

"Bad new first, Todd," Julia replied, reading the young man's name badge. "Please."

"Someone accessed your files at these times." He slid a printout across the counter.

"How do you know it wasn't me?" They hadn't told the tech anything other than she needed the laptop examined.

"I, um, I assumed," Todd stated. "Your system is set to automatically link to specific IP addresses and at these times, the IP address was different from the two most commonly accessed addresses."

She leaned over and peered at the printout. "Those are my home and office."

Todd nodded, giving her a smile as if she was the star pupil today. "Usually, yes. For most people." She listened to him explain the technicalities, her heart sinking with every word. Her career at Marburg was over as soon as they discovered the breach.

"There's good news, Ms. Cooper." Todd's smile felt too bright, glaring in vain against her increasing despair of the stalker's unpredictable behavior. "No viruses or malware. Your system is perfectly clean."

"Great." Todd had no idea that news wasn't much cause for celebration. It did beat the alternative of investing in a new laptop. Her laptop wouldn't blow up or infect the rest of Marburg's network when she logged in again. "Thanks for your help."

"Sure thing." He handed her a card and a protective neoprene sleeve for the device. "Be sure to come back anytime."

"I think the kid has a crush on you," Mitch said when they were back in his car.

Julia wasn't in the mood for teasing. "I think the kid is barely old enough to work." She sighed as she buckled up for the drive back to the law firm. "None of this makes any sense. He's got us running in circles."

"Maybe that is the point," Mitch said thoughtfully.

"Then why target me? Why threaten me or anyone else?" Her voice rose with her temper. "He said he wanted to know who Falk was naming, but I'm *not* privy to that part of the case. It's a fruitless approach."

"Maybe taking your laptop has proved you can't help him and he'll leave you alone."

"Forgive me if I don't hold my breath." Knowing the stalker had people to help him sent her anxiety skyrocketing. She wouldn't be able to hide it much longer. Not from Haywood and definitely not from someone as observant as Mitch.

She plucked her old phone out of her purse. The device felt dirty in a way that had nothing to do with where it had been found. "There might be something to your distraction theory," she said. "Why take my computer when he so easily seized control of my financial life from a distance?"

He reached over and trapped her hand between his warm palm and her thigh, ending the rapid drumming of her fingertips. "You're not alone. I won't let you be alone in this, Julia."

The way he said her name sent a ripple of awareness through her system. Not the time, she scolded her wayward hormones. She couldn't allow her attention to be diverted from the primary goal of catching the creep who'd twisted up her life.

Mitch parked the car, a half block closer to the office this time. "I could manage this on my own," she said as they hurried toward the IT department. "You should come back for me after you meet with Carson."

"I won't let him divide and conquer again. We're sticking together until further notice."

She halted in the middle of the corridor. "Mitch, come on. You can't stay glued to my hip indefinitely."

Using her elbow, he nudged her along. "One step, one day at a time, okay?"

She gave him a skeptical glance but withheld her argument. With her computer under another evaluation, she went upstairs to bring Haywood up to speed in person. It was quickly evident her boss's mood hadn't improved much in her absence. He pointed to a stack of folders on his receptionist's desk and ordered Julia to start reviewing the witness statements.

"You're looking for repetitive wording and any overlapping dates and times," he said.

"All right." She understood he wanted to find any instance of witnesses being fed the same answers that would incriminate Falk or those working within the car-theft ring. "Can I take this home? In case I don't get through them all before my laptop is ready?"

"Nothing leaves the building," he said, his gaze as flat and cold as a sheet of black ice. "Except you." Haywood drilled a finger in Mitch's direction. "Her personal life can resume in a month or two."

"I won't bother her." Mitch's smile was cold.

"You're bothering *me*." Haywood squared off with Mitch, his hands on his hips. "Get out of my office."

Julia watched as Mitch took in his surroundings, obviously weighing his options and searching for a way to satisfy Haywood and maintain his obligation to her. She didn't want the men to clash and she needed to stay on the case for a multitude of reasons. Contrary to her bravado near the IT department, she knew she'd be battling fear if Mitch left. Haywood's corner office had too many windows and she felt the stalker was already out there, keeping tabs on her.

"Mitch is feeling a little overprotective after last night, Mr. Haywood." Her statement drew the attention of both men. "I admit, I'm a little jittery, too. I'd be more comfortable and get through this faster if he stuck around. He won't be in anyone's way if he waits for me right there." She pointed to the glass-walled waiting area between the offices and the elevator.

"You'll rush through it."

She forced her lips into her mild courtroom smile. "If I had that reputation, you wouldn't have added me to the case."

Haywood's eyebrows climbed his forehead. "Your confidence doesn't hurt, either." He backed down. "Just get it sorted out."

"I will," she promised. "Quickly and without rushing," she whispered when he was out of earshot. She flicked her fingers at Mitch, sending him to the other side of the glass.

As he settled into one of the leather club chairs that faced her, she opened the first file in the stack. At least she was doing something more productive than researching precedents. As the afternoon ticked by and dusk fell outside the large windows, she focused on the task at hand rather than how this was one more impediment to Mitch's potential identification of the stalker.

It was just past six o'clock when Haywood stepped out of his office to tell her the IT department had decided her laptop was clean and she could have it back.

"Any progress on those statements?"

"I've been through all of them twice."

Haywood narrowed his eyes. "You said you wouldn't rush."

She smiled through her perpetual annoyance with him. New associates were propelled to the top or tossed into the trash based on these tense encounters. "I did not rush." She tapped the two statements that had felt like misfits. "These two witnesses claim to have seen their cars being stolen by Falk's crew."

"And?" Haywood's gaze landed on the folders she held out.

"Their phrasing is too similar based on their differing neighborhoods and backgrounds. Additionally, the cars stolen weren't standard to Falk's operation."

"You think the prosecutor is piling on?"

Julia wanted to stretch the kinks out of her shoulders and neck, but it would have to wait. "That's something only you can decide," she said, stroking his ego. She stood up, caught the movement in her peripheral vision as Mitch did the same on the other side of the glass in the lobby.

For the first time since she'd been hired, she couldn't wait to leave the building for longer than her lunch break. "I'll see you on Monday," she said to Haywood as she walked away.

"Answer your phone."

"Yes, sir." To stay on the case, she had to remain available to Haywood's every demand.

In the lobby, Mitch dropped his arm over her shoulder in a blatantly possessive gesture. "You're not helping," she said through clenched teeth while they waited for the elevator.

"Don't care. Your boss is an ass."

"Comes with the territory." She hurried onto the elevator and slid away from Mitch's tempting embrace. She had to maintain her distance before she gave in and just let him sweep her out of this mess. "Junior partners land in a grinder that's worse than the associate obstacle course."

"How is that?"

"No one expects much success out of a new associate," she said. "A high percentage of new associates at Marburg simply burn out. A few become effective workhorses. Fewer still get the right opportunities to move up." The Falk case was her next step on the ladder, but it was at risk of snapping and sending her tumbling down to the bottom of the heap. "Partners have to hire the right associates, bring in more billable hours and log more victories than losses in court to maintain the stellar reputation."

"Hard to believe you willingly signed up for all of

that." He shook his head, but a smile lurked at the corner of his mouth. "What's the fastest anyone made junior partner?"

"The Marburg record is three-and-a-half years. The Falk case—if I managed to contribute something that helped them win it—would've accelerated my personal schedule."

"You planned to break the record."

She shrugged. It was silly to confirm or deny his statement. What had been a lofty goal might be forever beyond her reach if the stalker didn't relent soon. They didn't discuss anything else while they retrieved her computer and walked out to his car.

Her stomach rumbled loud enough to be heard over the souped-up engine. "You must be starving, too. I'm sor—"

"Don't apologize for doing your job, Julia. Want me to pick up a pizza on the way home?"

Home. The word sounded so nice it set off warning bells in her head. "Sure. You don't have to tend bar tonight, do you?"

"No."

Once they decided on toppings, she sent a text to the number logged into his phone, and then a comfortable, peaceful silence filled the car. Julia watched the city go by, wondering when Mitch would share whatever was on his mind.

Close to his neighborhood, he stopped in front of an Irish pub. "My cousin's place," he explained. "Don't let the shamrock fool you, they have excellent pizza." She caught a few speculative looks while he paid for the pizza and a six-pack of beer. Good wishes for his parents followed them out the door.

His world was full of that vague unity she'd been looking for all her life. She'd seen glimpses, of course, but when she'd dared to try to become part of it, it crumbled around her. Only at Marburg had she truly felt like she fit, and that was a cutthroat environment.

"Oh, my word," she said suddenly. "I'm an idiot." She didn't have a real stalker, not someone connected to Falk anyway. She had an enemy inside Marburg, another associate willing to take her down in order to secure her place on the case. She bounced a little in her seat as Mitch pulled into the driveway. "I'm never this naive," she said. "Whoever is doing this must be laughing himself to sleep at night."

"Julia? Could you let me in on the joke, please?"

"Sure. Over pizza." Her stomach rumbled in agreement. "Come on."

"The stalker has to be one of the associates from Marburg," she said as she set the pizza box on the counter. "It could be someone who's been passed over for a big case or someone who generally resents female lawyers. Good grief, it's so obvious it's embarrassing."

"Right." He handed her the plates. "Why don't you walk me through it as if I'm the idiot?"

She put two savory slices of pizza on each plate and carried them to the table while he popped the top off a cold beer and poured it into a glass for her. "I'm an attorney, not a princess," she said, inexplicably charmed by his thoughtful gesture.

"From where I'm standing, you're both." He turned away before she could respond, grabbing the napkins.

"You've cooked for me twice today," she said as they sat down. "I'll handle the cooking tomorrow."

"This doesn't count." He passed her the Parmesan

cheese. "Who at the firm could hate you so much that they'd go to these lengths to get you off a case?"

"I don't know yet, but it makes complete sense."

"To one of us. Where I work, coworkers who try to take someone out are booted off the job."

"I would hope so. Our jobs have different risks," she replied. "Law school has a high dropout rate and a cut-throat approach among the remainder."

"Guess I'm glad to be a simple guy. I'd rather know the people around me are loyal." Mitch raised his beer bottle to his lips and took a long pull before he continued. "Firefighters aren't perfect and there have been issues," he allowed. "But for the most part, I can count on the people around me having their heads on straight. Especially in a crisis."

"You're not a simple guy," she said with a chuckle. "And my head is on straight, thank you very much."

He tipped back in his chair, balancing it on the back legs. "Convince me."

"First, all those pictures proved he has close access to my schedule and he clearly knows that part of Philly as well as I do. Second, having my computer linked to the firm's network must have made it a breeze to tap into my finances and passwords. He could have picked up the bank information through the payroll."

Either the beer or the excitement of a workable theory—finally—had her feeling flushed and warm. She scooped her hair up off her neck and held it there for a moment. Mitch's gaze dropped, trailing over her throat. The effect was as effective as a touch, heightening the sensation that she'd spiked a fever. She shifted abruptly, her hair falling to her shoulders, relieved that the tension snapped, on her side of the equation anyway. No one had ever looked at her quite the way Mitch did, as if he saw through her tough facade without underestimating her capabilities.

The man could kiss as if his life depended on it, in a way that made her want to forget everything else. That spark between them was tempting her. She struggled to remember that physical attraction wasn't what had brought her here.

"Third." She paused to clear the rasp of desire from her throat. "Third," she repeated, "and most important is that he hasn't asked for anything that would truly jeopardize Falk's defense. The notion of a competing lawyer explains what doesn't add up between the threats and demands and the actions that put me in the hot seat."

Mitch had listened intently as she delivered each point, his brown eyes going dark as he concentrated on her.

"Well?" she prompted when he didn't say a word.

"If it is someone from the firm, he's spending a ton of time away from his desk."

Resigned, she conceded that point.

"More than that," he continued. "If the stalker is inside, why steal your laptop when he had easy access via the network you mentioned?"

"That move was designed to scare me and make Haywood see me as a risk, putting me a step closer to being off the case."

"Okay." Mitch dipped his chin in agreement. "Are there pictures of the lawyers anywhere? I got a good look at the guy yesterday."

She perked up again. "Everyone has to have a new head shot done when they're hired. They're on the firm's website."

"Let's get to it."

She retrieved her computer and set it up on the table for him, pulling up the website. "I'll handle the dishes while you start searching," she said, stacking their plates.

"You don't have to do that."

She smiled down at him. "Haven't you noticed I'm no good at doing nothing?" He'd noticed just about everything else about her.

He answered with a smirk that made her heart speed up as the rest of her body froze in place, anticipating what might come next.

What did she want to come next? Before she could stop herself, her mind spun a delicious fantasy of Mitch sweeping her up into his arms and carrying her to bed. She bobbled the plates, and the clatter of silverware as she caught them brought her back to reality. "Did the website load okay?"

"Yes." His brow furrowed as he studied her. "Why don't you sit down, Julia. The dishes can wait."

"No, thanks. I don't want to influence your search." She took a step back, distressed by the sense that she'd made another wrong move. An ill-advised retreat. *Into the kitchen*, she scolded herself. She couldn't have stood there indefinitely, tempting fate. There was a stalker to find, and exploring this sizzling chemistry between them wouldn't make the task any easier.

She wanted to ask him a dozen questions about the man he'd seen, but any description would have her jumping to conclusions about who'd put this in motion. She recalled the note that had been tucked in with her mail that first night, the stalker's attempt to use people close to her as leverage. Her stomach pitched.

Just by pretending to be her new boyfriend, Mitch was putting himself in danger from the stalker. If the stalker was a coworker at Marburg, Mitch already had a target on his back. In the brief time they'd been forced together, she already cared for him. She'd learned the hard way her emotions were too intense to be trusted and easily twisted up into something that drove people out of her life.

Her lousy track record with people had started at home and progressively worsened as her world expanded. After one bitter disaster after another confusing lust for love in high school, Julia used college to effectively run away from home. Thank goodness there had been one teacher who believed in her, who'd kept helping her with college apps and scholarships despite her mother's repeated attempts to malign his reputation.

Therapists during her undergrad years had cleared the way for her to have a healthier emotional life, until the stress of her first year of law school had resulted in a pitiful backslide. She'd struggled that first year, trying to figure out how to coexist as a decent person and an ambitious law student.

She glanced at Mitch. Impatient and cocky, he was a good man, a man who didn't deserve to be saddled with her baggage. Hot kisses and mutual attraction aside, surely she could keep her hands off him until they could return to his regularly scheduled life. He might be assigned to protect her, but she wouldn't hurt him in the process.

Chapter 10

Mitch could practically hear Julia thinking while she did the dishes. She'd been energized by her new theory about the stalker's identity as a coworker, then she'd abruptly gone quiet. He hadn't indulged himself and kissed her again, though resisting had been a challenge. When she'd pulled up her hair, he'd yearned for a taste of the creamy skin of her neck, to feel the pulse at the base of her throat beat gently against his lips and tongue.

Astute as she was, receptive as she'd been to his kisses, it would be stupid to think she hadn't noticed his desire. Maybe he'd been so forward and his desire so obvious, he'd scared her away before he had a chance to do things right.

Rather than dwell on that small misery, he gave his full attention to the computer. It wasn't a bad theory that someone at her office was the root of this mess. Julia wasn't the only lawyer he'd known, just the first from Marburg's notorious ranks. If most of her fellow attorneys took after her rude boss, Julia's sense of decency must be a rare commodity inside that building.

Scrolling through the pages of pictures on the website, he noticed a scarcity of female attorneys. Apparently, the managing partners—all male—weren't worried about maintaining their equal opportunity stats. He'd watched his dad's generation deal with similar issues in the fire department. The rigorous training was compounded by a steep gender bias. Few women qualified to work fires and those who did usually had to overcome all kinds of doubt within their firehouses. He couldn't imagine adding backstabbing to their list of daily concerns. He glanced over his shoulder at Julia with a new appreciation for her unfailing composure.

He ignored the women and older men and those listed in satellite offices across the country. He spent more time on the younger men, reading through the bios in case the pictures weren't current. When they all started to look alike, he pressed the heels of his hands to his eyes.

He heard her poking around the cabinets and allowed it to distract him. At some point he had to tell her they were having dinner with his family tomorrow. He sure hadn't figured out how to tell his mother he *wouldn't* be there.

"Any luck?"

"Still looking," he replied, reluctant to dash her hopes. He twisted around in his seat. She'd pulled up that glorious red hair again, securing it with a clip. He flexed his hands, wanting to let it down and sift it through his fingers. "Do you work with anyone you know from law school?"

She shook her head. "I'm the first in a long time to be hired by Marburg straight out of my school."

"First woman, too, based on the bios I've read."

"Yes." Her chin came up and her hands twisted the dish towel mercilessly.

"The dish towel isn't the stalker, Julia."

Her eyebrows dipped in a frown, then her expression cleared with a spate of nervous laughter. "I would like to get my hands on the right target." She tossed the towel over her shoulder. "I did a quick inventory for tomorrow. How does a pot roast sound? You have a slow cooker and—"

He held up a finger to halt her. "We won't have to worry about dinner tomorrow." Coming to his feet, he removed the towel from her shoulder and returned it to its hook on the side of the refrigerator. Just like pulling off a bandage, it was better to spill the news all at once. "We're having dinner with my family tomorrow. One o'clock at my parents' house."

She rocked back on her heels, the color draining from her face. "Family dinner." She sat down hard on the counter stool. "You can't seriously mean for me to join you."

"That's exactly what I mean. I'm not leaving you alone. It's not a big deal," he promised. "It's more like a weekly requirement built into the Galway DNA."

"Do you and your siblings show up with guests often?"

"Often enough," he hedged.

Her eyes narrowed with suspicion. "When was the last time *you* brought a guest of the female variety?"

He should've expected her to see through that answer. The first time had been in high school and everyone had known she was only a friend. Just over a year ago he'd brought the woman he'd expected to marry. "A while ago."

"I see. Does anyone other than your brother know I've moved in here with you?"

"No. Stephen wouldn't open that can of worms."

"You have to go?"

"I missed last week. *We* have to go." How could he explain it to her without sounding like some lame man-child who should still be living in his parents' basement? "Missing two weeks in a row without a valid excuse is akin to an unforgiveable sin." He stepped closer and leaned forward, bracing his elbows on the counter and pouring on the charm. "The food is amazing and since it's your first time, you don't even have to help with the dishes."

"First time?"

Her green eyes were wide and troubled, and all he wanted to do was take her in his arms and erase every bit of stress clouding her features. "I expect we'll go back until this stalker thing is resolved."

She groaned, covering her face with her hands. "This is crazy."

He gently drew her hands away from her face. "Why?"

"Mitch." Her gaze dropped to where he drew his thumbs in slow circles over her palms. "Stop."

"In a minute." *Maybe.* He liked the feel of her soft skin, the sound of her voice. "Tell me why it's crazy." *Trust me*, he added with his eyes. Her breathing was quick and shallow. She was a private person, used to being alone. He hadn't expected her to be thrilled about dinner with a bunch of strangers, but he hadn't antici-pated her panic.

"They'll get the wrong idea," she said. "I'm a client, not a date."

"You could be both." He brought her hands to his lips and feathered kisses over her knuckles. He knew she appreciated the direct approach; he preferred it himself. "I'd like it if you were both."

Her lips parted for a moment, then clamped shut. He thought he caught a sheen of tears in her eyes before she closed them and lowered her head.

"Forget the family and focus on the dinner part," he said, still holding her hands. "The food will be amazing."

"I can't separate the two," she replied, meeting his gaze again. "What if…"

Her expression blanked and he followed her unspoken thoughts down the dark spiral. "You won't be putting any of us at risk."

"I wish I could agree. It's not smart, Mitch."

Her worry strengthened his resolve. They were going to dinner. She needed a break from this mess. Though his boisterous family aggravated him frequently, they were good people who believed in laughter, hard work and common sense. "No one will start humming a wedding march when we walk in."

He'd meant it as a joke, something so absurd it would shock the worry and fear right out of her. Instead, she swore, yanking her hands from his grasp.

"You can't just tell your mom you're working? Working a new job, I mean."

"Not this week." He tried to laugh it off. "She knows I'm suspended and I lied about a closing shift at the Escape to get out of last week. Typically, the only valid excuse for missing dinner is being on shift. Which might explain why so many of Myra Galway's children have chosen public service careers." That earned a small smile. Finally. "All that to say I think you'll like her. Honestly, she would have my head if she heard what a hash I've made of this."

"I'm sure she's a lovely woman." She turned her back on him. "Don't ask me to crash your family dinner. I'll be safe enough here. I'm the last woman any mother wants her son to bring home," she finished quietly.

He came around the counter, laid his hands lightly on her tense shoulders. "What makes you say that?" When she remained there, letting him touch her, he kneaded the knots in her muscles, working gently to loosen them.

"Off the cuff?" She held up one finger. "Redhead." Another finger rose. "Lawyer." A third finger joined the others. "Representing one of the biggest criminals in city history."

Did she think he was blind? None of those were her real reasons. "You're making this a bigger issue than it is." Far bigger than he'd meant to make it. His reasons for being agitated about how his family reacted to her made sense. He worried they'd see through him and realize how much he cared about her before he was ready to broach the subject with her.

Her increasing desperation had him scrambling to make things right. Despite everything that had brought her to the club, everything they'd encountered since, she'd never shown this type of insecurity. "Take a breath. Tell me what's really bothering you."

She shook her head quickly, setting wisps of her gorgeous hair free of the clip to curl at the nape of her neck. "Pretending you're my new boyfriend at the office is one thing. They don't matter. Don't ask me to deceive your family."

"That was never the intention. I'll introduce you as a friend, though. Calling you a client would be a tougher sell. They don't know what Grant does at the Escape."

She slipped away from his touch, facing him once more. He was pleased to see the resolve return to her eyes, along with that determined lift of her chin. Why did he find that angle so enticing?

"And bringing home a *friend*—" she used air quotes "—implies so much more. I'll stay here."

Her voice was rock steady now. She'd fought off whatever had stirred up her anxiety. Inexplicably Mitch felt shortchanged that she hadn't needed his help to get over the problem or trusted him enough to share it. He rolled his shoulders, trying to dismiss the weird feeling. "No."

"No?" She folded her arms over her chest and her eyes lit with a fight.

He tucked his hands into his back pockets and met her gaze. Held it. "We stick together until we identify your stalker *and* he's in custody."

"Mitch."

"Discussion over. End of debate." He returned to the table and sat down to resume his search of the attorneys she worked with. "Let's start eliminating suspects."

Eventually, she joined him at the table and they pulled together a short list of possible suspects that resembled the man he'd seen in the coffee shop. Four men who had been difficult since she'd joined the firm. It was far from definitive, but it was progress. "See, we do great work together," he said.

"Yeah." She closed her laptop and rested her hands lightly on the top. "I hope we're on the right track," she murmured, her brow furrowed as she gazed through the window to the dark street.

"Worried I'll knock the wrong heads together before we have evidence and facts?"

"No." She turned her attention to him and her lips curved into a sly smile. "If it comes to that, I know a great attorney who can help you beat assault charges."

He laughed, pushing himself out of the chair, pleased she could make jokes about the situation. "Let's get some rest." He stretched his arms high over his head, regretting he'd kept her up so late.

She didn't budge, just stared at him with a gaze that mirrored the hunger and longing churning inside him. "I overreacted earlier," she stated. "About tomorrow."

"I know." He grinned at her. "I'll get you through it unscathed. I have a lifetime of experience."

Her lips twitched but she didn't smile. "I just… I don't have the best track record with family dynamics," she stated. "You've helped me and I don't want to create problems for you or your family."

He pulled out the chair and turned it so he could straddle the seat, stacking his arms across the top rail as he sat down again. "Do you want to tell me what happened?" The answer shimmered in the depths of her green eyes.

"No. Not right now," she added quickly. "Dwelling on my past…um…failures will make me more nervous than I am already."

He didn't press the issue, yet she didn't seem ready to call it a night. "What do you need, Julia?"

The question seemed to startle her. She fidgeted in her chair and gave her attention to the water bottle on the table as she avoided his gaze. "Sleep, I suppose," she said, shutting him out once more.

He could take a hint. He stood up once more and slid the chair in properly. "Then we have a plan." In a perfect world she'd sleep beside him, but he had to settle for across the hall. *For now.* Although her circumstances had forced them together, he wanted more. He refused to rush it and blow his chance to thoroughly explore what was simmering under the mutual attraction and heart-stopping kisses.

In the hallway between their bedroom doors, he said good-night, but she hesitated. "Mitch, why did you kiss me?"

"Which time?"

He liked the way her lips quirked as she thought about it. It was all he could do not to kiss her again while he waited for her reply.

"I'm not talking about those little pecks at lunchtime." She turned the water bottle around and around in her hands. "I know those were for show."

Maybe the first one, he thought.

"I'm referring to the kiss when we were leaving my apartment."

"Because I needed it," he confessed. She'd needed it, too. "Pulling up, seeing all the first responders…" He pushed a hand through his hair. "The bomb squad. Julia, the whole scene scared the hell out of me."

She nodded. "Me, too."

"I never should have left you. Grant raked me over the coals for the assumption." He breached the narrow gap between them and smoothed a wayward lock of hair behind her ear. "You're so warm," he murmured. Nothing like the cold-blooded-shark attorney she had to be in the office. "You were chilled, by the weather and the attack. I needed the reassurance that you were alive and well."

"I've been so focused on my career I think forgot I needed that, too." She moved into him and looped her hands around his neck. "Thank you." Her lips brushed his. "For the reminder."

A white-hot bolt of need blazed across his senses and he seized control of the kiss, slanting his mouth across hers. He wrapped her in his arms, her breasts soft against his chest. At her little, pleasured gasp, he took full advantage, his tongue dueling with hers.

Still, he wasn't close enough. He stroked his hands over the curve of her hips, and boosted her up until her legs came around his waist. Almost. Almost close enough.

With her body caught between his and the wall behind her, he flexed his hips. She answered with a soft moan, grinding the sweet juncture of her thighs against his erection. Mouths still fused with heat, he eased his hands under her sweater, inching higher until his hands were full of her lush breasts. Her legs tightened around his hips. He thumbed the pebbled tips of her breasts, relishing every sweet response she gave him.

He could hardly believe this woman, the one who resisted any invasion of her personal space, was practically molding her body to his. Open and eagerly granting him access to all of her. *Too good to be true.*

He kissed the shell of her ear, felt her shiver and absorbed it with his body. Kissing her jaw, he worked his way down that elegant throat until he felt her heartbeat racing under his lips. Better than he'd imagined.

"Mitch, wait." She fisted her hands in his shirt and pushed a little, the effort creating hardly any distance.

He managed to stop kissing her despite the demands for more surging through his body.

"I let this go too far." She brought his mouth back to hers, the kiss soft and slow. Sweet enough he might die from it. Cupping his face, she held him just out of reach, those green eyes smoldering. "We need to wait. I'm so sorry." She shifted and her legs slid down his hips so she could stand on her own.

He marveled that she was steady when he wanted to crumple from the loss. "Okay." Hell, he wanted to beg her to reconsider. He couldn't get his brain to push the rest of the words, the right words, out of his mouth.

"Don't be mad. I just can't. Not…not tonight."

"Okay," he repeated, his voice rough as a hasp. There was no hiding the erection straining the limits of his button-fly jeans. "I'm not mad." Frustrated? Definitely.

"I'm sorry." She laid a hand over his pounding heart. "This—" she wagged a finger between them "—is so fast, so good, it scares me."

Who had screwed her up so badly that she resisted affection and trust? Why did he feel the soul-deep need to fix it? "Then we slow it down." He stepped out of reach before temptation obliterated the last of his common sense. "Whatever is between us is good." And worth waiting for. "Fast or slow," he added, "I want you. You need to be sure."

She nibbled that full lower lip with her teeth. "I'm sorry," she said again.

"Don't do that. Don't apologize to me." *Trust me!* He thought his jaw might crack if he didn't make a quick exit. "Good night," he said, somehow managing to close his bedroom door gently when he was on the other side.

He leaned back against the door, listening as she made her way to and from the bathroom. He didn't breathe easy until he heard her bedroom door close one final time. As he stripped off his clothes and slid between the sheets, he knew he was in for a long night. He might not have her in bed, but he knew she'd be starring in his dreams.

That wonderful temptation would have to satisfy him until she was ready to open up to him, body and soul.

With a Beethoven sonata lilting through the car's speakers, Leo drove through the tidy working-class neighborhood and circled the block looking for the right opening. No one took any notice. People were too damned complacent.

His computer genius had alerted him to the activity on Julia's laptop, confirming the boyfriend had gotten a look at him in the coffee shop. Leo couldn't let that go, even if their search wasn't even warm yet.

K-Chase had earned his pay when he'd tracked down the pair, and earned another bonus as he gathered intel on the boyfriend. Julia and her suspended fireman thought they were clever, moving out of her apartment, but they weren't out of his reach. If Leo had his way, she never would be. He knew she'd recovered her belongings, having watched her do it, and he gave them points for keeping her cell phone turned off. The challenge would only make the outcome more satisfying.

After reviewing the report from his computer genius, Leo had decided the new man in Julia's life was certainly not an investigator or even much of a bodyguard. He was more an inconvenience. Adding another body to the rising count didn't worry him, though he was considering all his options. His goal was reaching his brother before disaster struck. The prize was Julia.

She'd surprised him, enlisting help and disguising it as a love interest. The move kept her firmly in the category of potential long-term asset. A shrewd and fierce defense attorney was helpful, and this one was nice to look at.

He'd shifted his tactics with that in mind, testing her to see how hard she'd scramble to stay on the biggest case of her career. She had yet to cave and confess her troubles to her superiors, but he sensed she wasn't quite ready to cooperate.

That was fine. He appreciated her fortitude. He didn't trust people who caved too quickly. According to his sources, his brother was merely posturing to keep the prosecution interested in dealing. Until Danny had to put up or shut up, Leo was free to toy with Julia and test her limits.

Leo's phone rang through the car speakers, interrupting the sonata. "Go," he answered.

"It's done," the female voice on the other end of the call responded. "You are secure."

"And you are a day late." He'd hired her to make sure the men who'd been arrested for impersonating policemen were silenced, swiftly and permanently. Leo would cut her pay by a third, knowing she was too desperate to complain.

"Were they interrogated?"

"No. Mug shots, fingerprints, then a holding cell." the woman confirmed. "You are secure," she repeated.

Leo disconnected the call and hummed along as the sonata resumed. These were the decisions his brother struggled to make in a timely manner. People were necessary to a successful operation and yet every last one of them was replaceable.

He checked the addresses K-Chase had provided and resumed his study of the neighborhood. Leo preferred keeping the spitfire attorney on edge and learning how she reacted. She'd demonstrated a protective streak—and loyalty, too, currently applied to the wrong people. He'd thought she might be someone he could trust one day, assuming she accepted his offer. Then they could unlock her full potential and safely add her to his greater plan.

Chapter 11

When Sunday dawned in perfect autumn fashion, Julia wished she could simply climb out the window and run away. She couldn't believe she'd agreed to attend family dinner this afternoon. Well, she hadn't exactly agreed—Mitch had declared the debate over. Not a good sign. If her brain hadn't been so muddled by his mere presence, she surely would have found a way to win the argument.

Thank goodness she'd mustered up the common sense to stop before they'd gone past the point of no return last night. Her body heated and her pulse skipped, remembering the feel of his mouth and hands and the remnants of the steamy, sensual ideas that had chased her in dreams.

It would be enough of a challenge hiding her feelings for Mitch from his family today. If she'd given in last night, it would have been certain disaster. She understood how important those bonds were to him and she didn't want to give the people he loved any false hope or reason to doubt him when she was out of his life.

She rolled to her side, wondering if she should fake a stomach bug. Mitch didn't know it, but he'd be better off that way. Maybe she should just tell him the whole damned story so he'd stop tempting her. If he knew how damaged she was, he'd be smart and run the other way as soon as possible.

The last time she'd been invited to a family dinner—her second semester of law school—it had gone so poorly her boyfriend had dumped her on the drive home. His parents had rooted out all of her secrets, embarrassing both of them, and he'd found creative and hurtful ways to retaliate during the remainder of their classes together.

The ugly memories sent a chill sliding over her body. That was when she'd shifted her focus into criminal defense. No one should be accused over appetizers, judged during the main course and declared guilty by dessert. She'd been blindsided, labeled as gold-digging trash and denied any chance to counter the allegations.

She rolled out of bed and quickly made it. At the door she paused, listening. Hopefully, Mitch was still sleeping. She wasn't looking forward to facing him after last night's attempt to climb his body like a strong tree. Battling against the urge to be a coward, she decided to reclaim her dignity and face him with self-respect and confidence.

She showered and dressed in jeans and a zip-up fleece and headed for the kitchen to make coffee and breakfast. There would be plenty of time to change into appropriate clothes and apply her makeup before they headed to the dinner.

Because she managed to think about it without cringing, she mentally gave herself a high five. She'd spent enough time with Mitch to realize he wasn't anything like the jerk who'd screwed her over in law school. Surely those flaws would've shown up by now if he had that capacity for cruelty.

Resentment and shame from that terrible evening coursed through her, alongside fresh anger for letting the old baggage dictate her actions last night. She'd been afraid that if they'd slept together, his mother would know and call her out.

But Mitch wasn't like the other guys she'd dated. He'd said she'd like his mom.

"Stupid," she muttered. She thought she'd packed those old weaknesses away, yet here she was, cycling through them once more. What did Mitch see in a mess like her? And had she killed this chemistry between them by shutting down the passion last night?

She gathered up ingredients for pancakes. Hopefully, food was a positive strategy for putting them back on an even keel before she met his family. A special gesture might take the sting out of last night, though she avoided searching for a deeper meaning in her rationale. She could use a friend, that's all. This was the wrong time in her life for a real boyfriend.

Great. As if being stuck in the stalker's vise wasn't bad enough, she'd managed to work her way into a romantic quagmire. "You know better," she whispered as she measured out milk and oil. "Mitch knows better."

Haywood was right about personal lives. Young associates wanting to move up didn't have time to invest in relationships. Young associates on major cases were little more than ticking time bombs. She was seriously attracted to Mitch, leaving her struggling against herself and the nature of her job not to wreck his life with her complications.

Hearing his footsteps in the hallway, she braced for disaster.

"Morning," Mitch said, his sleep-roughened voice teasing her senses.

"Good morning." She gave the mixture in the bowl one last whisk with the fork and then set the bowl aside to fill a mug with coffee for him. It wasn't easy to meet his gaze when she turned around.

He hadn't shaved and the golden whiskers highlighted his strong jaw. The snug, long-sleeved thermal shirt emphasized every angle and plane of his chiseled torso. She felt the blush heating her cheeks as the sensual dreams raced to the front of her mind, taunting her. She wanted him, badly, and if the cautious look in his eyes was any indication, she'd made a critical error last night.

Her fingers tingled when they brushed his as he accepted the coffee mug she offered. "I'm making pancakes," she said after an awkward moment soaking up the delectable view.

"I like pancakes."

His smile wasn't quite as warm today. She gave herself a mental kick for ruining a good thing before it really got started. That had to be a new one for the record books. He watched her steadily over the rim of his mug as he sipped the coffee. Unable to withstand the speculative glance, she turned back to the batter and set the griddle to heat.

"Can I help?" he asked.

Oh, she'd like that. She could imagine the feel of him all around her, crowding the galley kitchen with his size and heat, setting her hormones on fire. A ripple of an-

ticipation danced down her spine despite her best efforts
to ignore it. This was about becoming friends again or,
if not friends, at least two people who could muddle
through the crisis without hurting each other.

Time and place, she reminded herself, tossing a drop
of water on the griddle to test the heat.

"Who does that?" Mitch asked from behind her.

"Does what?"

"Tests the griddle that way."

What was he talking about? "It's how you're supposed to do it."

"Huh."

She shot him a look over her shoulder. "How do you
do it?"

"Mom taught me to use a spoonful of batter for pancakes."

Julia shrugged and resumed her task. Everything
she'd learned about cooking had come from the inter-
net or cooking shows. Her mother hadn't been into domestic bliss, unless it was to impress the newest man
she needed for one purpose or another. "If you don't
want pancakes…"

"I do," he said quickly. "I'll be quiet."

She could hear the grin in the eager rise of his voice
as she carefully poured circles of batter onto the griddle.

When they were seated at the table with a stack of hot
pancakes on each of their plates, he seemed to hesitate.

"What did I forget?" It seemed everything they
needed had made it to the table.

"Nothing. It smells delicious." He lifted his gaze from
the plate and the blatant heat in his brown eyes startled
her.

"Okay, good." She dropped a pat of butter on the top

pancake and watched it melt down over the others. He still stared at her. "Dig in."

"In a minute." He reached for the syrup pitcher as she did and curled his fingers around hers. "No one's ever done this for me before. Thank you."

That couldn't be true. She could not be the only woman in the world consumed with the urge to spoil him. "I don't believe you." When his eyebrows shot up, she stuffed a bite into her mouth before she blurted out another insult.

"Your doubt doesn't change the facts," he said, his smile back to full force now.

This had to be another ploy to get her to open up. He was too curious to drop that agenda. From the beginning he'd been asking about her past. What had been for the sake of the case felt far more intimate now. Thank goodness they hadn't slept together.

Yet. She'd be happy if that pesky voice went mute.

"These are amazing," he said after he'd downed half his breakfast. "What's your secret?"

"If I told you it wouldn't be my secret."

His gaze turned serious. "You can trust me with any secret," he said. "Big or small."

She thought of one of the cooking show hosts talking about love being the best seasoning of all. *Love* wasn't in play here. Only chemistry. *Food chemistry*, she corrected quickly. Julia had added a splash of orange juice and some nutmeg to the batter. "I wanted to do something nice for you," she said. What an understatement.

"You don't owe me anything, Julia."

They would have to agree to disagree on that. She gave him a smile and felt it wobble. "I…" She tried again.

"I wanted us to be comfortable with each other again before we head to dinner."

"Comfortable?" He sat up straighter, his thumb moving slowly over the curve of the handle of his mug. "Why would we be uncomfortable?"

The motion reminded her of the way that same thumb had traced the curve of her breast last night. Oh, good grief. That was exactly the place her thoughts should not go. "What's the dress code?" she asked, ignoring the breathy little catch in her voice.

Mitch's gaze narrowed as he focused his attention on her face. "Relaxed. Dad always changes as soon as they get home from church."

She sputtered. Could his family get any more traditional?

His dark eyebrows arched high. "Got a problem with church, too?" The flash of humor in his eyes softened the challenging question.

She rolled her eyes, exasperated with both of them. "No." She had a problem with her general lack of religious experience and education. Attending church regularly had been another college experiment as she'd tried to figure out who she wanted to be. The services and events had been nice. Calming. But she'd put her faith and focus into the practicality of law. "I'm glad you didn't insist we join them. It would have been tragic if a lightning bolt meant for me singed you."

He grinned and then finished his breakfast. Clearing their plates, he paused and gave her a heart-stopping look. "You can quit wasting time trying to convince me you're some kind of amoral shark disguised as a beautiful, compassionate woman. I know better."

The compliment left her speechless. She wasn't sure

what he thought he knew or how she felt about the words he aimed at her. "Mitch—"

"You're overthinking it again," he said, running water over the dishes. "I can hear the gears in your head turning all the way over here."

"You don't even know what I was going to say," she protested. How could he? He didn't know her, didn't know how utterly wrong she was for him. She didn't even understand why she wanted to be right for him. For anyone, she amended. Alone, she could accomplish her goals without fear of hurting anyone. Staying single meant she didn't have to worry about her money-grabbing mother or the shadows in her past spilling over onto someone else's life.

Only a mysterious stalker had shifted her out of her preferred state of being perennially unattached and Mitch was hip deep in her problems. "You're a good person," she began, searching for better words.

"So are *you*." He whirled around, his eyes flashing with temper. "Thank you for breakfast," he added, visibly pulling himself together. "I've got a few things to take care of out back. Call me if you need anything."

Startled into silence, she stared after him. How could she make him understand she only wanted to keep the fallout to a minimum?

Mitch cussed himself out the rest of the morning. Why couldn't he crack Julia's hard shell? She'd made him breakfast and he'd snapped at her. How had she put it? That making pancakes was her way of being comfortable again together. He'd liked the sound of that, until he realized she'd meant it as a penance.

She didn't owe him any gesture for stopping that

heated embrace last night. While he was definitely eager to break through those massive walls she'd built, he was a little unnerved to realize he wanted her secrets as much as he wanted her body. *More*. Sure, she trusted him to shelter her from the stalker. Why couldn't she trust him with the real woman under the layers of education and sexy-as-hell business suits?

He'd washed the dishes, worked out back, cleaned up for dinner, and still not been able to shake off the feeling of being cared for and valued just for being present. And she still didn't seem to understand what a gift that was. A gift she'd given him. He wasn't the only good person in this equation.

After changing clothes twice, she'd settled on snug dark jeans and a soft, pale green top that subtly emphasized her delectable figure. She wore sleek boots with enough of a heel to bring her lips within easy reach. He wanted to mold his hands over each amazing dip and swell of her body. And if he kept thinking about it, he'd be exceedingly uncomfortable as he introduced her to his family.

He cleared his throat. "This could get dicey," he warned on the short drive over. "No one in my family really knows when to shut up or stop asking questions."

"I promise not to sue anyone for nosiness," she replied.

"Ha-ha." The reply irritated him. "You know damn well that's not what I meant."

Julia turned that stoic, knowing gaze on him, the one he imagined would leave a prosecutor sweating through his suit in a courtroom. "You're nervous."

"A little." No sense denying it. He hoped his candor helped unleash hers. "Not about you," he said, with a smile. "My siblings have a tradition of pestering the one who brings a guest."

She jerked in her seat, as if he'd thrown more than words at her. His hands flexed on the steering wheel.

"Do me a favor?" she said, her gaze straight ahead.

Anything. "What do you need?"

"Don't say another word about your family before we get there."

The request startled him. "Can I ask why?"

"You won't get an answer."

He bit back another terse response at the sound of her cool, composed voice, though it cost him. Waiting didn't come easy and she'd been pushing the limits of his curiosity. When would she open up? "Will you tell me on the way home?" he asked, parking behind a line of cars at the curb.

He caught the soft gasp and saw her press a hand to her stomach. "What's wrong?"

Instantly, her face smoothed into the emotionless mask she'd employed with her boss. The same look she'd worn when she'd aimed a gun on the fake cop. "I'm fine." She reached for the door and he stopped her.

"Julia." Beneath his fingers, he felt her trembling. When she met his gaze, her lips parted on a hiccup and then she pressed her shaking hands between her knees. That did it. He shoved the key in the ignition and started the car again. "We'll go." He pulled out into the street without looking. Someone honked, but he didn't care. He floored it. "I'm a jackass," he said, downshifting to stop at the sign on the next corner. "We're leaving. Just breathe."

"Mitch. Go back. I'll manage. It's just—"

"All the people," he finished for her. How could he

tease her about *not* being a callous shark and then ignore her fear of putting anyone else at risk? *Stupid.* He
wanted her to meet his family, to share that side of himself with her. *Too soon.* "I'm sorry."

"No, it's me," she said. "I'm being ridiculous. Your
mother's expecting you. Us."

"You're shaking."

"I know." She deliberately flattened her palms on her
thighs. "It's not all about the stalker, though he does
worry me."

"He should." Mitch had to agree. Although neither
of them said it, they both knew, with the resources he'd
exhibited, the Galway family was on the bastard's radar
whether they went to dinner or not.

"Go back," she said. "I won't let the past trip me up
this time."

He held his breath, refusing to ask, refusing to make
her share something she clearly wanted to keep buried.
She had to *want* to share those secrets with him.

"You're different," she murmured. "I'm different."
She spoke the words over and over as if reciting a meditation. "Thanks for the valiant effort," she said, smiling
a little. "I'll tell you all the gory details later and we can
have a good laugh at my expense."

He didn't think he'd be laughing over a story that had
nearly induced a panic attack. "Whenever you're ready to
share, I'll listen," he replied. This time when he parked
he was behind Stephen's truck. Maybe his parents would
have their hands too full with his brooding brother to
worry about the guest he hadn't warned them about.

He knew she didn't want to give his family the wrong
impression, but he took her hand as they walked up the

sidewalk to the porch. She still looked a little pale. "We'll leave before dessert," he promised in a whisper.

Mitch wasn't a bit surprised when the front door flew open before he touched the handle. "You're almost late," his youngest sister accused.

"Nice to see you too, Jenny." He caught her in a tight hug until she smacked at his back to get him to let go.

Her eyes lit on Julia. "Who's this?"

"Let us in and I'll introduce you."

In the muted light of the foyer, he took Julia's coat and made introductions. First to Jenny, then to his siblings, Megan and Andrew, and their respective spouses and children as everyone trickled in at the commotion near the door. "You remember Stephen," he said at last. "And these are my parents, Samuel and Myra Galway."

His parents stepped forward and greeted Julia warmly.

"A pleasure to meet all of you," Julia said. "Mitch claimed I wouldn't be any imposition."

"No, no imposition at all," Myra said as a smile bloomed across her round face. "Come in, come in." Myra waved a hand to give them room to walk into the house. She poked Jenny in the shoulder. "Go set another place at the table."

Her astute gaze landed on Mitch next. "This is an interesting surprise," she whispered as the rest of his family caught up Julia and led her to the family room.

He silently pleaded with his mother to let it go. She hesitated, then stepped back and tipped her head toward the family room. More than a little concerned, he peeked around the corner, ready to charge to Julia's rescue. But she showed no signs of the earlier anxiety, her smile open and easy as she answered questions as quickly as they were tossed out.

"You'll help me with drinks." His mother tugged him along to the kitchen.

He knew better than to argue. As he passed by, he caught Julia's eye, sending her an encouraging smile. Fifteen minutes later, when his rowdy family had packed around the dining room table, he was relieved she hadn't run away screaming yet.

He tried to see it all from her perspective and wanted to cringe. Meals and conversation at her apartment and even his house had been quiet, primarily case related. He'd grown up with this disorderly process that bordered on crazy. He was used to hearty meals and loud voices talking over one another as food was passed and devoured.

They'd quickly learned she was an attorney and her chin had only come up a little, daring them to have an opinion when she told them she was with Marburg.

Although his father had raised a curious eyebrow at that, no one challenged her or asked about the Falk case. Mitch exchanged a look with Stephen and realized they'd been warned. He'd have to thank his brother later for smoothing the way. With every conversational topic and rambling tangent, he learned a bit more about Julia. Not about where she'd come from, but who she'd decided to be now.

"She fits in pretty well," Stephen said as he helped Mitch carry dishes into the kitchen. "Mom likes her."

"Mom likes a lot of people," Mitch replied. When Stephen only gave a noncommittal grunt, Mitch changed the subject. "You haven't had any trouble at the garage?"

"No." Stephen scowled. "Should I expect some?"

"Doubtful, but stay alert. The guy hassling her is focused on *her*, but something's off." Hearing Julia's laughter, he leaned over to catch a glimpse of her.

"Your focus, if I had to guess," Stephen grumbled.

Mitch was about to elbow his brother in the ribs when a thunderous boom sounded, shaking the house. For a split second, they stared at each other and then both of them bolted for the front of the house at the same time. Stephen shot straight for the front door and Mitch took a route through the dining room. His first priority was Julia.

She stood at the window with the rest of his family, staring at a fireball engulfing the hood of his car. He swore when he saw Stephen racing closer to the swelling blaze.

"Call 911!" he ordered. "Mom, take Julia and the others to the basement." The gun rack was down there and all of the adults knew how to handle the firearms. If the stalker got into the house, he'd have a war on his hands.

Everyone moved at once and Mitch ran back through the kitchen, grabbing the fire extinguisher on the way.

"Give me that one," his dad snapped.

Mitch obliged. Bursting through the back door, he went for the bigger fire extinguisher his dad kept in the workshop behind the house.

Another explosion sounded as Mitch reached the front of the house. He watched, horrified as Stephen and Samuel were tossed back by the blast. The bed of Stephen's truck went up fast and came down again in slow motion.

He rushed forward against the fire, focusing his effort on stopping the destruction at Stephen's truck before it spread in a chain reaction down the street. Behind him, he heard shouts and car engines revving. His family and neighbors were moving cars out of harm's way. A siren cried from a distance as others came outside to watch the commotion. The crisis was almost over when the first fire truck turned into the street, lights and sirens tearing up the quiet Sunday afternoon.

The firefighters put out the blaze and paramedics checked them all for injuries, taking a few minutes to chat with Mitch, his brothers and their dad before they left.

His dad looked around. "Where did Myra and the girls go?"

"I sent them to the basement," Mitch replied, thankful they'd stayed there.

Stephen shook his head, his expression grim, while he studied the charred remains of the vehicles. "I'll call in a tow truck while you deal with that." He raised his chin toward the police cruiser rolling to a stop at the driveway.

Mitch was about to ask his dad to keep Julia out of it when she stepped out onto the porch. Her eyes wide, she clapped a hand over her mouth as she took in the scene, then she ran straight for him. "Are you hurt?" She looked at Stephen and their dad. "Are any of you hurt?"

"Not a scratch." Samuel pressed a hand to his hip. "Maybe a bruise or two."

"Oh, I'm so sorry." She leveled an accusing glare at Mitch. "I warned you."

His dad gave him a quizzical glance before shuffling off to hug his wife.

Mitch pulled her aside before Julia said something she might regret. "This isn't your fault."

She folded her arms over her chest. "So cars blow up around here after dinner every week?"

"Not every week," he teased. She wasn't amused. "You did not cause this."

"You can't believe this is unrelated." She sucked in a breath, her gaze darting over the damaged vehicles. "Your car. Oh, Mitch. Without me, your house, your family would have stayed safe."

"Hush," he said, pulling her into a hug and tucking her head to his shoulder. He knew this was the work of the stalker. They were on display out here. "We're all alive and we're all going to stay that way."

Mitch and his dad delivered the initial report to the police officers. The officers split up, one taking names and statements from the Galway family, the other canvassing the neighborhood for any witnesses. Myra served coffee and dessert during the interviews, always hospitable to any guests. It was such a mom thing to do and yet Mitch knew it made Julia feel worse.

By the time they were free to go, the burned vehicles had been hauled away to the forensics lab. Julia fell into a tense silence, her hand linked with his, as they rode in the backseat while Samuel drove them to the garage to pick up loaner cars.

He longed to comfort her, to let her vent every crazy theory brewing in her stormy green eyes. He could see her shoulders sagging under the weight of the misplaced guilt and blame she was carrying.

With a renewed sense of purpose, Mitch silently vowed that, one way or another, they would stop the bastard tearing up her life before he destroyed her.

Julia never dreamed she'd consider a nightclub safe haven and yet by name and reputation, the Escape was becoming just that. The knotted muscles at the base of her neck loosened as Mitch drove east toward the river rather than back to his house.

Once they were alone, she'd tried to apologize, but he'd cut her off, refusing the notion that she was to blame. It was more than gracious, it was silly. Hopefully, Grant would set him straight, maybe assign her to someone else or...

She slid a glance at the square jaw of Mitch's strong profile. She didn't want anyone else. "When you sent me to the basement with your mom I was pissed," she confessed. "I wanted to be out there, helping you."

"I had help. Qualified help," he pointed out. "It helped me more knowing you were safe, out of his sight."

"Mmm-hmm. Still, I could've looked for that damn orange hat while you did your thing."

"This wasn't your fault."

"So you've said." Countless times.

He parked at the far end of the employee lot and turned off the engine of the boring beige compact sedan Stephen had loaned him.

She climbed out, resigning herself to another Q&A with Grant that likely wouldn't put them any closer to the stalker. "I hate this." She leaned against the closed door, staring at Mitch over the roof of the car. "I'm going to call my boss and just relinquish the case. Take a vacation to Siberia or somewhere equally isolated."

"I think today is a good sign."

She snorted. "You must be rewriting the definition of 'good.'"

"I'm not. We must be getting close if he's pulling stunts like this."

"Stunts? Mitch, he's proving he can do anything, get to us anywhere we go. That should scare you."

"He doesn't hold all the cards," Mitch insisted.

She watched him come around the car, his stride easy

and his brown eyes full of the sincerity she wanted so desperately to believe in. It couldn't be real. He just didn't know her well enough to push her away. Being around her had turned his world on end and it surely wouldn't be helping his chances for reinstatement. "You must hate this car," she said, kicking the tire. "You must hate me for losing that classic."

His hands gripped her shoulders and his mouth claimed hers. Rational thought fizzled. She gripped his jacket and pulled herself closer to the kiss, her body instinctively seeking the comfort and distraction he offered.

He leaned back, his gaze inscrutable as his big hand sleeked down her hair. "I don't hate you. Don't say that again. Ever."

The words brushed her cheek. "Okay," she whispered. As his body pressed her back to the car, his arousal was obvious. If they were anywhere but here, she'd give in, toss caution aside and drag him to the nearest flat surface. She smoothed her palms over his chest under his jacket. "Am I allowed to say I told you so?"

"That depends."

Her eyes locked on the tilt at the corner of his mouth. He had such a sexy smirk, full of sinful promises. "Depends on what?" The words came out all breathless and fluttery and she didn't even care.

"I don't remember." He nudged her aside and opened the passenger door. "Get in."

She grinned, liking this bossy side of him too much. "Isn't Grant expecting us?"

He pushed her gently into the seat and shut the door. Her heart leaped as he raced around to the driver's side.

"Grant can wait. He has friends on the police force. We don't know anything new anyway."

"We know he knows all about you." Playing devil's advocate kept her from crawling all over that gorgeous body while he was trying to drive. That kind of move would cause all kinds of problems for both of them—well beyond the obvious traffic violations. "Hurry," she said.

"I am." His knuckles turned white on the wheel. "Trust me, I am."

He swore when he reached his house and realized the remote for the garage door had been blown up with his car. She giggled—an absurd reaction, considering the circumstances.

"Keep it up and we'll do this right here in the car."

She licked her lips, contemplating the potential of that idea. As combustible as she felt, it was better to do this inside. One car explosion was more than enough for one lifetime.

He leaned across the seat and gave her a tender, bone-melting kiss, completely at odds with the need and excitement surging through her system. "You're sure?"

She nodded, not trusting her voice. At the moment she didn't care what had brought them together or what was propelling them forward. Adrenaline, attraction or simple survival response, she wanted Mitch. Now. Desperately. The relationship analytics could wait.

His smile teased her senses as he took her under with another slow, dazzling kiss. "There's more where that came from," he said, nudging her toward the door she hadn't noticed him opening.

By some miracle, her legs managed to hold her up as they left the car and hurried into the house. Once they were inside, Mitch slammed the door and locked out their troubles. Here, now, it was only the two of them and the need arcing like lightning between them. Coats, shoes and clothing disappeared between hot kisses and tantalizing touches, leaving a trail through the house from the back door straight to his bedroom.

She sighed when her hands met his bare skin, and she paused to admire the view of his powerful chest and sculpted abs. The soft evening light caught on the dusting of hair on his chest. She pulled her hands back, suddenly scared to touch him, scared the moment was too good to be true and he'd simply evaporate before her eyes.

"You're stunning," he murmured, his gaze raking over the lavender lace of her bra and panties. "Better than my dreams."

His confession made her bold. "You dreamed of me?"

"Every night." The buttons of his fly popped one after the other and he pushed his jeans and boxers down to the floor. Nude, he pulled her close, his erection snug between them, his heat and masculine scent surrounding her in a cloud of desire. "You didn't dream of me?"

"Yes. From that first night." She'd never been so open with anyone before. "I worried my tossing and turning kept you awake."

The grin was all masculine pride and pure sin. "It did." His palms cruised up and down her back, erasing any judgment out of the statement. With each touch, he made making her feel beautiful and feminine. Her body went soft and pliant, eager for every hard inch of him.

Words were forgotten as a needy kiss took her deeper into new pleasures. He unhooked her bra and eased her back to his bed, nudging her down and stretching out over her. She grazed her short nails up his biceps, over his shoulders and down his back, pleased when he arched into her touch.

The give and take of discovery melted her from the inside out, smoothing every jagged ache from her past. He rained kisses over her face, feasted on her throat, then moved lower to learn the shape and feel of her breasts. With fingers and lips, tongue and teeth, he brought her to the very edge of a climax, kept her perched there, deliberately spinning out every sensation.

She ran her hands through his short hair, across his shoulders. No need to rush anything. There would be time enough to return the favor. His hands teased her thighs and her legs fell open for him. "Love me, Mitch," she murmured, bucking her hips against the fingers sliding over her slick center.

His big body rose over her, his sexy grin replaced by such open need that she thought she could hear the last of the walls around her heart crumbling. Lifting her hips, he entered her in one smooth thrust. She cried out, delighted, her body clutching his. She hugged his lean hips with her legs, her hands reaching for his shoulders while he rocked in and out of her.

The pleasure swelled, amplified by nuance as they found that precious, sensual rhythm. Faster and wild, she clung to him, her breath fractured on gasps of passion. The orgasm rocketed through her system. His body shuddered a moment later and he fell forward, bracing himself on his elbows to kiss her thoroughly before he rolled to the side.

She nestled into his embrace, utterly content as his heart beat under her cheek. It felt so perfect and true, she snuggled deeper, trusting him enough to give in to the exhaustion and sleep right there in his arms.

Chapter 12

Mitch listened to her fall asleep, smiling to himself as her breath settled into a gentle, intermittent breeze across his skin. Her silky red hair sifted over the back of his hand as he caressed her shoulder. Did she have any idea what she'd done to him?

Love me, Mitch.

God help him, he did. The signs were obvious; there was no sense lying to himself about it. He didn't plan to say the words anytime soon, but he knew they'd be true the moment she was ready to hear it. She might not realize what she'd said in the heat of passion.

He kissed her hair, telling himself to slow down. As a firefighter, he'd been trained to avoid the misplaced infatuation of rescued victims and still managed to get tangled up with the wrong woman. Julia was different, despite how they'd met. She wasn't a victim looking for a hero—she was a fighter. Falling in love with her wasn't a mistake.

Not like Leann. Despite knowing better, he'd accepted an invitation from a rescued woman to have coffee after shift. They'd made it a weekly habit and after a couple months, it seemed completely natural to ask her out on a real date. For six months he'd been sure Leann was "the one." His mom had disagreed, though not outright. Those conversations had been left to his dad and older brother.

Mitch had ignored every warning from his family until it was nearly too late. Fortunately Leann's true nature showed itself just before his sappy plan to propose on Valentine's Day. Looking back, he could see what a nightmare he'd escaped. He tensed at the memory, and in her sleep Julia's palm smoothed over his chest. She had a lovely, compassionate instinct that warmed him body and soul. Behind those sharp heels and cool gazes, she had a generous, tender heart.

Everyone had scars and secrets. In her profession, he'd assumed she'd realized that basic fact of life. He wasn't afraid of showing his to Julia. Good grief, if he had proposed to his cheating ex in February, he wouldn't be free to help Julia now. The idea of her dealing with her trouble alone, or with someone else from the club, made him want to punch holes in the nearest walls. He couldn't stand the idea of another man teasing that bright laughter out of her or making those green eyes go dreamy with a kiss or passionate touch.

She'd resist the concept out of habit, but he could convince her they were good together. Not just together until the stalker was in custody, but for the long haul. He could happily spend a lifetime helping her shelter and protect that soft center hidden under the shark-lawyer layers.

He rubbed his foot along her calf and felt the chill on her skin. Carefully, he shifted enough to catch the edge of the sheet and pull it up over them. Julia sighed, her arm sliding around his waist, keeping him close. He liked that innate reaction. He wouldn't do either of them the disservice of thinking it was too much. It felt exactly right.

When she woke, she'd likely return to that tendency to take the blame for bringing her stalker so close to his family home. It was nonsense, of course, but she had that big, caring heart deep inside her. Mitch's mind raced, wondering how to expose her stalker. If—*when*—he identified the jerk, would she agree to trust him enough and let him stick around? Maybe for life?

He pressed a kiss to the top of her head, breathing deeply. The spicy fragrance of her shampoo reminded him of Thanksgiving and autumn leaves blanketing yards in a riot of sunset colors. She'd fit in around that boisterous dinner so naturally.

He could kill the stalker for ruining the day before she had a chance to realize it. Reluctantly, his thoughts drifted back to her case. Since his car had been the initial target, the police questions had revolved around him. Julia's relief at being ignored had been palpable. She wouldn't have wanted to lie to the police, but she could hardly give an honest answer that wouldn't piss off the stalker or her boss. How long did she expect to hold out against this threat?

Although he respected her theory of a disgruntled coworker, he didn't think it was the right direction. The men they'd identified were borderline matches, not exact enough to give him confidence. Based on the bios and the work ethic he'd encountered at her office, he didn't think anyone at Marburg had the wherewithal to bomb a car on a quiet Sunday afternoon.

Yes, people could do crazy, irrational things. He'd put out more than one fire started on purpose and he'd seen enraged people try to prevent rescues out of spite or vengeance. That bomb hadn't been placed or detonated by an irrational person. He recognized it as a message—a direct threat against him for coming between the stalker and Julia.

Why had the bastard fixated on her?

In his arms, Julia stretched languidly, her short nails tracing a path down his side, over his hip. "You're awake," she murmured against his chest.

"You, too." Her voice, husky with sleep, slid right into his bloodstream, giving him more of a jolt than a double shot of espresso. He forgot the stalker as she rolled on top of him. Her hair tickled his cheek, his chest as she scattered kisses over his face, throat, and lower still. She straddled his waist and sat up, the sheets pooling at her hips. Under the sensuous ministrations of her mouth and hands, he wasn't a bit cold. Inside or out.

With a sultry smile, she gave and gave, every touch setting off fireworks through his bloodstream. He'd never been so completely entranced. She took him deep into her body, bringing his hands to her breasts as she rocked up and down in long, tantalizing strokes.

Mine, he thought. Letting her set the pace, he savored the view, his body taut as a wire. When she arched her back, his name a low moan on her lips, he knew there was nothing in the world as glorious as Julia reaching a climax and bringing him along with her.

* * *

Julia felt a disorienting contentment waking in Mitch's arms, and it made her happy to have the feeling follow her throughout her morning. Even the expected check-in text messages on her new cell phone couldn't penetrate this strange happiness. She'd had no idea her life could sparkle this way.

They'd shared a shower before breakfast and on the way in, Mitch explained his plans to stick close to her building when he couldn't actually be in it. She still didn't trust herself not to say or do something that would break this fragile, budding relationship, if that was even the right word. It must be, since her heart had fallen right into his hands from the moment he'd woken her with a warm smile and tender kiss.

She was in her cubicle, trying to keep her mind on the case when her original cell phone hummed with a text message.

Don't be upset. The car was empty. The gloating words didn't bother her nearly as much as the picture of Mitch that came through a moment later.

Mitch had found a spot at the bistro just up the street, watching the building as promised. From the angle it seemed as if the picture had been taken not far from Marburg's front door. She forwarded the message and photo to Mitch, hoping he had some idea how to handle it.

His message came back to her original cell immediately. Perfect. A smiley face followed, along with a note that Grant was sending the sketch artist to meet Mitch at the bistro.

Julia applied herself to the case work her boss had assigned, though it felt like a futile exercise. This morning, after looking at all the possibilities, she had to agree with Mitch's assessment that no one she'd known in law school or met here at the firm would blow up a car.

It was hard to believe someone other than the stalker would choose this particular moment to blow up his car. And the closest thing to an enemy in Mitch's life was a bully from high school and the allegedly negligent father who'd picked a fight with him at a fire.

No, it had to be her stalker making it obvious he was in control, making it clear others would be hurt if she didn't cooperate. As if she needed a reminder. She'd tried and failed again this morning to regain control of her financial accounts. The credit card payment date had come and gone, and an email had arrived this morning about the late payment. Thank goodness Stephen was subletting the apartment.

The stalker had proved his control and ingenuity time and again. He could clear a building with a single phone call just to access her computer. Although no one found any evidence of tampering, she was sure he'd searched her laptop. The timing of the car bomb, just after they had a potential identification was no coincidence.

Another text message set her phone vibrating on her desk again. She braced herself before she swiped the screen to read it.

Her entire body relaxed at the sight of Mitch's cell phone number. Hey beautiful. How about dinner at Baglio's Riverview and dancing after? Escape is hosting that band you love.

Her heart did a silly pirouette at the endearment. Dinner out sounded like a real date. The club afterward for dancing, that must be code that Grant required a face-to-face update. There weren't any local bands she knew well enough to love.

It's a date, she texted back immediately, wishing it could be. Mitch must be laying a trap for the stalker. She hoped whatever he had in mind involved sufficient backup. Yesterday had proved to her that they weren't strong enough to stop the dangerous creep.

She headed downstairs at lunchtime, meeting Mitch in the lobby as planned.

"We've got to make it quick today," he told her as they passed the information desk. "I have an appointment this afternoon."

"No problem. I can use every extra minute today." She paused on the sidewalk just beyond the door, her gaze sifting over the faces near the bistro across the street, before Mitch took her hand and guided her in the opposite direction, toward the park.

She ordered a salad at the food truck, anticipating a delicious, indulgent dinner. "You saw the picture, right?"

He nodded, biting into a cheesesteak sandwich. "Has he demanded anything?"

"No." The single syllable carried the weight of her mounting frustration. "Did Carson show up for the sketch?"

"That was just a line to annoy your stalker," Mitch replied. "I'll catch up with him later. We'll get an ID."

She nodded, poking at her salad. "When do you think he'll force my hand?" When that moment came, she was increasingly afraid she would cave to the right leverage.

"I don't know," Mitch replied, his voice grave. "You're not alone in this. We won't let him win, Julia."

"I just want it over with," she admitted. "I'd like to get back to my routine."

"Careful what you wish for." Mitch slanted a grin at

her. "I'm walking you back, all the way to your desk today," he said when they finished eating.

She couldn't hide her pleasure at that gallant declaration.

When he held her hand, she felt as if she were protected by some invisible shield. Nonsense, of course, but she wanted to tuck the feeling deep in her heart so she could take it out later, when he was gone. At her desk, he gave her a sweet kiss goodbye and headed out quickly, as if he really had somewhere to be.

She sank into her chair, relishing the warmth of his touch lingering in her hand, and the gentle tingle on her lips. Her foolish heart had fallen right at his feet and the rest of her was eager to join it. She'd grown accustomed to having him around, with his wit, thoughtfulness and determination. Her sudden wish that it could last, that they could hold hands and grow old together, sent her heart knocking against her ribs.

They were so different, yet the more time she spent with him, the more she noticed what they had in common besides the sizzling, satisfying chemistry. People thought of firefighters as community heroes and often lumped defense attorneys into a heap labeled *community scum*. People weren't entirely wrong about either generalization, she thought, frowning at how unlikely they were as a couple.

She'd enjoyed meeting his family, enjoyed discovering that families could be warm and sincere, thoughtful and kind, instead of cold and calculating. She'd been shocked that they'd been warm to her, even after hearing where she worked. And she'd repaid them by leading a car bomber to their street.

Swallowing the lump in her throat, she reached for

the phone to call Stephen's garage. Directly responsible or not, her problems had spilled over into his life and she wanted to apologize for the destruction of his truck. The phone rang and rang, but no one picked up. She hoped that meant he was working, rather than avoiding her. Assuming she was invited back, she could get used to spending Sundays around the Galway dinner table.

She waited for the dread to rush in and chase away the idea, more than a little shocked when it didn't. This was risky thinking, though she couldn't seem to stop the formation of a gentle, muted picture of being with Mitch beyond the purpose of her safety. As if there'd been any doubt, her racing, erratic thoughts proved sex changed everything. What would happen if she told him she was in love with him?

Her desktop computer chimed with an incoming email, drawing her away from the daydream of life with Mitch as a real boyfriend. As she opened the message, she thought about how quickly he'd left after lunch. She hoped his appointment had something to do with his suspension.

Every time she thought about that incident it bothered her knowing Mitch was paying an unfair price for another man's negligence as a parent. Mitch's situation was one more example of why she'd chosen to practice as a defense attorney. People needed someone to help them navigate life's raw deals. From everything she'd been able to learn about that fire, the fight at the scene and the disciplinary action against Mitch, he'd gotten a raw deal all around.

Mitch's problems were pushed to the back of her mind as she read and reread the email. Her boss had called an emergency meeting on the Falk case. She had less than an hour to prepare an update on her research progress.

With an oath, she shifted into high gear to meet the new demand. Unwilling to take any chances this time, she gathered her personal belongings and took them upstairs with her.

In the elevator her phone sounded another text alert. She swiped the screen, sure it was Mitch, only to find a picture of them in the park today, edited with an X over his face.

Julia's knees turned to water and she leaned against the elevator wall for support. The two other people in the car gave her an odd look. "Excuse me. Turned an ankle." She knelt down and fiddled with the strap on her shoe while she tried to catch her breath. The stalker was taking direct aim at Mitch.

Her heart pounded, knowing there was nothing the stalker considered out of bounds. If he'd just tell her what he wanted, she could do something. This limbo, where her imagination filled in the blanks with progressively more horrible options, was breaking her.

In the waiting area on Haywood's floor, she opened the text message again, this time reading the instructions under the awful picture. I know where you're going. In the rush of panic, Julia looked around for that dreaded orange cap. Give me the names Falk is exchanging for his freedom or romance is dead. You have one hour.

A shiver rattled her body from head to toe as she aimed for the conference room. Her confidence gone, she swallowed a useless surge of tears and suppressed the desperate urge to run. Despite the stalker monitoring her cell phone activity, she forwarded the terrible text messages to Mitch and Grant. He'd told her repeatedly he could take care of himself. Now she had no choice but to trust him.

Just outside the conference room, she muted her phone and did something she hadn't done in years. She prayed for a miracle.

Mitch had argued with Grant by text and phone about leaving Julia alone, even behind the limestone facade of Marburg's ostentatious building. Grant won, evidenced by Mitch's arrival at Escape to meet with Carson for the sketch. They needed the ID, sure, but Julia needed him to stick close.

He entered the club at the back door, his temper on the rise. "Look at this." He shoved his phone at Grant.

"She sent it to me, too," Grant said. "I've got a friend from the police department near the building in case something happens."

As if Julia would trust a cop she didn't know. "I need to get back there," he insisted. "She needs me."

"I've got her covered," Grant insisted. "You are the one he threatened. Hurry up in there." Grant gestured to the office. "Carson's waiting on you."

Mitch swore under his breath. Grant was right. They needed an ID to circulate around the city so someone could nab this guy. The sooner they got this done, the sooner he could get back to Julia. Despite the protective walls of her professional persona, he knew the picture and message had filled her with dread and worry.

Carson asked Mitch several questions about the encounter on the street and inside the coffee shop, making notes and adjustments with pencil and paper.

Mitch did his best to cooperate, racking his memory for any detail he might have overlooked in the heat of the moment. Carson continued to work as Mitch talked, then turned his sketch around. "What's right and what needs work?"

Something at the jaw was off. "More rounded through here. He wasn't fat or overweight. More filled out."

The adjustment made, Mitch studied it again as it hit him. "He had a scar," he said as it dawned on him. "Close to his ear." He pointed to the spot on the picture. "And another one right here, that interrupted the whiskers on his chin."

Carson made the changes. "Now?"

"That's him."

"Nicely done." Grant clapped Mitch on the shoulder.

Mitch stared at the picture. "Do you recognize him?"

"No, but someone will. I'll get it circulated."

Carson tore off the sheet of paper and handed it to Grant. "Anything else you need from me?"

"That'll do for now. Thanks again."

Mitch stood up and shook Carson's hand, watching the other man depart, a limp visible in his stride. "No one saw anything suspicious yesterday." He balled his fists in his jacket pockets. "Have the cop impersonators said anything?"

"They're both dead," Grant said quietly. "Heart attacks two nights ago."

"Both of them?" Mitch sank into a chair. The stalker was taking no chances with witnesses. The thought made his blood run cold. "I have to get back to Julia."

"Make a copy of that picture and take it with you." Grant rocked back in his desk chair, one hand working a spot at his shoulder, just under the collarbone. "I want you to show it to Julia at the first opportunity."

Mitch pulled out his phone and lined up a clear snapshot of the sketch.

"Not that way," Grant said, grabbing the piece of paper. He grumbled as he wrestled with the printing and scanning device. "I don't want him to know we have this yet. We need him to keep operating as if he's untouchable."

"Did it occur to you he might be untouchable?" Mitch took the copy Grant offered, folding it carefully and tucking it into his pocket. "I need to get back over there. He made the demand as soon as I was out of sight."

"He made the demand because he has reason to suspect she will cave in to save you."

"Then he doesn't know her very well." Mitch scrubbed at his face. "Or me. I won't let her throw away her job or her pride for this scumbag."

"When you see her," Grant continued, "if she didn't do it already, encourage her to give him something legitimate."

"She'll lose her job," Mitch said, coming out of his chair. "It means everything to her. There has to be a way to end this without her being disbarred."

"Lives mean more. Hers, yours and others, too. We have to reel this guy in."

"Right." Julia didn't deserve to have to sacrifice everything she'd worked for to this sneaky bastard. It annoyed the crap out of him to have some nameless, faceless criminal running around dictating the rules of the game, changing them on a whim.

The screen on his cell phone lit up with an incoming call—his mother, calling from home. His stomach pitched at the dreadful implications. Had the stalker done something worse? "Hi, Mom," he said for Grant's benefit, trying to keep his voice light and casual. Myra picked up on the tiniest inflections and then picked them apart until she knew every detail of what was going on with her children.

"There's a fire at the Franklin house." His mother was too distracted to notice Mitch's tension. He heard his rock-steady mother fighting back tears. "Your dad is out there, thinking he can help."

Mitch stifled a groan. He wasn't supposed to be anywhere near a fire while he was suspended. This would make twice in two days. "Did you call Stephen?"

"Of course I did, but he didn't answer. I left a message. I need you both."

"Dad isn't an idiot, Mom." Mitch had to trust Grant to cover Julia for a little longer. He lifted his hand in farewell as he left the office.

Myra vented her concern and dire, hypothetical threats against his father. "He misses the action and you know it," she was saying as Mitch jogged across the street.

"I'm on my way," Mitch assured her. "I have to hang up. No good hands-free options with this loaner car."

"Okay, okay." But she didn't hang up. "Where are you?"

"At the club." He switched the phone to speaker as he started the car. If he was lucky, it would wreck the connection and he could drive in peace.

"And your new girl?" Myra never missed a chance to nose around in his social life.

"She's at work."

"I like her."

Mitch rolled his eyes. "Me, too, Mom. I'm heading

your way right now. The speaker is lousy on my end. I'm hanging up now."

He ended the call as she thanked him, and focused on the shortest route. When he arrived, the street was blocked with emergency vehicles, reminding him too much of the night the Marburg building had been evacuated. He parked a block down and paused long enough to text and confirm Julia was okay. Leaving the car, he jogged to where his mom waited, in the middle of the front yard, presumably keeping an eye on his dad.

Quickly he snapped a couple of pictures and sent them to Grant. The old adage to divide and conquer ran through his mind as he took in the scene. What would the stalker do while Mitch was so far from Julia?

He hugged his mom as he asked about his father.

"He's over there. Too close." Myra pointed to the fire trucks flanking the burning house. "If the man had his gear, he'd be in the thick of it."

"There's your silver lining," he said with an unrepentant grin. Striding forward, he hoped no one pushed him too hard about being there.

The blaze wasn't yet under control, burning hot and leaping through the roof. Mitch did a quick head count and assumed there were teams around back.

"You're giving Mom gray hair," he said, tapping his dad's shoulder.

"She's tough." Samuel spared Mitch a quick glance. "Gray looks good on her anyway."

"Not the point, Dad."

"You shouldn't be here, son. Go on back to the house."

"Mom will disown me if I go back without you," Mitch replied.

"Fine." Samuel watched the blaze for another minute. "This was arson," he said under his breath as they walked back to the house.

"You sound awful sure about that." Mitch turned around, wondering what had tipped off his dad.

"I'm positive." Samuel gave a solemn nod. "I was in the kitchen when the corner of the roof lit up like a Roman candle. Arson all the way."

"Hard to believe anyone would target Mr. Franklin's place."

"He was visiting his daughter in Connecticut. Planned to be home Saturday night. I'm glad he was delayed." Samuel shook his head. "No man deserves to see his house go like that. He helped build it, you know."

"I know." A prickle of unease raised the hair at the back of Mitch's neck. Mr. Franklin always checked in with the neighbors when he traveled—they all did. A delayed return on Saturday night, a car bomb on Sunday afternoon and a fire today. "When did he tell you about the delay?"

"He didn't." Myra slid her arm around her husband's waist, as if that would be enough to keep Samuel from wandering back into the action. "No one's heard from him. I asked around." She waved an arm up and down the street. "I tried his number as soon as the fire started, but he isn't picking up."

"Probably driving," Samuel said. "He'll be heartbroken."

As Mitch listened to his parents chatter on, that prickle of unease grew into a terrible theory. The man stalking Julia knew how to pry open bank accounts, hire cop impersonators and blow up cars. A criminal with those skills or connections wouldn't hesitate to kill an elderly man for being in the wrong place at the wrong time.

"The cops didn't speak with Franklin yesterday when they canvassed the area about the bomber?"

His mother stared at him as if he'd lost his mind. "Of course not. He wasn't home."

"Right." Mitch blew out a long breath. "I need to borrow Dad a minute."

Myra narrowed her eyes. "One minute."

"Maybe five," he amended, giving his mom a peck on the cheek as a preemptive apology.

He and his dad walked around the house, toward the awning beside the garage where Samuel kept the retirement RV ready to go at a moment's notice. "I want you and Mom and Jenny to leave town for a few days."

Samuel scoffed. "We can't do that. Jenny has classes and—"

"This is serious, Dad. If you can't leave town, at least get away from the house."

"What's going on, son?"

"I'm worried that arsonist is also a murderer. I'll tell you the whole story when this is settled, but my gut tells me it's the same person who blew up my car and now burned down the house to get rid of any evidence on Franklin's body."

"Franklin would've called when he got home." His dad peered beyond his shoulder toward the street, as if recalling every detail of the explosion yesterday. "With that hedge, Franklin's house would be a great hiding place to set or detonate an explosive device."

"That's what I'm thinking." Mitch hated being right on this. "Can you tell the chief what you told me about Franklin's travel plans?"

Scruffy gray eyebrows knit into a deep scowl. "Should I tell him I think there's a body inside?"

"No. Just the timing." Jumping the gun could backfire if the media caught wind of it and tipped off the stalker.

"Fine." Samuel raised his hands in surrender. "I know you have to keep your nose clean until the hearing. And after." He sighed. "Your mother will tan my hide, and yours, if she sees me over there again."

"I'm sorry, Dad."

"This has to do with your new girl?"

"It might." Sex didn't make her definitively his, not beyond reasonable doubt anyway. "She's a good friend." It bothered him to keep putting her in that box when he wanted to proclaim his feelings for her, *to her*. She was more than that to him and he didn't want to hide that from anyone. "She is in a predicament. We met at the club and I'm helping her out. I think her problems followed her here."

"Thought you'd learned that lesson, son." Samuel scrubbed the thick whiskers on his chin. He'd started letting his beard grow in for the cold winter months ahead.

"Uh-huh." Mitch ground his molars and filled his lungs with a calming breath. Losing his patience or protesting the issue wouldn't help his credibility on this topic. His family would just have to wait and watch him win Julia's heart.

"Give me a minute."

Hands in his coat pockets, shoulders hunched up, Samuel crossed the street again. A few minutes later he returned, two spots of ruddy color on his cheeks. "Already found a body. Arson's on the way."

The confirmation of his suspicions didn't give Mitch much comfort. Only putting the stalker away would do that. "Now will you go? As a precaution? I figure the guy giving Julia trouble knows he can get her cooperation by hurting people she cares about."

"Humph." Samuel folded his arms over his barrel chest, weighing Mitch's statement. "How'd this bad guy get the idea you mean something to her?"

Mitch waited out the intense scrutiny without a word. A tough task on several levels. If the stalker thought his family had witnessed something incriminating, they were all in jeopardy. "You need to move quickly. Please, Dad."

Samuel dropped the defensive posture. "Come on. I'm not telling your mother any of this nonsense on my own."

Mitch fell in beside him, wishing it was nonsense. Repeating his request for his mother's benefit, he shoved his hands into his pockets, enduring another long, speculative gaze. Damn it, Julia was nothing like Leann, couldn't they see that as well as he did?

"I'll call Jenny," she said in a tone that meant business. "We'll do as you ask." She glanced past him through the window to the street. "And Stephen just pulled up." Her shoulders relaxed a fraction. "We'll fill him in, too."

"Thanks, Mom. Dad." He gave them each a fast hug, then danced out of reach, eager to see for himself that Julia was safe.

"Be smart!" His mother's voice followed him out the door.

Mitch smiled as he blew past his older brother and ran for the car. Once his family got to know her, they'd understand why he refused to let the way they'd met undermine their future.

Chapter 13

The restaurant wasn't crowded, though there were enough people to make Julia simultaneously nervous and comfortable. The people around them couldn't all be tied to the stalker, and while it shamed her to think it, she appreciated the buffer of extra bodies. Surely the stalker wouldn't attack where there were too many witnesses to kill.

She tried to be happy that they were both here, alive and well, but guilt swamped her. An innocent man had died, a neighbor the Galways had known for decades, because of her. She played with her silverware until Mitch reached across the table and covered her hand with his. "It will be okay. We have the sketch," he said. "We're closer to catching him now."

She had her doubts, despite his confidence. When Mitch had insisted she leave the office early, she'd learned the grim news about Mr. Franklin. Reluctantly, she'd explained that the emergency meeting had lasted forty minutes and when her hour was up, she'd made the only possible choice and given the stalker one of the names Danny Falk planned on trading for his freedom. The stalker had yet to reply, but no one else had been attacked, so maybe things were going their way.

Mitch hadn't expressed any judgement about her decision and when they'd arrived safely at his house, she'd studied the sketch, miserable that the man was a stranger to her. She wanted an ID to take to the police, even if it meant confessing that she leaked details on the case.

She turned her mind to more important factors. "Your parents and sister are safe?"

He nodded. "Jenny can telecommute for the week, so they took an impromptu vacation."

"What about Stephen and the others?"

"Stephen is too grumpy to become a victim."

The outrageous statement brought a smile to her face.

"Everyone else is on alert for trouble. We'll all be fine."

"You said that about family dinner," she pointed out. Glum, she sipped her wine. "And now I'm ruining our date."

"Not from where I'm sitting. Have I told you how beautiful you look tonight?"

Only enough times that she was starting to believe it. She'd worn the little black dress she'd packed on a whim when they'd moved from her place to Mitch's house. It was a good piece she could dress up or down for the office or for a night out. She hadn't anticipated a hot date, but it worked for that, too.

The lightweight shawl on her shoulders was shot with

silver and gold threads, and she'd chosen big gold hoops at her ears and bangles at her wrists. Black heels pulled the look together and lifted her almost to eye level with Mitch.

Her hot date. Mitch had pulled out all the stops to make what had started as a ploy into a real date. She smiled at him over the candle centerpiece, determined to show him how much she appreciated his effort.

His cell phone hummed on the tabletop and she looked at him expectantly. "Email," he said. "From my chief." He looked up and smiled. "My hearing is scheduled for tomorrow morning."

Finally! "Now we really have something to celebrate," she said. She left her chair and came around to his side of the table to give him a hug, ignoring the onlookers. "We needed good news."

His brow furrowed. "It leaves you exposed at the office."

"I'll be fine." Her mind drifted to all the ways they could celebrate, privately, once he was reinstated.

"Grant will send backup to keep an eye on you," he said absently. "No way I'm leaving you unprotected."

"I've never felt safer in my life," she admitted. "Thank you, Mitch." Her mood considerably lighter, she enjoyed the meal and easy conversation with a man she'd fallen in love with. She felt so light and happy she'd nearly said those three little words as they shared dessert.

No, she knew the perfect place to tell him she loved him. "Can we stop at Boathouse Row again?" she asked when they were on the way home. They'd decided not to stop in at the club so Mitch could be well rested tomorrow.

"Sure."

She could tell his mind was working overtime. Maybe this wasn't the best time to dump her feelings on him. She waited until they reached the overlook and were leaning against the car to enjoy the sparkling view of the white lights across the river. Reaching for his hand, she asked what was on his mind.

"I don't know." He brought her to stand in front of him, drawing her back to lean against his chest. "I want to believe I'll be reinstated, but I can't go back to work until I know you're safe."

"You're suspicious of the timing?"

She felt him shrug. "He's manipulated everything else—why not a hearing."

"It's possible," she allowed. "Unlikely, but possible. Why don't we assume the best for now?"

He shrugged again.

Julia delighted in his embrace, in spite of his somber mood. "There's something I need to tell you," she began.

"Do I get to hear a Julia Cooper secret?" He kissed the back of her neck. "You never did explain why the family dinner terrified you."

"Oh." With everything else, she'd forgotten her promise to tell him about that. It wasn't what she wanted to share, but it might demonstrate what was in her heart more than three small words.

"What if we trade secrets?"

She nuzzled into his warmth, liking that idea. "Do I have to go first?"

"I will." He kissed her temple. "The last time I brought a date to Sunday dinner, it was a woman I'd rescued from an office fire. It's taboo to go out with a rescued victim. I knew better, but did it anyway."

She twisted in his arms. "That's a big secret?"

"It left a mark," he admitted. "My family saw through her, but I nearly proposed before I saw the light. It's embarrassing to know she made a fool of me."

"That's on her for abusing your good nature."

He snorted in a half laugh and kissed her nose. "Julia Cooper, my champion."

"Believe it," she said fiercely. Oh. That made it her turn now. She kissed him quickly, just in case her secret ruined everything. "Last time I was at family dinner with a boyfriend was law school. His parents were royalty-level wealthy and they'd done a full background search on me." She bit her lip, her gaze locked firmly on the second button of his dress shirt. "They didn't like what they found. His mother said the most terrible things about me and the things my mother did."

And now she'd opened herself up to share that secret, too. Well, at least she didn't have to worry about the big "I love you" anymore. "He broke up with me and made life miserable at school for a time."

Mitch lifted her chin and kissed her softly under the starlight, in front of Boathouse Row. "I know."

She frowned, then remembered he'd gone digging through her law school life. There had been at least two disciplinary write-ups after that fateful dinner. "Of course you know. That terrible day is sort of why I chose criminal defense."

"Not that, Julia. My second secret. I know about your childhood." He held her chin when she tried to look away. "We all have scars, but you? You have so much courage it slays me."

"Huh?" The statement was so foreign, so unexpected, any anger over his invasion of her privacy dissolved.

"Look at where you landed." He spread his arms wide.

"On courage, grit and hard work, you made yourself into this amazing, independent woman." He brought those arms around her and held on tight.

Had anything ever felt better than his absolute acceptance? "You don't cringe thinking about where I came from?" He shook his head. "Mitch, my mom accused a teacher of sexual assault just so he'd stop helping me get into college. She didn't want him polluting my head with more impossible dreams."

"That's what really set you on the defense path, isn't it?"

"No. Maybe." She supposed this is what she got for letting him melt her defenses with hot kisses and kindnesses.

"You have the most beautiful heart," he murmured.

"No, I think you take that title," she argued.

He laughed, turning her toward the sparkling lights once more. "There she is, Julia Cooper for the defense."

Hours later at his house, Julia slipped out of bed once she was sure Mitch was asleep. She dragged on the first piece of clothing she found and smiled as she buttoned up the dress shirt he'd worn to dinner. His scent enveloped her, restoring her confidence that they would find a way through the nightmare created by the stalker.

They had to. Mitch knew everything about her and loved her anyway. Well, he hadn't said it in those precise words, but she felt it in the way he touched her and made love to her. She wouldn't relinquish that treasure without a serious fight.

Tiptoeing out to the kitchen for a bottle of water, she paused to study the sketch again, cursing the man for the terrible things he'd done. She was ready to take the picture outside and use it for target practice when her eyes locked onto the scar on his chin.

"No way." She pulled up her computer and searched through old media reports and arrest records. When that didn't help, she took a chance and logged into the Marburg cloud to search through old cases. Haywood wouldn't be happy, but if it resulted in bringing a murderer to justice, she'd ask forgiveness later. Hell, Haywood could represent him and take the credit for bringing in a whale of a client.

"Hey." Mitch joined her, covering a yawn with his fist. "What are you doing?"

"I recognized the scar." She keyed in a search and turned the screen for him when the face popped up.

"Whoa. That's a dead ringer."

"I know, right? I'm an idiot for not seeing it sooner. Meet Leo Falk, Danny Falk's older and apparently not-so-deceased brother."

Mitch pulled her to her feet and spun her in a circle. "Way to go!" He kissed her soundly and set her back on her feet. "Now what?"

"I guess I'll tell Grant and then take everything we know to Haywood in the morning." She reached over and closed her laptop.

He frowned. "Let's sleep on it." He raked his hands through her hair. "I'd rather be with you when you start sharing."

She was tempted to argue, but he had to be up early and fresh for his hearing. "Your protective side is showing."

He grinned at her, placing her hands on his chest. "Do you like it?"

"I might need some convincing," she replied, anticipation thrumming as she followed him back to bed.

Leo heard his window of opportunity slam shut. According to Julia, his brother had given up at least one important name in the higher echelon of the organization. He'd sent the order to eliminate her boyfriend in case she remained stubborn and called them off when the name had been confirmed with his source in the prosecutor's office.

It was time to cut his losses and move on. Danny had brought this on himself. "Pack it up," he ordered his computer genius. "Leave nothing behind."

"Sir, we have a problem."

K-Chase was swiveling the desk chair from side to side. It must be serious. "So fix it."

"I'm not sure I can."

"What the hell are you talking about?"

"Cooper's computer just searched through your old case file on the Marburg cloud."

"Meaning what?" he bit out each syllable.

"I think she's managed to identify you."

"That's impossible." He came closer, livid when he realized the kid was right. "Okay." He walked away, thought it through, reviewing a short list of lousy options. "Here's what I need you to do." He outlined his plan, tweaking it as the genius made technical suggestions.

If he hoped to escape the authorities and maintain his influence and operations on the East Coast, he had to take immediate action. Of all the people available, he couldn't believe his future was riding on the skinny shoulders of this sun-deprived kid.

"Fair warning, kid. Fail me or try a double-cross, and you'll die, too."

"Yes, sir." K-Chase started hammering at his keyboard.

Chapter 14

This was his day, Julia thought, giving Mitch a kiss when he dropped her off early at Marburg's side door. He'd be reinstated by noon and she couldn't wait to send him off to his first shift back on the job he loved.

Unfortunately, she still had no response from the stalker, and no control of her finances. Thanks to the confidence and support of Mitch, and Grant by extension, she was done playing games. By noon, she would have her timeline ready and her arguments prepared to expose Leo Falk's most recent crimes to Haywood.

Julia said good-morning to Bethany as she breezed by the desk, slowing down when she saw Bethany's frightened expression. "Mr. Haywood called for you."

Julia glanced at her watch. Of course her boss would come in early today. She forced her lips into a smile. "Great." No one needed to know that the summons sounded like a death knell in her ears. "I'll just get my notes."

Bethany shook her head. "He said you're to go straight to his office. Only to his office." She jerked a thumb over her shoulder. "He sent an escort."

"I see." Julia noticed the security guard standing between her and the primary access to the cubicles. He wasn't part of the typical security team of white-haired men with blazers and rounded shoulders. This man was bigger, younger and armed with more than a stern smile. "Have a nice day, Bethany."

Julia turned on her heel and aimed for the elevator. The numerous possibilities for the summons and the guard cartwheeled through her mind, none of them good. Her phone chimed and her heart skipped, though it was far too soon for news from Mitch. Just anticipating his sexy smile and the celebratory kisses in her future helped settle her nerves.

She waited to check until she had a moment's privacy in the elevator, then wished she hadn't. The message iced the blood in her veins and sent the elevator car into a slow spin.

Thanks for all your help, Julia.

What in the hell had Falk done now? She didn't have time to respond or forward the message as the elevator doors parted and the guard urged her out.

She pocketed her phone and rolled her shoulders back, determined to handle with dignity whatever Haywood had to say.

Haywood didn't even stand as she was shown in and the office door closed behind her. On reflex, Julia's gaze swept the view outside his office windows. She didn't see anything, didn't expect to. A master criminal like Leo Falk wasn't dumb enough to stand on a nearby rooftop in a bright orange ball cap so she could point out the root of her recent trouble.

"Good morning, Mr. Haywood."

"Oh, no, it isn't," Haywood barked. "Sit down, Cooper."

She obeyed, keeping her coat over her arm and her purse in her lap. As he stared at her with that unrelenting courtroom gaze, she knew she was facing the worst-case scenario.

"You're off the Falk case," he said suddenly, his voice full of an unarguable finality.

"Why?" He didn't have to tell her, but she would not leave without an answer.

"Why?" Haywood repeated, incredulous. "Because you're no longer a Marburg associate, for starters."

"I beg your pardon?" Why would Leo put her off the case when she'd cooperated? What the hell was his end game? "You can't be serious."

"I am serious. You're terminated, effective immediately. Don't expect severance or a glowing reference. Don't you even dare to take so much as a paper clip with you. Get out."

"No."

"No?" Haywood's face turned dangerously red. "I have no qualms about hauling a criminal out of this building by force, regardless of gender."

"Oh, come on." She stopped the furious tirade dancing on the tip of her tongue. "You've been pleased with my work. I'd like to know on what grounds you're terminating me. I deserve that much."

His eyebrows plummeted into a terrifying scowl.

"You *deserve* jail time, Cooper. Your belongings are waiting for you at the information desk. The security guard will walk you out." He reached for his phone.

She refused to budge. "Please. This isn't making sense."

"We hired a cyber team to audit the Falk case," Haywood said. "Thank God."

Cyber team? She'd never heard of such a thing. There was no reference in the case file.

"One of Marburg's cronies claimed the service could pinpoint information leaks or security risks." Haywood pressed his fingers to his temples. "We're test-driving the group as a new precaution since the witnesses on this one keep dying."

Julia thought of Mitch's inside-man theory. "That makes sense," she murmured. Leo had a hand in this, she was sure. It would explain the ease of access the stalker had to her banking and personal information if he was controlling someone on the cyber team. She was furious with herself for caving to his threats.

"Gee, Cooper. I'm so happy you think so. The team found several emails from *you* to a reporter, referencing confidential information on the Falk case."

"I would never." Except for the moment yesterday when she'd caved and shared the one name. One out of four mentioned. A name previously linked to Falk in an inquiry last year. Then it hit her, he'd said "emails" and she'd only sent a text message.

"We have the evidence, Cooper. Not only that, we caught the payment moving through your bank account. The Falk case was tough enough without your greedy, conniving stunt. We'll be damn lucky to get out of this without sanctions. It will all be moot if Falk dies."

"Sir, there's been a mistake."

"Don't try and sell me some load of crap about how you'd never do this or that." Haywood tapped a folder in front of him. "You get points for hiding the seedy side of your nature behind the heels and smile. I vouched for you."

"Mr. Haywood, please hear me out."

"Get out." He was turning red above his crisp white collar. "I'll see you disbarred for this."

"But, Mr. H—"

"Get out!" he bellowed.

She jumped to her feet and scrambled backward for the door.

He came out of his chair and stalked after her, trailing her down the hall. "If our client dies because of your greed, Cooper, I guarantee the next time I see you it will be in a courtroom as accessory to murder!"

She pushed through the door and aimed for the stairs. The security guard assigned to her caught her and bodily ushered her to the elevator. As the car moved toward the ground floor, she felt the futility of her fight pressing in on all sides. Her dream job was over in a flurry of false accusations and manufactured evidence. Leo Falk had set this in motion, but why? They had evidence he had assistance from other sources, sure. What purpose did this stunt serve?

The elevator stopped on the first floor and the guard led her to the security station at the rear of the building. At least Arthur wasn't there to see her disgraceful departure. The older man had been friendly to her from day one. The security guard at this desk shoved a banker's box into her hands. She tried to peek under the lid for a quick inventory as they pushed her to the door.

The guard swiped his card and pushed opened the rear door. She stopped short at the threshold. "I can't go out there," she whispered. Mitch was at the hearing. Alone and exposed, Leo could do whatever he chose with her. Was that the purpose of this stunt?

"You can't stay here," the guard said.

"Just let me make a call first." She shifted the box, reaching for the alternate cell phone in her pocket.

"Do it outside."

"No. Wait."

He grumbled a curse and forced her through the door and into the alley.

Julia could only stare as the door locked with finality, terror rooting her in place. She expected to hear a squeal of tires or a gunshot. She expected a team wearing black, on the orders of a man in an orange ball cap, to toss her into a panel van and speed away.

When none of it happened, she couldn't muster up much relief. Leo had warned her she was useless if she was off the case. She didn't hold out much hope that he'd leave her alone or fix the parts of her life he'd tampered with.

Her life. It was silly to stand here waiting to be attacked. She was still breathing—she'd best make the most of every minute until that status changed. Reluctantly, her feet cooperated, propelling her closer to the corner of Walnut and Sixth. She walked to the park where she'd enjoyed so many lunches and dropped the box on the first open bench. Pulling out her alternate cell phone, she sent a text message to update Mitch and Grant.

After that, she used her original phone and called her credit card company to file a fraud report. The call dropped before the computerized voice could direct her call. Checking that she had a good signal, she tried again. The call dropped and a moment later a new text message arrived, interrupting her third attempt.

You're wasting time. I'll fix everything if you share what you know.

As if she'd believe anything Leo said. She turned off her phone, too aggravated to play this game. Let him drive his other sources crazy. He was about to learn how scrappy she could be. She moved the box to the ground and propped her feet on it. Pulling out her tablet, she opened up an outdated email app. She hadn't used this address since high school, when she'd needed to hide scholarship correspondence from her mother.

With the occasional glance around the park for an orange cap or Leo in all his arrogant glory, she composed her message. It would carry more weight if she could add the attachments, but she didn't want to access anything linked to the accounts Leo had compromised. She filled in the recipient's address from memory and hit Send, hoping for the best.

What now? A cab to the house or the club? She felt safer out here in public, among people who would notice if she got attacked or shot.

Somewhere along the line, before she'd made the ID, they'd misread Leo's motives. Marburg represented Danny Falk, who was reportedly cooperating with investigators in several branches of law enforcement. All the witnesses who'd previously turned on the car-theft operation had been killed. Falk, in an undisclosed safe house, was out of reach. She'd read and reread the case. She'd talked it through repeatedly with Mitch. They agreed Leo must have something significant to lose if Falk exposed him, and yet Leo Falk was not among the names Danny offered up in exchange for his freedom.

A man with a criminal record as long as Leo's wouldn't put all of his hopes for success on one associate. He'd exhibited tremendous resources and access to hack into her life, yet he didn't hide behind a computer. He'd personally followed her and persevered even after Mitch had nearly caught him.

"Pardon me. Are you Julia Cooper?"

The soft-spoken question startled her. She glanced up, expecting Leo, and found a skinny twentysomething kid with dark hair and black-framed glasses smiling at her. Physically, he didn't pose a threat, but something in his eyes contradicted the quiet tone and slight smile.

"I am, yes."

"Here." He thrust a note card at her. "Have a good day."

"Wait!"

He didn't. She ignored the note in favor of watching him hurry off. He didn't speak with anyone else before he was out of her sight.

Damn. Resuming her seat on the bench, she opened the note card. Turn on your phone.

She crumpled the note and shoved it into her coat pocket, refusing to obey him while she debated her options. In an hour, if she hadn't heard from Mitch or Grant, she'd catch a taxi to the club. Until then, she'd wait and see what card Leo played next.

With a sigh, she donned her sunglasses and studied each and every person from behind the dark lenses. If he was close enough to get a handwritten note to her, he was close enough for her to spot him.

And when she did…

She would do what? Drag him up to Haywood's office and force him to tell the truth? Hold her fingers like a gun and make him fix everything? Maybe she could persuade him to tell her what the hell was going on. All while pigs flew formation in the sky.

"That's an expression designed to keep anyone at a distance."

This time the voice was familiar. She smiled a little as Grant sat down beside her. "You're on backup detail today?"

Grant nodded. "Simplified the scheduling issues. I got your text. This is an interesting place for a pity party. Didn't Haywood believe you?"

"I never got a chance to say a word," she replied. "And I thought staying in a public place would make things more difficult for *Leo*," she raised her voice on the name. "Plenty of witnesses out here."

"Fair enough," Grant allowed.

She pushed her sunglasses up into her hair. "I called my credit card company to report the fraud. The call didn't go through. Instead, I got a text from him."

"And you turned off your phone."

"Yup. Both of them."

"That could've been disastrous."

"Any more disastrous than what's already happened? He's here, watching me right now. Us."

"You're sure?"

She nodded. "He had some geeky guy drop off a note ordering me to turn on my phone."

"But you haven't done that."

"No." She knew she sounded belligerent, on the verge of a childish tantrum, and she didn't care. Every time she thought the situation couldn't get worse, Leo did something more foul. She filled in Grant on the bits of pertinent information from her disgraceful exit. "He gets nothing now that I'm fired." She didn't give Grant time to share an opinion. "He's forced me out of my apartment, managed to screw up my career and my finances, and still he wants to know what I know. At this point, I only know Leo is alive and in Philly, which isn't news to him."

Grant laughed. "There are far better places for an attorney like you than Marburg."

She snorted. Two weeks ago she would have pointed out all the good she could've accomplished in her dream job as she worked her way up the ranks. Now she'd have to take whatever position she could find just for the cash flow. "Is the public defender's office hiring?"

"If not, I always am."

She laughed at that. "Please. I waited tables through college. Customer service isn't my strong suit."

"Come on." Grant reached down and pulled the box from under her feet. "It's like I tell everyone who spends much time at Escape, this too shall pass."

She walked with him out of the park, wondering how all of this would pass for her. "Did Mitch say anything about his hearing?"

"Not yet. I let him know you're safe. He can meet us at the club when he's done."

"All right." She felt a little guilty for turning off her phones. "I didn't mean to make him worry. I was just so pissed off."

Grant unlocked his truck and slid her box behind the

seat. "I might've made a mistake assigning him to your situation," he said, holding the passenger door open for her.

"How so?"

He shrugged a shoulder and urged her into the truck.

"Why would you say that?" she demanded when he was in the driver's seat.

"Neither one of you is the patient sort."

She frowned. Mitch had an impatient streak, she'd noticed that, but he'd demonstrated a wealth of compassion and patience with her. "I admit we both want to get back to our respective careers without all the drama."

"That's good."

His tone didn't match the words. "Ambition and determination are good things," she said, going on the defensive. Mitch deserved to get his job back and she sure deserved better than being tossed out on her ear for a breach she had been forced to commit.

"Trying to convince me or yourself?" Grant asked as he merged with traffic.

"Could you just state your point clearly?" She sighed. "Please? I've had enough mind games for one lifetime."

"I'm just saying it's not enough to set a goal—you should know why you want to reach it."

She wasn't in much mood for philosophy, either, and she turned the conversation back on Grant. "You have good reasons to detest Marburg and I'm glad you didn't leave me hanging because I worked there."

"Do you have good reasons for wanting to stay with that kind of firm?"

"Yes! There's no shortage of opportunity at a firm with Marburg's reputation."

Grant pulled into the reserved space behind the club. He turned off the engine and pulled the key. Shifting, he faced her. "My first career is over, but I don't blame Marburg, his partners or anyone in that musty old building, Julia. If you keep your eyes open, you'll find life is full of opportunities regardless of the circumstances." He pushed open his door. "Come on. I could use some help with inventory. My supplier's waiting on my order."

"Counting is one of my many useful skills," she said, hopping out of the truck. If nothing else, it would keep her brain busy while she waited for Mitch's good news.

Grant smiled. "That's great. Thank you."

During the afternoon break, Mitch felt the vise on his chest loosen when Grant's text came through that Julia was safe. He knew his mind should be on the hearing—his career was on the line, after all. But since the moment he'd dropped Julia off at the office, he'd been plagued by a bad feeling.

No, the bad feeling had started last night when he'd caught a glimpse of her stalker in the restaurant parking lot. He hadn't wanted to hide it or lie to Julia, but he'd also refused to alarm her. She'd been so happy about his hearing, so sure it would go well. At the time he had decided notifying Grant was enough.

Now that he knew they'd been that close to the notorious Leo Falk, he couldn't stop worrying about why she'd been fired. It helped knowing Grant was watching over her, but Leo was a dangerous piece of work with who-knew-how-many criminal connections around town.

When his hearing resumed, he answered questions from the board members who weren't sure about reinstating him, while part of his mind worked on the trouble dogging Julia.

"We have a reputation to protect, Mr. Galway," Chief Johannson said.

Mitch nodded.

"Community is at the core of what we do."

He nodded again. He understood the philosophy, having firefighters all over his family tree.

"We expected you to serve your suspension without incident and yet you've managed to create more trouble with this car fire and another fire the next day."

Mitch waited until he was sure they wanted him to reply. "I had nothing to do with either incident. The police report stating the same fact is in the file."

"I've read it." Chief Johannson tapped the paper on top of Mitch's file. "It boils down to fact versus public opinion and perception. That's a difficult hurdle when trust has been violated."

Trust? What exactly did they expect him to do? He'd defended himself against an unruly, negligent father. He thought of Julia's poker face and tried to mimic her sphinx-like expression. "I understand, sir. All I've ever wanted is to do my job well, with the highest integrity and commitment to the department and the people we serve."

"Uh-huh." Chief Johannson stacked one hand over the other on the table. "Those are the right words, Mr. Galway. Did your attorney help you rehearse them?"

"No, sir." What the hell was going on here? He bit back the rant building in his chest. Losing his temper would undermine any progress. He couldn't afford another setback. The better he played the game here and now, the sooner he could get back to unraveling Julia's problems.

"Mr. Galway, we'll review your case and have a decision for you by tomorrow. You may go."

He stood tall and made eye contact with each of the five members on the disciplinary committee. "Thank you for your time." He tried to mean it.

The moment he was out of sight, he checked his phone. Nothing new from Julia. Damn it. He broke into a jog and took the stairs two at a time to the ground floor. Knowing Grant was there helped, but he wanted to hear her voice or imagine her voice as he read one of her text messages.

Leo must be intercepting messages again. He started the car and used his speaker feature to call Grant.

"She's fine," Grant said in lieu of a greeting. "We're doing an inventory."

"Inventory?" A vision of Julia, dressed in the white flowy blouse and the sleek black skirt and heels, traipsing around after Grant, filled his head.

"You're on speaker, Galway."

"How was your meeting?" Julia asked. "Did they reinstate you?"

His entire body relaxed at the sound of her hope-filled voice. The ridiculous reaction didn't faze him. Much. For good or bad, he was hooked on this woman. In his career, he was exposed frequently to how fragile and short life could be. Whatever came of this relationship, he planned to enjoy every minute. That way if she walked out of his life when her situation was stable, he wouldn't be left with any regrets. "Not yet," he replied, smiling.

"What is the holdup?"

He grinned at her instant outrage. "There was talk of trust, community and department reputation."

"Oh, please," she snapped. "You're the poster child for community dedication."

Mitch could hear Grant smothering a laugh with a fake cough in the background. "You think so?"

"As if none of them ever made a mistake," she continued. "Who do they think created the reputation and trust issues in this city?"

"The board will come around," he said, trying to appease her. He wasn't at all sure he wanted to be reinstated right this minute. He'd feel better about returning to work once they had Leo behind bars with no hope of bail.

When he reached the club it felt like a ghost town. The lunch rush was over and the kitchen staff had left. He strode into the empty club and turned a circle, his pulse kicking with apprehension. Had Leo made a bold move on the club?

He called out Julia's name, then Grant's. When neither answered him, apprehension morphed to dread. He'd seen Grant's truck in the parking lot. They should be here counting beer or glassware or something.

He pulled out his phone and dialed Grant's number. Mitch's stomach sank when the call went straight to voice mail. A clatter from behind the stage had him jogging that direction. If Leo had his hands on Julia—

Mitch skidded to a stop as Grant leaned against a door, his arms full of boxes, holding it open for Julia, who was equally burdened. Mitch stepped in and relieved her of the load, giving her a kiss on the cheek as he did. "What are you doing?"

"We finished the inventory," she said, dusting off her palms. "And started shifting things around back here."

Her cheeks were pink and her hair curled at her temples from the exertion. Her clothes were a mess, but she looked beautiful and relaxed. Something inside his chest unfurled, suffusing him with happiness. "You do have a gift for organization."

She tipped her head to the side, thinking about it, then laughed. "Order is good for the soul," she replied. She circled her finger at him. "This will go over there."

When things were in place, he rounded on her. "Why did they fire you?"

"Haywood claims I leaked sensitive case details to a reporter. Oh, and they claim I took money for it, too," she added, avoiding eye contact.

"What?" He glanced at Grant over her shoulder and got no help. "Didn't you tell Haywood about Leo being alive?"

She laced her fingers together, squeezing tight. "No. I've been waiting to tell you both at the same time." She stepped back so she could include Grant. "Haywood told me they hired a new cyber team for this case. Leo must be manipulating someone on that team. It's the best explanation for the thorough access to my financial information and how they planted false email evidence against me."

"Then why not use the cyber team to access the case? Why would Leo need you, too?" Grant asked, his gaze narrowed in thought.

"I got the impression the cyber team is only tracking Marburg employees for leaks," she said. "The dying witnesses worried people."

"It still doesn't make sense," Mitch said. "You can't help if you're fired."

She nodded in agreement. "It's been circling through my head and I still don't have an answer. He can't expect my help if I'm out, and yet it's clear he does." She handed Mitch her cell phone. This time when he gave it back, she left it on in case Leo tried again.

"We have to do something," he said.

Grant agreed. "I'll ask a friend to take a look at the cyber team company. Maybe there's a money trail that leads back to Leo." He stepped aside to make the call.

"In the meantime?" Mitch asked.

She came in close for a fast hug and kiss. "In the meantime, we're almost done with this reorganizing. I want to see it finished, for sanity's sake."

"Fine," Mitch said on a heartfelt sigh. He wiped a smudge from her cheek. "Let's knock this out."

Chapter 15

Julia's phone vibrated in her pocket with a social media update and she ignored it. It had been a wonderful break to work on organizing the space backstage. Nothing here had anything to do with the law, witnesses and evidence, or unpredictable, not-so-dead stalkers.

When Grant's phone sang out a few bars of the *Rocky* theme and Mitch's phone glowed through his back pocket with an alert, she knew the break from trouble was over. All three of them paused to check their devices. Instead of the social media update as she'd assumed, her notification was for a news alert she'd set up to keep her apprised of any mention of the Falk case.

She swore at the breaking news headline that Falk's safe house had been breached and shots were fired. "Haywood," she murmured. "H-he said he'd bl-blame me," she stammered, *accessory to murder* echoing in her head. "This can't be happening."

Mitch's arm came around her waist, steadying her. The warmth of his arm filtered through her silk blouse and pushed back against the sudden chill that skated over her skin. "Blame you for what?"

She had to pause for a breath, as well as courage. "Accessory to murder." There she got it out in a rush. It didn't make it any better. "If Falk dies."

"That's crazy," Mitch said. "You didn't do anything."

"He said the cyber team can prove otherwise."

"That's all fabricated." He pulled her tight to his chest and just held her, his heart beating under her cheek. Here in his arms she felt safer than ever, despite the world crashing around her ears. "I'm taking you home."

"Not yet," Grant said. "We need to know what we're dealing with first. My office," he said, leading the way.

"He's right," she murmured, looking up at Mitch. His eyes were dark with frustration and she was more than a little afraid of what he'd do on her behalf if Leo threw one more problem on the heap.

"I don't care about evidence," Mitch said, his voice low and lethal. "Whatever his motives, I won't let him destroy your career. I promise."

Her career at Marburg was beyond saving, but she gave him a watery smile anyway. She laced her fingers through his and followed after Grant. "I'll take that promise," she whispered, leaning into his arm a bit. "If you'll give me one back."

"Anything."

"Don't ruin yourself or get hurt in the process of protecting me."

He stopped short and planted a hard kiss on her lips.

"That sounds like a woman who might care about her man."

Her man. The words shot through her with all the speed and destruction of lightning. She barely suppressed the shiver as she recognized the sudden spark in his eyes. He was teasing, wanting to distract her and make her laugh. It was almost more disconcerting that she saw through his ploy. "Just promise me."

His lips were soft against her ear as he whispered the words she needed. "I promise, Julia."

Grant had the television on and the police scanner going when Julia and Mitch reached his office. "First reports are conflicting. Either Danny Falk's been killed or he's been captured while they were trying to move him," Grant said, his voice as hard as his eyes. "According to my source, it sounds like someone from Marburg warned the FBI his location might have been compromised."

Her legs going weak, Julia dropped into the nearest chair. "That's what he wanted all along, a clear shot at Falk and a patsy to take the fall."

Behind her, Mitch rested his hands lightly on her shoulders. She soaked up the comfort in his touch while the scanner crackled and the breaking news team gave relatively useless information. Maintaining contact as he moved, Mitch pulled the other chair up close to hers. His warm palm swallowed hers, infusing her with his strength.

She hated the feel of tears stinging her eyes. "He used me." The man who'd orchestrated all of this had pinned her in a corner and all the fight had gone out of her. "I mean, we knew that, but he used me t-to find and kill his brother."

"Shh. The facts will come out," Mitch said. "It's too soon to panic."

Julia disagreed. In fact, it might be too *late* for all-out panic, too late to run. Leo Falk was nipping loose ends to make his escape. She knew too much for him to leave her alive.

"Watch the coverage," Grant said. "Look for Leo in every shot."

She did her best to obey the request, searching every wide angle for a glimpse of that brutal face or the orange ball cap, on the off chance he still wore it. Mitch's hand clasped hers, a point of comfort as they watched the dramatic images from the safe house.

Gunfire rang out and the reporter flinched. The police radio came to life with chatter as the teams on-site sorted out who had fired and how to respond. Shouts of "Agent down" came through the mics.

Julia knew Falk was dead before the ambulance moved closer to the house, before any confirmation came over the radio or TV. Leo was plugging the leaks, trying to save the organization before it collapsed.

If Haywood had his way, she'd be charged as an accessory before Falk's body reached the morgue. And if Leo got to her first?

Grant muted the television and radio. "Take her home," he said to Mitch. "I'll make a few calls and see what I can do from here."

Their voices barely penetrated the thick fog of self-recrimination hemming her in. She hardly noticed the sunshine on her face as Mitch walked her out to his car or from his car into the house. The drive in between was little more than a blur.

"Stop beating yourself up," Mitch said, helping her out

of her coat and hooking it on the peg by the door along with her scarf. "He used you, that's all." He pegged his jacket next.

Wasn't that enough? "Another man died today."

"A guilty man with terrible enemies determined to silence him and protect themselves."

She tried to cling to his logic, but it didn't ease the guilt coursing through her. She closed her eyes and clamped her lips shut to keep from screaming. She should have done something. Something more. Something else. Every detail from the first creepy text message to the last one this morning ran through her mind. She let Mitch pull her into a hard embrace. "Can I panic now?" she muttered into the solid warmth of his chest.

"No." He smoothed a hand over her hair. "Not on my watch."

"Mitch." Reluctantly, she pushed out of the sweet comfort of his arms. They'd exhausted their resources last night after his near miss. "Admit it." She reached around him for her coat. "We're out of time and options. Get me to the police station so they can take over."

Mitch shook his head. "If Grant thought that was your best choice, he would have said so."

"We've been fighting a losing battle from the start." It actually felt better to admit it now that it was over. "Grant knows that as well as you and I do. Leo played me and got what he wanted—access to his brother." She shivered. "My best hope now is to beat Haywood to the police—" her voice cracked "—and tell my side of the story before he can smear me."

He took her coat and hung it on the peg again. "We'll sleep on it first. If you still feel the same way in the morning I'll take you first thing." He turned her toward the kitchen and nudged her along when her feet refused to cooperate. "For now, we lay low."

That panic he claimed she didn't have time for tried to surface again. "Fine." She sat at the table while he placed a bottle of water and a glass of merlot in front of her.

"You didn't fail your client." Mitch brought a beer and a bag of potato chips to the table when he sat down. "Say it."

She tried, but the words caught in the knot of grief and worry in her throat. "Haywood—"

"No." He gently tilted her chin so she had to face him. "You didn't fail your client. Hear me, Julia. Believe me."

"I'm trying." To her horror, the tears she'd been holding back spilled over her lashes and down her cheeks. "Sorry." With a sniffle, she pulled away from him and swiped at her face. "You're right. I'm being an idiot."

"Pressure needs an outlet," he said. "Tears happen." He got up and walked away, returning after a moment with a box of tissues. "Let it out."

"If we don't have time for panic, why is there time for crying?"

He shrugged. "Maybe you'll think better after a good cry."

"Right." She snorted. "Because I've been such an asset throughout this entire situation." It was easier to believe she hadn't failed the client. "It's not like I knew him." She reached for another tissue, dabbing at her eyes, blotting her nose again. "And you're right, he was guilty by more than association. I'm just feeling sorry for myself."

Mitch nearly choked on his beer. "Now, that's a crock." The last person in the world Julia would cry for was herself. She'd been little more than a limp noodle since Falk had been declared dead. "You might not have known the guy, but you cared."

"About my job, sure."

And so much more. "Drink your wine." The agony and guilt weighing on her had been obvious long before Leo had twisted up evidence so she'd take the fall for today's stunt.

He understood why Grant wanted them flying under the radar for now, but he hated sitting here waiting for the police to knock on his door and haul her in for questioning.

He muttered an oath, aggravated with all the things he couldn't do to help her. He didn't have the chops to help unravel the computer angle, and storming into Marburg for the sole purpose of busting Haywood's nose wouldn't help either of them, though he'd feel better.

"I overheard my dad one night after a fatal fire. He must have called Mom before he left the firehouse, because she was waiting up for him." He picked at the corner of the label on his beer bottle as he remembered that night. "It's the only time I heard him cry." He risked meeting Julia's gaze. "They'd done everything right and he didn't know the man who'd died, but Dad sobbed on Mom's shoulder for a good long time." He swiped at the condensation on the dark bottle.

"Never saw him cry for a fallen firefighter, but he cried for that stranger. Nothing upset him more than the moments when doing the job well wasn't enough."

"That's terrible."

"Sometimes it is, Julia." He tipped back his beer, draining it. "Life is crap sometimes and people get hurt. It's one thing for us to pay the price when we're doing

the job right. That's part of the risk we signed on for."
He caught her gaze, held it. "It's something completely
different when you lose an innocent person you're sworn
to protect."

Though he hadn't made any declarations to her, he
was discovering a challenging new pain as he watched
the woman he loved hurting. "I'm not letting you throw
everything away on misplaced guilt." He shoved back
from the table as anger shot through his system. "Leo
did this, not you. You did everything right to protect
yourself and your client."

He wouldn't let her dedication go to waste and he
sure as hell wouldn't let the bastard get her, too. They'd
worked within the law, with the information they had,
and lost the battle, but not the war.

"I'll get over it," Julia said. "Minor setback."

"You will." He'd make sure of it. "There are other
places to be a lawyer in this town."

Her lips hitched in a wobbly smile. "Grant said the
same thing."

"Then it must be true. The man knows practically
everyone in this town." What she needed was a respite
from everything. "Why don't we go down for pizza—"
His suggestion was cut short by the loud trill of the ringing house phone. No one used his landline anymore and
he was tempted to ignore it until he saw the number on
caller ID. "It's the firehouse."

"Pick it up," she urged him, her smile brightening.

When he heard his chief's voice informing him he was
reinstated and back on duty as of tomorrow morning, he
wanted to break out a serious fist pump. But he couldn't
go back to work unless Leo was located and in custody.

"Don't you dare say no," she whispered, a fierce scowl on her face.

He smirked, his own personal champion. Wrapping up the call, he replaced the phone and stared at her. Any celebration felt wrong, with her grieving the loss of both a client and a dream job.

"Well? Was that the news you've been waiting for?"

He nodded. "I've been reinstated. They want me back on the morning shift."

She threw her arms around him, her joy for him bubbling over in her touch and effervescent congratulations. He paused to revel in someone so invested in what made him happy.

"I knew it!" she exclaimed again.

"Why were you so sure?" He held her at arm's length, suddenly worried she'd called in a favor on his behalf.

"Oh, don't give me that look. I didn't have anything to do with it." She came close for another hug. "How do you want to celebrate?"

"With another day off," he replied. "I can't leave you unguarded."

"Mitch, it's your job. You've been cleared—don't jeopardize that on my account. Leo is probably halfway around the world by now. He can't stay in Philly. I can't stay here—"

He pulled her into his arms and kissed away the words. "Don't say it." He couldn't bear the suggestion that she leave. It would undo any small progress they'd made as a team. "I'll call Grant. Maybe he has news, too."

The owner of the Escape was happy to hear Mitch's good news, but he didn't have anything new they could take to the police. He did however promise to send backup to cover Julia while Mitch was on duty tomorrow.

She insisted it would be enough, that he needed to get back on the job. He decided to stop arguing, take her out for pizza and then be home early to bed.

Mitch rolled over when his alarm went off and sat up in a rush of fear when Julia's side of the bed was empty. A moment later, he caught the scent of bacon frying and smiled. His favorite attorney was making him breakfast.

He showered and dressed in record time and hurried downstairs. "This is a scene I could get used to."

"Yeah, well, I advise you to consider it a one-time deal."

He leaned in for a kiss to distract her while he swiped a crispy piece of bacon from the top of the serving plate. She looked so domestic in her yoga pants and one of his thermal shirts, with her hair piled up in a messy knot on top of her head. The words were right there, ready to launch from his mouth and he bit them back. She didn't want to hear that he loved her. She wasn't ready for him to ask her to stay in his life forever or until she got sick of him, whichever came first.

"I don't think I can do it," he said, wrapping his arms around her waist and nuzzling her neck. "I can't leave you when you look so delectable."

"Please. I've passed by a mirror this morning. Besides, we went over this last night. It's your first shift back, you have to go."

"*Have to*. Strong language from the queen of bacon." He stepped back and held out his arms. "How do I look?"

She fluttered her eyelashes. "Like a hero." She pressed up on her toes and kissed him.

Damn if his chest didn't puff up with pride.

She laughed and the normal, delighted sound rippled over his skin. He let her fix eggs while he made toast for both of them. When they sat down at the table, he knew he'd never want to share this kind of intimacy with anyone else. She was the one. It didn't even sound strange in his head. It sounded right and true. It might take him a lifetime to convince her to stick with him, but what else did he have to do that was more important than her?

He raised a toast point in salute. "Perfect breakfast. Thanks."

"Least I could do after, well, everything."

He didn't care for the note of farewell in her voice. "You'll follow Grant's orders and stay here until I'm off shift, right?" They'd discussed it repeatedly last night and the minute he thought he had her convinced to wait, she'd presented a new reason to act first. Why did he like the way she argued?

She nodded now, her green eyes focused on pushing the next bite of egg onto her fork. He recognized the meaning behind her evasion. She intended to turn herself in the minute he was out the door. The idea of her going to the police alone gave him chills.

"I'll call in and check on you every hour unless there's a call. The number for the firehouse is on the refrigerator if you need me."

"Great. Thanks." She pushed her food around her plate. "I'll be fine."

He waited for her to clarify her definition of *fine* while he devoured the food she'd prepared. He cleaned up his plate and the skillet while she finished. A glance at the clock proved he had to get out of there or risk being late his first day back on the job.

He pulled his coat off the peg and returned to the kitchen. "Grant sent a text that someone else is keeping an eye on the house," Mitch said, tapping his phone before he slid it into his coat pocket.

Her gaze drifted to the front windows, though the curtains were drawn. Thankfully, she didn't ask to see the text. "Stay put, babe. My shift will be over soon."

"Babe?"

Finally, he had a reaction out of her. "Too soon?" He winked.

"It will *never* be time for that word."

His heart kicked in his chest and he couldn't stifle the cocky grin creasing his face. "Never is a long time." He was going to hold her to that. "How do you feel about *sweetheart* or *honey*?"

"Go to work." Her sharp retort didn't dull the sparkle in her eyes. "I know what you're doing."

"You do?"

She walked right up to him and fisted her hands in his coat. "You're absolutely transparent." She gave a tug and pulled his mouth to hers for a kiss. "Have a great shift," she said, her lips brushing his. "I'll be fine. And I promise I will be right here when you get back."

"No better motivator than that." He gave her another brisk kiss, looped the strap of his duffel over his shoulder and walked out the door.

It felt so damned wrong to leave her as he drove down the street. If he stayed, he'd lose his job and his identity. He was a firefighter blood and soul. He wanted to believe Julia would stay put. She was probably right that Leo had skipped town. It didn't help.

Neither did the idea of backup doing his job protecting her. Though they'd agreed about it last night, he was cir-

cling back to all the reasons he should put off his return
to work until she was out of danger. They were too alike,
he thought with a caustic laugh. Lately they were both
making decisions only so they could second-guess them.

He tried to settle his thoughts. Falk had killed his
brother and plugged the last leak in his organization. It
was reasonable to assume the mastermind would move
on to his next pet project. Unless he felt the need to snip
the remaining loose ends here in Philly.

Mitch's stomach dropped at the thought. At the next
corner, he turned back for home. She'd just have to work
from the firehouse today. He'd think of some excuse for
the chief. Backup or not, Mitch refused to leave her hanging out there like bait.

Once Mitch left for his shift, Julia set to work. She
couldn't sit there twiddling her thumbs and pacing until
he returned. Playing house this morning should've
freaked her out; instead, she was far too content with
the idea of making breakfast for him on a regular basis.

Silly, but true. She hadn't recognized the signs when
she should have, and now she was irrevocably in love
with the man. Consumed with the case and Leo's motives, she'd made excuses and ignored how serious her
feelings had become.

She wasn't infatuated with Mitch because he was convenient or kind when he wasn't being cocky. The sex
was amazing and what should've been a fast, physical
release had blown past her smart defenses and touched
her heart and soul. Hopefully, when he got home from
his shift, she and Grant would have a lead on Leo's location. Once that last detail was handled, she vowed to

lay her heart on the table for him to pick up or leave behind as suited him.

She didn't want to take any chance that he'd believe she was sticking around simply because she was scared or had developed some weird hero complex. She wanted no barriers, no excuses, to come between them.

All this cycled through her brain as she carefully pieced together every encounter with Leo. Contrary to Mitch's worries, though the guilt still niggled at her, she had no intention of playing into Haywood's hands and going anywhere near the police until she had more than a few text messages to prove Leo Falk was alive and the author of a personal crime wave.

Where had the creep been hiding before Philly? Where had he stayed while he'd upended her life to find and kill his brother? And where would he go next?

In school, she'd studied cases of jury tampering, of the shady crews with zero morals available to the highest bidder. That was what Leo felt like to her, an edgy mercenary who knew what buttons to push and when to push them to get his way. Where did a man like that hide?

She pushed her hands through her hair and tugged a little. Checking the clock, she realized Mitch had missed his first check-in call by ten minutes. Telling herself that calling him would be the worst demonstration of clinginess, she forced herself to go get a shower and put on real clothes.

Once she was dressed in jeans and a simple cable sweater, she dried her hair and put on her makeup. No sense giving in to all the clichés and spending her first day of unemployment in a sloppy funk.

She walked into the kitchen and her fresh wave of determination disappeared on a terrified scream.

Leo Falk sat at the kitchen table, scrolling through her laptop. Her heart lurched in her chest and telling herself to run, she found her feet rooted to the spot, frozen by fear. "You look lovely," he said with frightening familiarity. "Better than I expected. I can see what he finds so appealing."

"Get out of my house!" She weighed her options as adrenaline and the will to survive kicked in. Could she reach the phone and dial 911 before he caught her? Could she make it to the bedrooms and climb out a window?

"Your house?" He chuckled, turned the laptop toward her. "I thought it was his."

She clapped her hands over her mouth at the sight of Mitch slumped over the steering wheel of the loaner car. "What did you do to him?"

"I arranged an effective, one-car accident."

Tears stung her eyes, but she would not give Leo the satisfaction of seeing her tears. She had to believe it wasn't as bad as it looked.

"You have a choice, Julia. A pleasant death, or a messy one. Which will it be?"

Her temper boiled over and she lunged at him. He knocked her to the floor and pulled a gun she hadn't noticed. "Messy it is."

"You won't get away with this," she said, looking for an opening as he tied her wrists and ankles to a chair and dragged her into the kitchen.

"Of course I will. This isn't my first fire."

"Mr. Franklin wasn't your first, either, I'm betting."

"Safe bet." He tested the ties. "For what it's worth, I thought you had excellent potential."

"As what?" she asked, horrified.

"Permanent legal counsel." He touched her jaw, forcing her to meet his gaze. "I've watched you for some time. Shame your true talents will be wasted." He set the gun on the counter and hummed tunelessly as he poured kerosene over the kitchen floor.

She made a futile attempt to curl her toes up and out of danger. "I never would have worked for you."

"Yes." Leo smiled sadly, lighter in hand. "I did figure that out."

Her gaze transfixed on his thumb as he sparked the flame and lit the trail of kerosene. "Any last words?"

The kitchen door burst open and Mitch staggered through. The miracle of his appearance shocked her and she wasn't sure she could trust her vision. But Leo saw him, too. "Gun!" she shouted as Leo reached for it. Mitch knocked it out of his hand and they went crashing over the counter stools.

The flames flowed across the kitchen floor, lapping at cabinets and circling her chair. She had to do something to save herself. She tried to stand and scoot, and made little progress with either approach.

She heard Leo and Mitch fighting on the other side of the counter as furniture splintered and fists and grunts were exchanged. She had to help Mitch.

Ignoring the flames, she wriggled her legs up and down against the chair legs, to loosen the bindings. Rocking the chair back, she slipped her feet free of the chair legs. Her wrists still bound to the chair, she tucked her nose and mouth into the collar of her sweater and braced herself to run through the fire blocking the only exit from the kitchen.

The smoke stung her eyes and throat. She knew she had to get low, but the floor rippled with fire.

"Julia, this way!"

Hearing Mitch's smoke-roughened command, she turned to see him reaching over the counter. No sign of Leo. She tried to cooperate but the chair made it impossible.

She couldn't make the jump and if she didn't run, she'd be stuck. He moved before she did, coming over the counter and hauling her up off the floor, chair and all. He grabbed a knife from the block and sliced through her bindings, then pushed her back over the counter. "Go!"

Leo emerged from the smoke, blocking her path and aiming the gun at her face. Mitch shoved her to the floor, covering her body with his. "Straight ahead is the door." He groaned as Leo attacked again. "Run. I'll be right behind you."

She made it out and looked back just as Leo dragged Mitch deeper into the burning house.

She screamed his name and reversed direction. She couldn't let him fight her battles alone. A firefighter caught her around the middle and hauled her toward the front yard. "You have to save him," she begged. "Please, save him!"

Julia stood in the street, the cold pavement easing the minor burns on her bare feet and the acrid smell of smoke billowing into the sky, marring what had been a beautiful morning. Firefighters from Mitch's shift surrounded her, battling the terrible blaze chewing through the house. It was obvious Leo hadn't limited the accelerant to the kitchen floor. She prayed they found him in time. If he died...

No. He'd promised her he wouldn't sacrifice himself to protect her. Any minute he'd come striding out, a cocky grin on his face. She wouldn't tolerate anything less. Mitch had saved her, pushing her clear before Leo Falk could pull the trigger and make his escape.

It was hard to believe "alone" had ever been her preference after shedding her childhood troubles. If Falk managed to kill Mitch, Julia knew she would be irreparably broken by the loss. She took an involuntary step toward the house.

"He'll make it," Grant said, holding her back.

"Yes, he will." The world just couldn't be so cruel as to show her the love of her life and then snatch him away. He was a miracle. Everything about him showed her every good thing within herself. "Leo showed me a picture of Mitch dead in a car."

"They found his car a few blocks away." Grant held her in half a hug. "Looks like he was ambushed on the way back to you. Whatever they gave him to knock him out wasn't strong enough."

Pressing her hands to her lips, new worry surged over him fighting a criminal mastermind in a fire with an unknown drug in his system. And no gear. Still, she had to believe. They'd come this far, and she refused to give up on him now.

"He'll make it," Grant said again. "He knows what he's doing in there."

Then what was taking him so long to get out of there? "You're right. He will make it." No doubts allowed. "And Leo Falk better come out of there alive enough to be prosecuted, as well." A litany of potential charges rattled through her mind, along with all the ways to prevent him slipping through any loopholes created by a good defense team.

"Sounds good to me," Grant agreed. "You need shoes," he observed.

"I'm fine." She was alive, thanks to Mitch. She'd wait right here until he joined her.

"At least move back to the grass."

She shrugged away from Grant. "He said he'd be right behind me." She was *not* leaving this spot until Mitch made it safely out of that blaze. "He doesn't lie."

But he wasn't there. What had Falk done to him?

Firefighters shouted and paramedics moved closer to the front walk. She watched, holding her breath as a firefighter emerged from the smoke, a limp body over his shoulder. Too short to be Mitch, her heart sank.

"Is he dead?"

"I'll find out," Grant replied.

Her thoughts reeled, thinking of the fight, the terrible blows exchanged before Mitch had cut her free and shoved her out of harm's way. She wrapped one hand around her other fist, refusing to cry, refusing to believe Leo had won.

"Come over here, Julia." Grant tried again to take her away from the fire.

"No."

"Leo Falk is dead," he said.

The news took a while to register. No trial or just punishment, but his victims had closure. That was probably better for all concerned, unless they tried to blame Mitch. She turned to Grant. "How?"

"I'm no doctor, but he has a chunk of glass embedded in his arm. They found him around back near a blown-out window. Between the cut and the smoke..." She stopped listening. If they charged Mitch with any crime, she would oversee his defense. All that mattered now was that he came out of that fire alive.

At last another firefighter appeared, arm around

Mitch, and his oxygen mask pressed to Mitch's face. Julia raced forward to shore up his other side, ignoring orders to stay out of the way. She was less than effective, being smaller than him, but she wasn't about to leave him.

"Thanks, Jennings," Mitch rasped as the firefighter handed him off to paramedics.

Julia ran her hands over him, seeking any injuries. "He was in a fight. There was a knife," she explained to the paramedics. She stayed at his side while he was treated with more oxygen and his minor scrapes were addressed.

"I'm okay." He reached for her hand, giving it a squeeze. "Tougher than I look."

"Don't talk," she ordered. "Just…just breathe."

He nodded and laced his fingers through hers. She brought his battered knuckles to her lips, kissing every abrasion. He'd saved her. Not just from Falk. In sheltering her from a stalker, Mitch had irrevocably changed her life. He'd saved her from her old fears, giving her the courage to let go of those burdens and be her best self.

Tears welled in her eyes, but she wouldn't cry. Not out there. As soon as he was feeling better, she'd cook him dinner and thank him properly for setting her free, for loving her enough that she knew how to love him back.

He pulled the oxygen mask down and gave her a devastating smile. "I'm okay."

"I can see that."

"Can you?" He sat up, swinging his legs to the side of the gurney so his face was only a few inches from hers. His lower lip was split from Falk's lucky punch and there was probably a black eye welling under the soot stains.

She nodded, though it felt shaky. "I love you," she

whispered. So much for waiting for the proper setting. She kissed him, carefully avoiding the injured spot. "You're stuck with me now."

"Promise?" Joy and love radiated back at her from his gorgeous brown eyes. "Don't tease me now, Julia."

"I promise." She swallowed another swell of tears and gripped as much of his big hands as she could hold. "Don't let go. Please." She'd flounder without him.

His laughter was rusty from the smoke as he pulled her into his arms. "You'll have one hell of a challenge finding any quiet time again," he said, raising his chin in the direction of his family, already trying to talk their way past the line of first responders blocking the street.

"I'm up for it," she said. "Together we can tackle anything." She ran her hands over his face, reassuring herself he'd really survived. They'd survived.

"You say that now—"

"And I'll say it fifty years from now. Mitch, do you think we could—"

He held her at arm's length, eyes wide. "Don't you dare propose to me here."

She bit her lip, trying to hold back the sudden ache around her heart. "Too soon?" Love took time. Just because she'd gotten there first didn't mean he wouldn't. Eventually. "Okay. I get it. We can—"

"Julia, hush." He laughed again, hard enough this time to start coughing. A paramedic pushed an oxygen mask over his face. Mitch shoved it away. "You've got your heart on your sleeve, sweetheart."

"Only for you," she admitted. "No one else can see it."

"I know." He drew her close to stand between his knees. "It's safe with me."

She leaned against the gift of his calm strength, accepting the unconditional support she'd longed for her entire life. "I love you," she whispered again.

"I love you, too, Julia."

The sweetest words she'd ever heard fell like a soft rain over her head, sinking in, a soothing balm over scorched nerves.

"Call me traditional," he said, "but when *I* propose to *you*, it won't be in front of a crime scene."

She leaned back, beaming at him. "I won't argue with that."

Laughter shook through him, along with another smoke-induced cough. "And I won't hold my breath."

Epilogue

Mitch sat with Julia at the end of the bar, applauding with the crowd as Grant finished his set as guest drummer. Not unlike the first night they'd met, yet so much had changed in recent weeks. He had his job back at the firehouse, and while the Falk murder fiasco was being hashed out, Julia worked here as Grant's assistant.

Her finances had been mysteriously repaired and restored, a feat they were both too relieved to question closely. With his uncle's house a total loss, his entire family had pitched in to transform an outbuilding near the garage into an apartment for Stephen, so Mitch and Julia could move back into her place. After feeling so cramped in September, now it seemed the perfect size for them as a couple.

As Grant emerged from backstage, Mitch took Julia's hand, smiling as the diamond ring he'd given her sparkled. Sometimes he still couldn't believe she'd said yes without a single argument. She'd be beside him at Thanksgiving dinner and Christmas, in the thick of it with his sisters, brothers, their spouses and kids. He couldn't wait for each and every day ahead of them.

They followed Grant to the office, only to find a pale, skinny kid in a black hoodie and ratty jeans and a Philadelphia PD detective in a crisp suit waiting for them.

"Mitch, Julia, this is Detective Bryant," Grant said as he rounded the desk to his chair.

The detective stood and shook hands with them, then offered his seat to Julia. Mitch stood behind her, hands on her shoulders. "Detective Bryant stopped by as a favor to me. I figured you'd appreciate an update, Julia."

"You," Julia said, her body going tense when she recognized the kid. "You gave me the note in the park."

The kid nodded, his gaze locked on his shoestrings.

"He goes by K-Chase as a hacker," Bryant said. "Took us some time to verify his story." Bryant jabbed him in the shoulder. "Talk, kid."

K-Chase leaned forward. "I apologize, Miss Cooper." He lifted his gaze to search her face. "You got your money back, right?"

"Yes," she replied, wary.

"You locked her out of her accounts?" Mitch asked. "You're responsible for the credit card fraud?"

"Yeah." The kid rolled his shoulders back, a little pride showing. "And I'm the one who fixed it all, too."

"And," Bryant prompted when he stopped talking.

"And I'm sorry for sending that picture to your boss, messing with your gear, and all the rest of it. Really sorry about the whole thing with you and the car," he said to Mitch. "He said he'd kill me if I screwed up his plan to escape."

"Leo Falk threatened to kill you?" Julia asked, incredulous.

The kid drummed his fingertips on his knee. "I got conned as much as anyone else. A few hacks for some easy money. It snowballed."

"What an understatement," Mitch grumbled.

"Hey, I can get in and out of any system in the world, but I'm not a killer. When I heard he died in that fire, I wasn't sure. So I stayed low awhile. He faked it once before."

"Yes, we're aware," Julia said. "You were supposed to kill Mitch?"

K-Chase nodded. "I did just enough to make it look good, then I ran."

At the memory of shaking out of the blackout and running back to find the house on fire, Mitch couldn't quite suppress the shudder. He couldn't decide if he wanted to throttle the kid or shake his hand. Julia reached back and laid her hand over his on her shoulder, making the decision for him. They'd survived. He'd focus on the positives.

Bryant shoved his hands into his pockets. "Kid offered a full confession if I let him apologize to you both."

"Thanks," Mitch and Julia said in unison.

"All right, time's up, kid." Bryant urged K-Chase to his feet. "Let's move."

Julia watched them go, and Mitch could hear the wheels turning as he took the empty chair. "Don't even think about it," he murmured at her ear. "You know that one's guilty."

"He's entitled to competent defense," she protested, her eyebrows furrowed thoughtfully.

Grant laughed. "I'm not sure the kid can afford a Marburg attorney."

Mitch held his breath, watching the reactions play across Julia's features.

"I can have my old job back? No one's reached out to me."

Grant shrugged a shoulder. "Based on the evidence Bryant is pulling out of that kid, your job may be the easiest situation to rectify. K-Chase didn't just hack for Leo, he hacked *into* Leo's operation. A kid like that will trade everything he knows to avoid hard time."

Grant had enough experience to know.

Julia reached out and caught Mitch's hand, lacing her fingers through his. "I suppose it's something we'll consider, if Marburg makes an offer." She gave him one of those smiles that just shot through him like a summer day, her eyes as bright as the diamond on her finger. "In the meantime, we have a wedding to plan."

"Well, if you need a band or reception venue, say the word and the Escape is yours," Grant offered with an easy smile.

"It's not a bad idea," Mitch said. Standing, he draped his arm around her shoulders, enjoying the way she leaned into him at every opportunity now.

"We'll think about it," she replied, wrapping her arm around his waist. "I had a different request for you, Grant."

"What's that?"

"Would you please walk me down the aisle?"

Grant's face blanked for a second, then gave way to

a brilliant grin. He came around the desk and wrapped her in a big hug. "I'd be honored."

"You're amazing, you know that?" Mitch pressed a kiss to the top of her head as they left the club. It was such a gift to be trusted with her big, tender heart. "You made his night."

"He's the closest thing I have to a dad, next to yours," she explained. She nestled closer into his embrace. "I get that from you," she added, her voice turning shy.

"What's that?"

"The courage to let people in. In close enough to feel like family." She pressed up onto her toes and kissed him. "I love you so much."

"I love you too, sweetheart." Just when he thought his heart couldn't hold any more, she gave him words like that. "You have plenty of family now." He laughed. "You're the most courageous woman I know and I'll be here to remind you today, tomorrow and always."

* * * * *

For a moment longer she just gazed up at him and looked
nothing like the fierce protector who had been ready to
shoot to protect her child.

He wanted to protect her. And Emma. He wanted them
both safe and able to grow and blossom as he knew they
would. He'd never felt the urge this strongly in his life.

Except with her.

He couldn't stop himself; he reached for her. She came
into his arms easily, and he realized with a little jolt she
was trembling.

"Jolie?"

"I'm scared," she whispered.

"They're gone, whoever it was," he assured her.

She leaned back again to look at him, gave a tiny shake
of her head. "Not that. You."

He went still. "You're scared of me?"

Again the small gesture of denial. "Of how I feel about
you. How you make me feel."

Making her feel was exactly what he wanted to do
right now. He wanted to make her feel everything he'd

felt, he wanted to make her move in that urgent way, wanted to hear the tiny sounds she made when he touched her in all those places, wanted to hear her cry out when she shattered in his arms.

On some vague level he knew she was talking of deeper things, but that reasoning part of his brain was shutting down as need blasted along every nerve in his body.

"I think we should check on Flash," he breathed against her ear.

He felt a shiver go through her, hoped it was for the same reason he was practically shaking in his boots.

"You think he might be getting in trouble out there?" she whispered.

"I think I already am in trouble."

"No fun getting in trouble alone," she whispered and reached up to cup his face with her hand. He turned his head, pressed his lips against her palm. And read the longed-for answer in her eyes.

He grabbed a blanket from the storage chest at the foot of the bed. Last time he'd been picking straw out of uncomfortable places. He supposed she had, too, but she'd never complained.

Jolie never complained. She assessed, formulated and acted on her best plan. It struck him then that she was exactly the kind of person he preferred to deal with in business. No manipulation, no backroom maneuvering, just honest decisions made with the best information she had at the time.

Like she had made four years ago?

Don't miss
COLTON FAMILY RESCUE by Justine Davis,
available October 2016 wherever
Harlequin® Romantic Suspense
books and ebooks are sold.

www.Harlequin.com

HARLEQUIN®

A Romance FOR EVERY MOOD™

Love the Harlequin book
you just read?

Your opinion matters.

Review this book on your favorite
book site, review site, blog or your own
social media properties and share
your opinion with other readers!

JUST CAN'T GET ENOUGH?

Join our social communities
and talk to us online.

You will have access to the latest
news on upcoming titles and special
promotions, but most importantly,
you can talk to other fans about your
favorite Harlequin reads.

Harlequin.com/Community

Facebook.com/HarlequinBooks

Twitter.com/HarlequinBooks

Pinterest.com/HarlequinBooks

THE WORLD IS BETTER WITH
Romance

Harlequin has everything from contemporary, passionate and heartwarming to suspenseful and inspirational stories.

Whatever your mood, we have a romance just for you!

Connect with us to find your next great read, special offers and more.

f /HarlequinBooks

🐦 @HarlequinBooks

www.HarlequinBlog.com

www.Harlequin.com/Newsletters

ⒽHARLEQUIN®

A *Romance* FOR EVERY MOOD™

www.Harlequin.com